A Streak Of Luck

RICHELLE KOSAR

A CORMORANT BOOK

THE CANADA COUNCIL   LE CONSEIL DES ARTS
FOR THE ARTS   DU CANADA
SINCE 1957   DEPUIS 1957

ONTARIO ARTS COUNCIL
CONSEIL DES ARTS DE L'ONTARIO

The publisher gratefully acknowledges the support of the
Canada Council for the Arts and the Ontario Arts Council
for its publishing program. We acknowledge the financial support
of the Government of Canada through the Book Publishing
Industry Development Program (BPIDP) for our publishing activities.

Printed and bound in Canada

National Library of Canada Cataloguing in Publication

Kosar, Richelle, 1950–
Streak of luck : a novel / Richelle Kosar.

ISBN 1-896951-47-3

I. Title.

PS8571.079S87 2003   C813'.54   C2002-905085-5
PR9199.3.K65S87 2003

Editor: Marc Côté
Cover and text design: Tannice Goddard
Cover image: Dolores Pitcher and Kelly Kyle
Printer: Friesens, Altona, Manitoba

Cormorant Books Inc.
62 Rose Avenue, Toronto, Ontario, Canada M4X 1N9

To Margaret Richardson Kosar,
who told me my first stories.

I

SIGNS

JESSE

Smoke and beer and a whiff of perfume,
Curve of white face, flash of gold,
My hands know just what to do,
Grab that old six-string guitar,
Play easy, play hard,
Play quiet, play loud,
Up to the roof, out to the air,
I'm rocking, I'm running,
I'm hammering, I'm thundering.
Listen to me howl,
Too crazy to stop,
Wild road.

Engine's roaring, tires are spinning,
Swig of 5-star whiskey
Tastes like honey going down.
Night flows round the car like water,
Clover in it, grass in it,
Dirt in it, gas in it,
Turn up the radio, shake the stratosphere,
I'm rocking, I'm running,
I'm hammering, I'm thundering,
Listen to me howl,
Too hot to slow down,
Wild road.

Moon and stars tear 'cross the sky
Life goes too fast and so do I
On to the next town, always the best one,
The one that I keep looking for,
So easy, so hard,
So near, so far.
Crash and walk away with sparks in my hair,
I'm rocking, I'm running,
I'm hammering, I'm thundering.
Listen to me howl,
Too lucky to die,
Wild, wild road.

— "WILD ROAD," BY JESSE MASARYK, 1980

MONA Sometimes I still dream of a glamourous city. I used to sit on our creaky swing, watching the road behind the house, thinking about how that road would join Highway 35, and Highway 35 would cross the American border and turn into US Highway 85, and if you kept going you'd end up in New York, all tall buildings and traffic and lights. I used to sit in the dark, bare feet kicking up dust, no sound except crickets, thinking of orchestras, taxicabs, men in tuxedos and women like Audrey Hepburn in *Breakfast at Tiffany's*, sleek and skinny in a black evening gown, smoking a cigarette in a mile-long holder.

Now, some nights when I'm taking a break in the alley behind the restaurant, I get a breath of cologne, as though someone's just driven past in a Cadillac. Or I'm waiting for a customer to make up his mind about what he wants to order, and I glance out the window and see a limo gliding by, one with clouded glass, so you can guess someone famous is inside. Then even this city seems fabulous, and I forget all the other crap. I start walking with a bounce, as though everything I do is being filmed, they're making a movie of my life. Okay, I'm a waitress, but I'm like Michelle Pfeiffer as a waitress — I've got a secret sorrow and soon I'm going to meet Al Pacino and he's going to fall for me big time.

"They totally destroyed the integrity of that play," Jimmie told me. The garbage cans in the alley were overflowing that night; you could forget about smelling any cologne. But we kept standing there anyway. "Know who played the part on stage? Kathy Bates."

"Oh, brother. Who'd ever believe Al Pacino could fall for Kathy Bates?"

"Why the hell not?" He always got excited when we talked about show business. "That was the point, it was about ordinary people, not glamourized, not young and beautiful, but they still suffer and live and fall in love and try to be happy! As far as Hollywood's concerned, once you're over forty, you can't be anything but an extra! Especially if you're a woman! Do you think that's good?"

I knew what he meant. But the truth is, I'd rather imagine myself as Michelle Pfeiffer than Kathy Bates. And he wasn't immune to beauty either. In another two minutes he said, big effort to be casual, "How's Rebecca doing these days?"

I'd seen it happen to him, the day she ran in for five minutes to bring me an umbrella. She had on a blue scarf, the same colour as her eyes. Don't think that was accidental. She gave him an indifferent smile, hardly looking, in a hurry, Wayne was waiting in the car. But Jimmie froze, holding a stack of dirty pizza plates. Only his eyes moved, lifting with her as she went up the stairs and out the door, shifting as she floated past the plate glass window and ran across Front Street, her scarf like a piece of blue sky in the middle of the grey afternoon. After that he mentioned her all the time, careless questions, offhand references: how old is she, where does she work, is she going out with anybody? It was always like that for Becky. All she had to do was breathe in and out.

"She's fine," I told him. I could have let him know he didn't have a hope, she'd never give a second look to an actor moonlighting as a waiter, but I liked it that he seemed so in love. I thought it was kind of romantic. I didn't want him to give up.

Back inside the manager, Dominic, glared at us and looked at his watch. I ignored him. He was always trying to be intimidating, but after some of the other places I'd worked he seemed pretty feeble. At Pete's Eats you didn't get any breaks, you had to have special permission even to take a pee. At Fandango if you sat down for five seconds the boss would be there handing you a mop or telling you to fill all the ketchup bottles. At Amici they docked your pay for broken dishes and everybody on staff would get called into the back once a week so the manager could tell you to shape up or else. But this is the thing: you can't ever let them scare you. Not even if your husband's out of work and your salary is all you've got. Not even if you only have a dime in your pocket. You have to act as if you're made of steel, as if no matter what they do you'll just laugh and walk out into the street without a backward look. Otherwise they've got you.

All the dishes at table two had been cleared away. The tabletop had been wiped until it shone. I walked over to Randy, the pimply busboy. "Did they leave a good tip?"

He gave me his blank look.

"Table two. They were running me off my feet. Did they at least leave a good tip?"

"Nope, nothing." He was the worst liar I've ever seen; even the rims of his ears turned pink.

I'd let him get away with it before, maybe that was why I felt so mad. I'd tried to be nice. I'd even given him his cut after every shift, as if I didn't suspect a thing. I guess I thought he was just a kid, give him a break. So to show his gratitude he wanted to screw me again. That's what you get.

"They had two rounds of drinks," I said. "They had an extra-large deep-dish supreme, three of them had dessert, the bill was eighty bucks, and you're trying to tell me they didn't leave any tip at all? Do I look that stupid?"

"There was nothing on the table," he said.

"Don't make me laugh," I said. "Come on." I was holding out my hand. It was surprising how loud my voice had gotten and how hot my skin felt. Even my knees seemed to be trembling all of a sudden. "I didn't say anything yesterday, but this is as far as it goes, okay? Fork it over!"

Jimmie came over to back me up. "Don't be a shit, Randy. We're in this together. Why cheat each other?"

But the little rat had gone too far to retreat. "She's paranoid! They didn't leave a cent, it's not my fault! What am I supposed to do? Now she has to throw a hissy fit!"

The next thing I knew I had a grip on his shirt and he was trying to shove me away and Jimmie's arm was in there somewhere too; I think it was Jimmie's elbow that knocked against my mouth and made my lip bleed. I had a vague sense that some of the customers had started craning their necks to see what was going on. My voice rang out, high and screechy, not like me at all. "Give it to me or I'll kill you!" I felt ready to tear his pockets open, maybe even tear his skin, anything to get at those dollar bills.

Dominic hustled us all into the kitchen. The swinging door bumped him in the ass just as he was folding his arms and trying to look like a big stern boss-man. If I hadn't been so worked up I might have laughed. "Keep your voices down, you're acting like schoolchildren! How do you suppose the patrons feel? They come in here for a pleasant meal and they're treated to a brawl among the staff!"

The three of us stood there, panting, hardly listening to his harangue. Jimmie kept trying to interrupt, to explain how I was being cheated out of my rightful tip, and Randy kept denying all knowledge. It finally ended with Dominic telling me that if I hadn't taken such a long break I could have collected the tip myself and then there wouldn't be any problem, would there, Mona?

I went into the washroom to dab at my lip with a wet paper towel. My face in the mirror gave me sort of a jolt. I looked so old and beat up. You never think of yourself as getting old, you feel the same as ever. Then in a certain light it hits you. My hair was messy, my lip was puffy, I looked fat, sweaty, ugly. I was forty. I never thought that's what I'd be in the year 2000: a greasy forty-year-old waitress who gets into a screaming fight with a teenage boy over a few lousy bucks. And loses. I knew damn well those people had left at least twelve dollars. He had it all, and I had nothing. And on top of everything else I had to stand there and get reamed out by a little tinpot manager ten years younger than me.

I cried a bit. Then I ran cold water and splashed my face. While I was pulling more paper towels out of the dispenser a bright glint of something caught my eye. It was a loonie, lying on the red tile floor in plain view. I picked it up and put it in my pocket. I could feel it right through my clothes, this little warm spot against my thigh. I know it's crazy, but I felt better. We were in the first year of a whole new century, so surely things were about to change. And my mother always used to say that finding money, even just a dime or a quarter, meant that something good was about to happen.

REBECCA   I made sure to take my time at dinner, even though it was obvious Wayne wanted to leave. I sipped my wine, nibbled at my chicken divan, held each mouthful of crème brûlée against my tongue for a count of ten before swallowing. He kept looking at his watch. I pretended not to notice.

In the car, he said, "I was supposed to pick the kids up at quarter to nine. I guess I'll just have to drop you off at the subway. Is that okay?"

"Of course," I said, staring through the windshield.

"You're not mad, are you? I just think it's a little early to be changing our living arrangements. We're doing great the way we are. Why risk screwing it up?"

"Right," I said.

"If you're mad why don't you just say so?"

"I'm not mad," I said.

In front of Christie station he tried to put his arms around me. I held him off.

"Aw, sweetie, don't be like this," he said. "Be nice to me. Come on." But I wouldn't kiss him. I wouldn't put my hand where he wanted me to put it.

"I need a hundred dollars," I told him. I didn't say why and I didn't pretend it would be a loan.

"Sure." He grabbed his wallet. "Sure, of course. Any time, just ask." He thought a hundred dollars was enough to get him off the hook. I wished I'd asked for two hundred.

As I was putting the bills into my purse he tried to stroke my arm, but I shook him off and got out of the car. He didn't sit there very long. I heard him drive away as I was pulling open the door to the station.

I could have cried. There I was, all dressed up in a new pink dress and matching shoes, my makeup perfect, my hair sleek and perfumed, and instead of stepping out of a limousine I was waiting on a subway platform, being gawked at by all the other nobodies, getting a blast of smelly air in my face as the train roared in. I had to stand up the whole trip because for some unknown reason half the people in the west end were travelling east that night. And of course the escalator at my stop wasn't working, so I had to climb two flights of stairs in a narrow skirt and heels. And of course there had to be a group of guys at the corner and I had to listen to their dreary comments as I went by.

And of course the hallway in our building was saturated with old cooking smells. When I was having dinner in one of our favourite restaurants, or spending the evening in Wayne's apartment, or even riding in the velvety front seat of his car, it was easy to forget about that stinking hallway. Six feet from our door I could already smell Jesse's cigarette smoke. He was supposed to quit but he couldn't. He had no willpower at all, he could never give up anything.

He was sitting at the kitchen table, a full ashtray in front of him, and a bottle of beer, of course. I didn't ask why he was sitting there in the dark. That's my rule: never ask him anything. I walked straight through the room without looking at the full sink or the sticky stain in front of the fridge. He'd sit there until the dishes were piled to the ceiling and a six-inch layer of muck had built up on the floor, and it would never occur to him to do anything about it. He had more important things on his mind.

One of Cory's dopey friends was with her in our room, both of them screaming and laughing the way girls that age do, a new burst of hilarity every sixty seconds, over nothing. "Karko likes you!" "He does *not!*" "Does too!" "Shut *up!*" There were pop cans and popcorn kernels everywhere, and the friend — a pudgy, gum-chewing black girl with nose rings — was sprawled across my bed with her feet on the quilt. I made myself a promise that someday I'd have privacy, a house with dozens of rooms, all with locks on the doors and windows overlooking a quiet garden. And everything would be clean, neat and orderly. And no one would be allowed to smoke. And the only drinks would be fruit juice, Perrier water and wine that cost at least twenty dollars a bottle.

"What are you doing back?" Cory wanted to know. "Don't tell me you and lover-boy had a *fight!*" She was just showing off, so I didn't bother to answer. Instead I climbed out the window and sat on the fire escape. The air was warm and the smell of french fries drifted up from the Burger King on the corner. In the gap between the buildings I could see people strolling along the Danforth. All of a sudden I imagined Jimmie Glenn walking into the alley and standing below, looking up at me. He'd see the pink dress, half in shadow, and my hair trailing around my shoulders. The railings would vibrate when he started to climb, I'd feel the tremor in the backs of my thighs. But I wouldn't move. I'd wait, absolutely still, my hair tickling my neck . . .

What an idiotic thing to imagine.

The house I'm going to have will be out in the country. It won't have a fire escape. There won't be any french fries or sirens. No one will get in without an invitation.

Cory was saying, "This was my dad. He was in a band." She'd taken out the photo albums. How pathetic.

"Wow," the dopey friend gushed breathlessly. "He was hot."

I knew which picture it was. Everybody's favourite: Jesse Maverick sitting on the ground in front of the crumpled fender of his '74 Chevy, the Saskatchewan licence plate dangling crookedly behind his shoulder. No shirt, just a vest. No socks, just scuffed black Oxfords. His bare arms crossed on his knees, cigarette smoke drifting upward to make a fuzzy halo around his punky, stand-up yellow hair. *Oh, he was so cool,* Mona used to say. She never had a brain in her head as far as men were concerned. *He was the coolest guy in the world.*

Yeah, and look where it got him.

"My mom said her knees went wobbly the first time she saw him," Cory babbled. Like it was some great story, like anyone who heard it would have to be mesmerized. "It was at the fairground in Walbrook, Saskatchewan, where we used to live. She almost didn't go to the fair that night. But then at the last minute something made her change her mind. She said later she must have been meant to go. On her way there, she found a five dollar bill. It was just lying on the sidewalk, waiting for her to come along and pick it up."

Someday I'll have hours of perfect silence — nobody talking, nobody watching television, nobody playing a boom box, nobody fighting or laughing or crying, not a single human voice. That would be like paradise.

"Ten minutes later she met my dad. He was taking a break between shows, standing behind the grandstand. He was wearing this vest with silver coins on it, and boots with shiny steel toes. She said when she laid eyes on him it was like being hit by lightning. He smiled at her and you know what he said? Get this. He said, 'Hi, beautiful.'"

That was the story that had to be told and retold until I got so sick of it I could have cried, all about the legendary meeting of those two clowns, the night they came together to live miserably ever after, clueless, careless and hopeless.

The bozo who lived downstairs was out on his fire escape too, standing there in a dirty undershirt and thongs, smoking something smelly and staring at me. So those were my options: either give a disgusting creep something to drool over, or sit in a tiny, hot, crowded bedroom with two teenage girls giggling like maniacs over a photo album.

I chose the fire escape. At least the creep was quiet while he jerked off. It was getting dark in the alley anyway, he couldn't have even seen me that well anymore. The sky had gone the colour of ink, and my blue shadow stretched across the grass toward the glow of electric light from the Danforth. I could smell perfume on my arm; Calvin Klein's Opium, a gift from Wayne. He could be a complete asshole, but at least he gave good presents. I promised myself that I'd always have the best things.

My grandmother told me once that if I looked at the new moon over my left shoulder and made a wish, the wish would come true. Of course I don't believe in crap like that, but I did it anyway. I wished that someday soon I'd be free.

CORY JUNE 10, 2000 I'm exhausted. All night I've been killing myself trying to entertain Brandi Shemar and it was absolute TORTURE! We used to be friends but lately it's like we have nothing to say to each other. Things got so desperate I was even happy to see Becky, but then she walked through the room without a word and went out to sit on the fire escape. People are always impressed by Becky because she's tall and blonde and acts like a princess tiptoeing through shit. So Brandi kept looking out the window to catch another glimpse of Her Royal Highness, and had even fewer interesting things to say than before. She didn't leave till nine-thirty! My whole body feels stiff from straining to laugh and come up with inane comments for about five hours.

I wish I could go down to Union Station and get on a train and go somewhere. I could change my name and dye my hair red and be someone completely different. Oh God, how wonderful to get out of this body and be someone else!

It's only when I'm alone in the dark with my music playing that I can feel myself disappear. If Enrique could just come here, sit beside me on the bed, whisper, "I can't get you out of my mind." Oh God, how lovely that would be.

I always remember the first time I saw him. I wasn't that interested in music, not like most of the other kids at school. Maybe because of Dad. Hearing a rock beat and seeing guys with guitars reminded me of things that weren't so happy. When my friends talked about 'N Sync or 98 Degrees or Enrique Iglesias I'd just tune out. But last April I was babysitting at Mrs. Ferrara's as usual, and she was late, also as usual, so I was channel surfing, trying to find something that wasn't totally dumb and boring. I hit Much Music by accident, and there he was. It's funny because I'd seen pictures of him before and I wasn't even impressed, I couldn't figure out why some of the girls at school were always drooling over him. He didn't look that great to me. Can you believe it?

It was the one where this girl is walking away and he's following her, singing with such passion that his whole body is vibrating, and then the camera zooms in on his face. It was like somebody hit me in the chest so hard that the wind was knocked out of me for a minute. He was singing to that girl, pouring out his heart. Some of the words were Spanish and they sounded a thousand time sexier and hotter than English, especially the way he sang them. It's weird, sometimes what's happening on the television screen seems more real than anything in my actual life. I felt as if I was the girl walking out onto that beach, looking back at him, listening to him pleading, saying he'd follow me anywhere in the world. That was when I first knew what it was like to be just crazy with love, to feel everything in my heart and soul going out toward this other person. It was a rude shock when the commercial came on and all of a sudden there were a bunch of dumb chocolate candies bouncing up and down and singing, "Yum yum yummy!"

By the time Mrs. Ferrara finally showed up the sun was already setting. The street was all red and gold when I looked out the window on the second floor landing. I imagined I saw him down there, walking in time to music, making a sort of dancing turn the way he did in the video, his hair blazing as if it was on fire with sunset light. The world was all changed for me, just knowing someone like him was in it.

Later I found out he recorded his first album right here in Toronto. He wasn't famous then, nobody even knew who he was. Maybe I walked right past him on the street. It's possible. If only I'd known he was in the same city, maybe I could have met him! Of course that was five years ago. I was practically an *infant* and probably too dumb to appreciate him.

Maybe he's sitting alone in his house in Miami right now, watching the ocean, feeling lonely, the same as me. I wish I knew him and could give him a call. He'd answer in that beautiful soft voice. He'd say, "Oh Cory, I was hoping it was you." He never answered my letter. Maybe he didn't get it. But maybe he's holding it in his hand this very minute. Maybe it's the best letter he ever read and he's been waiting for the perfect time to get in touch.

Sometimes I have this feeling that I can make the telephone ring just by wanting it badly enough. Concentrate hard, picture the phone in my mind, say to it, "Ring, ring, ring." I tried to do that for an hour last night, but it just hung there on the wall, dead, not a sound. Maybe if I try again now it'll work. Ring, ring, ring, ring. Maybe something wonderful is about to happen.

Guess what? Just after I wrote that last sentence, the phone did ring! I almost sprained my ankle jumping up and running into the hall. Of course Becky thought it was for her and yelled from the fire escape, "If that's Wayne tell him I'm not here!" It wasn't Wayne though. It was Kreepy Karko! Just because we're stuck doing a scene together in drama he thinks we're pals or something. If I'd had any choice I'd never have picked him as a partner. Just my luck to draw Kreepy Karko, the biggest loser in the school except me. Why am I always such a freak magnet?

He called to tell me he saw Majeska on the street this afternoon and she said that before school lets out for the summer he can use the drama room to put on his *X-Files* play, and of course I have to be Scully. I said, "Are you kidding?" He said no, I was the only one who could do it. I guess I laughed. I mean it was completely insane. But now he thinks I like the whole dumb idea and we're going to discuss it tomorrow before we rehearse *The Glass Menagerie*! Oh God, how do I get into these messes?

I hung up the phone and said, "Oh, shit!" I didn't think Dad was paying any attention. As usual he was sitting there in his own world. But he asked me, "Who was that?"

I said, "Oh, it was Kreepy Karko from school. He's written this *X-Files* play — although actually I gave him most of the ideas for it — and now he wants me to star in it! This is a disaster!"

Dad said, "Is it? You seem pretty happy."

I couldn't believe my ears. I said, "Happy! Are you kidding? I'd rather be strangled and shot and dumped in Lake Ontario than act in that play!"

He said, "Oh."

People never have a clue. They think that just because a person is laughing it means she's happy. God!

At least when Princess Becky bellowed from the fire escape, "Was it Wayne?" I had the satisfaction of bellowing back, "No, it was for *me*!"

I could pack a suitcase and take the subway to Union Station. Except I don't have a suitcase, or any money for a train ticket. I'm so sick of everything here. If the warehouse doesn't keep Dad on this time maybe we'll get thrown out of this dump and we'll have to live in the car again. If that happens I'll kill myself. How could beautiful Enrique Iglesias ever love an ugly loser whose home is the back seat of a Chevrolet? I don't even want to think about that. Think about something else. Think how wonderful it would be to have a suitcase, and money, and get on the train. It gives that lurch that means the journey is starting, and the wheels grind, and slowly it starts to move. I can picture it, coming out from under the roof of the station and seeing the night sky. Finally I'm on my way. The scenery is whizzing by. All of a sudden the sliding door at the front of the car opens. It's Enrique coming down the aisle! His gold earring gleams and his dark eyes give me a look that makes my body weak. He stops in front of me and says, "I told you I'd follow you anywhere."

Oh God, I would absolutely die.

But apparently Kreepy Karko is on the train too because I keep hearing his dumb voice. "You're the only Scully I want! No one can play Scully but you!"

I look over my shoulder and sure enough, there he is in the back of the car, with the lights flickering over his dumb baseball cap. What a freak! Of course, he's right — I could play stupid Scully better than anybody else in the whole stupid school. Enrique Iglesias wouldn't know that, but Karko does. I guess sometimes it takes one loser to know another.

MONA When I opened the door the first thing I saw was the red end of his cigarette. He was sitting at the kitchen table. For a second I felt this sort of terrible loneliness, worse than if I'd been coming home to an empty room. It was lonely just raising my arm to switch on the light.

I acted surprised to see him. "God, you scared me," I said.

There were three empty beer bottles on the table and he'd started on a fourth. I noticed, not for the first time, that his hair was going a little thin on top, and it had faded to a sort of soft sandy colour; gradually over the years it had lost that gleaming yellow richness it used to have. That made me sad. Or maybe it was something else. Maybe it was because my feet were sore and my back was stiff and I knew I was going to have to get up in the morning to pull a double shift. Maybe it was because walking from the corner I'd seen Becky high up in the shadows at the side of our building, first the splotch of her pink dress and then her bare arms and fair hair gleaming through the dark, a beautiful girl all by herself on a fire escape on Saturday night, a Juliet with no Romeo. Or maybe it was because on the subway coming home a tall blond kid had been sitting with his legs carelessly sprawled, reading a *Star Trek* paperback, and all of a sudden my eyes burned as though they were full of smoke.

"I'll be right back," I told Jesse. But somebody was already in the bathroom. That's what it's like when you have one bathroom for four people; you spend a lot of time hopping from one foot to another, rattling the doorknob and saying, "Are you just about finished in there?" The toilet flushed and Cory's voice yelled, "Just a minute!" Before I had time to step back the door banged open so hard it almost broke my nose.

"Sorry," she said. "What are you doing home so early?"

"It's not early," I said. "It's almost midnight." I lowered my voice. "How come Becky's home? Did something happen with Wayne?"

"How should I know?" Cory said sharply. "Why don't you ask her?"

I would have, but sometimes it wasn't a good idea to question Becky too closely. She'd bite your head off, shout that she just wanted to be left alone. "No, not right now," I said. "I'd better wait." Then I felt guilty, worried that maybe Cory was thinking I cared more about Becky, always put Becky's problems first. I tried to take her hand. "How are you doing? Come on and have some pizza."

She pulled her hand away. "No, thanks. I'm totally sick of pizza. If I never have it again in my life I'll be ecstatic."

I saw that she was holding a notebook. "Oh, good, you're using those journals. Are you writing a story?"

She rolled her eyes. "No."

"Well, what then?"

"I don't know. It's sort of like a diary or something, I guess."

"A diary? Oh, that's a great idea! I always wish I'd kept a diary. Think how much fun it'll be when you get older, reading what you wrote and remembering all the interesting things you did."

She rolled her eyes again. "Yeah, right. As if I ever do anything interesting."

"What are you talking about? What about *The Glass Menagerie*? Just tonight Jimmie was asking me how that's going. Monday's the big day, right? Can parents come?"

She twisted up her face in disbelief. "Are you kidding? *No way*! They're just stupid little scenes that we're supposed to do for the rest of the class! God!"

"But I'd love to see it. I'll bet Miss Majeska wouldn't mind. Maybe I should give her a call and ask."

"No, are you insane! If you call her I'm going to cut my throat!"

"Okay, okay. But I heard you practising some of the lines yesterday and you sounded really good."

It was like she had this hard shell all around her, equal parts exasperation, restlessness and disgust. But once in a while, if you were lucky, something you said penetrated through all that and hit her tender, vulnerable core. I saw a glimpse of it for one second before she ducked her head. "Oh, I did *not*! Get real, Mom."

She turned as if she meant to go back into her room. And all of a sudden I wanted to tell her. I couldn't tell Jesse; I didn't think he could take it. I couldn't tell Becky, she wouldn't want to listen. Cory was the only one left.

"You know what? I saw a kid on the subway tonight," I said. "He had blond hair and bright blue eyes and he looked about fourteen, and it just came into my mind that if Joey was still around, he might look like that."

She stared at me with her wide dark eyes. It seemed as if a sudden silence had fallen over the apartment, over the building, over the street — as though everybody was holding their breath at the sound of his name. In the stillness I could picture the subway disappearing into the tunnel, all its yellow windows passing slowly at first, then speeding up. I could see Joey sitting in one of them, a pale lock of hair dangling across his forehead, bending over his book, turning a page, absorbed in the adventures of the Starship Enterprise. I got a feeling in my throat, a sort of thick feeling as if I wanted to cry, or laugh, or maybe both at once.

Cory just kept staring at me, her lips moving slightly without making a sound. She had no idea what to say, but I didn't mind; it's not as if I'd really expected any answer. "Well, you'd better get to bed," I told her after a minute. "It's late. See you tomorrow."

When I walked back into the kitchen, Jesse hadn't moved. I sat across from him, opened my bag and took out a cardboard container of pizza. "There's cajun chicken and vegetarian tonight," I told him. "Go ahead. I guess no one else wants any."

It was one of his remote nights; he'd drunk enough to put himself at a distance from everything. I took a quick check of his eyes, and they were all right — a little hazy, but he hadn't had anything worse than beer. I drew a deep breath.

Sometimes in the past I'd come home and he wouldn't be there and, oh, the agonies of jealousy I suffered. But looking back on it, those times weren't so bad. It's better to imagine you've got a womanizer, a cheater, a sweet-talking liar, than to see a ghost sitting in the dark right in front of you, slowly and deliberately putting himself out of reach.

To be honest, the idea of his falling for someone else and leaving me wasn't completely terrible anymore. Sometimes it crossed my mind that it would be almost a relief. Then I'd feel ashamed, guilty. I'd have to erase that thought in a hurry before he read it in my face.

"My old man used to be an insomniac," he said. "You'd get up in the middle of the night to go to the can, and there he'd be, in the living room with the lights off, not making a sound. You'd say, 'Jeez, Dad, are you okay?' He'd say, 'Yeah, fine, thanks.' I remember thinking, 'What a sad old fart.' He worked for thirty years at the same job, Edmonton Transit, driving a bus. Never a complaint, not a word. One month after he retired he died of a heart attack, sitting on a bench in Mayfair Park. Even then he didn't make a sound. Croaked in silence like he did everything else. People walked past him for five hours, not even knowing he was dead."

He'd never told me that before. He'd hardly ever mentioned his father. You're with someone for twenty years, you think you've heard everything they have to say, and all of a sudden they come out with something new. After that he went quiet again.

I unfolded my newspaper. It was just habit, I was hardly paying attention. As I groped for the ticket in my purse I was looking forward to bed, sleeping, forgetting everything for a few hours. Three numbers matched, enough to claim ten free tickets for the next draw. That was the best we'd ever done.

He took a crumpled piece of paper out of his pocket. "I think I've got one, too," he said, squinting at it. "From last Wednesday, I guess. I forgot to check it."

"Last Wednesday? That won't be in this paper. Just a minute." A month's supply of old newspapers was piled up beside the fridge. Nobody ever remembered to take them out to the garbage bin. My legs were so tired they trembled when I crouched down. My neck was stiff, my lower back ached. I started leafing through the stack of newsprint, not finding the right date. I thought to myself, this is ridiculous, why am I bothering? But just as I was about to say oh, forget it, last Thursday's paper turned up.

He always picked odd numbers because he thought they were lucky, especially combinations including seven or nine. I sat down across from him and sleepily started circling the matches: 17 — yes, 29 — yes, 37 — yes . . . I stopped. Take a deep breath, I thought, you're hallucinating. It's past midnight, you've had a long day and you're exhausted. Make sure these are the Wednesday numbers. Check again, slowly. He'd lost interest; he was staring at the opposite wall. My hands shook. "Jesse," I said.

He looked at me. He didn't say a word; he didn't ask a question. It was as if he already knew.

CORY   JUNE 10, 2000 (LATER) It's impossible to get any privacy around here! I can't have anything to myself, I can't have anything that's secret and special. Someone else always has to be around sticking their noses into it. A while ago Princess Becky finally climbed in from the fire escape, looked over my shoulder, and said she thought Enrique Iglesias was just a "pretty boy." Well, who asked her? I told her he was NOT, and it was none of her fucking business anyway! So then she got mad and lay down on her bed with her back to me, sulking. I think she's asleep now.

In movies or TV shows, kids my age always have their own rooms and people always knock before they come in. The rooms are big too, with desks and computers and bookshelves and windows looking out on their own yards. The houses always have a downstairs and an upstairs and a basement and a porch. They're supposed to be just ordinary kids, but they have their own cars and boats and they go to Europe for summer vacation. They never live in small second-floor apartments, sharing a tiny bedroom with their sister, with their parents right on the other side of the wall, and the wall so thin everybody can practically hear each other's breathing. And only one bathroom. And a kitchen that isn't even separate from the living room. I can hear Mom and Dad in there right now, rustling paper and talking. In another minute they'll be arguing and it'll be about money, probably. The parents on TV never argue about money. When they do argue about something, it's in a great big kitchen looking out on a yard, and their kids are upstairs and don't even hear it. Sometimes when I'm watching TV I feel really lousy.

That's why I've started to like *The Glass Menagerie*. It was written a long time ago. I guess things were different then. The apartment the people live in sounds a lot like ours, and they're all sort of losers. It makes me feel like I'm not the only one in the world.

But that doesn't mean I want to do a scene from it with Kreepy Karko! I'm not going to be able to sleep all night, because whenever I close my eyes I start thinking about Monday and what a total *humiliation* it's going to be. I should have dropped drama. I hate it. I only took it because I figured it would be easy and fun, I didn't know it was going to turn out to be sheer torture! I hate Miss Majeska too, she's one of those teachers who always wants to shake things up, so I can never relax or just sit there daydreaming. I never know what dumb stunt she's going to force on us next! I should have figured she was going to be trouble when she showed up here in the fall. God, what a rude shock to open the door and see one of my teachers standing there! She had some dopey petition she was trying to get all the parents to sign, saying that if the drama program didn't continue at Eastend they'd all slash their wrists or something. She said to Mom, "Last year they cut back the music program because they claimed there wasn't enough money to buy instruments, and we're very much afraid that drama is going to be next on the chopping block. It's just CRIMINAL and they have to be STOPPED. The kids are being CHEATED out of what they deserve! The arts are NOT a frill, they're the absolute LIFEBLOOD of a society!" God, how could you guess she used to be an actress? Mom fell for it though, that's just the kind of thing she loves to hear. She practically grabbed the pen out of Majeska's hand, and while she was signing she had to say that once *she* wanted to be an actress herself, and Majeska had to pretend to be impressed. It was totally embarrassing. And then, as soon as Majeska left, Becky had to give her opinion, even though nobody asked her. She said, "These teachers make me laugh. One minute they're on strike, and the next they're pretending to care so much about the kids. All she really cares about is making sure her job's still there next year." Becky thinks people are all selfish pigs with sleazy motives for everything they do. I felt really disgusted with everybody, Becky and Mom and Majeska and most of all with myself for being associated with any of them.

A few weeks ago Majeska sprung it on us that we had to prepare dialogues and act them out in front of the class in June. As if that wasn't bad enough, she told us we couldn't even pick our own partners, we had to draw names out of a hat! She said that real actors couldn't always pick who they worked with, that they had to learn to adapt to new personalities and crap like that. Whoever said we wanted to be real actors? It's just a high school drama class for God's sake! She was a flop in the real theatre so now she has to try to make a big deal out of everything just to convince herself that she's still important.

Right before I stuck my hand into the hat I felt sort of sick. I knew it wasn't going to work out well, because anything that depends on luck is always sure to turn out terribly for me. I picked one piece of paper and then put it back and took another one. That was my big mistake. If only I'd gone with my first choice! But oh no, I had to change my mind, and who did I end up with? Kreepy Karko, the biggest freak in the entire school. Everybody hates him, he doesn't have a single friend. A couple of months ago some of the Grade Eleven boys held him down and made him eat mustard from one of those squirt bottles, and he didn't even fight back, he just swallowed it down and said, "Mmmmm-mmmm!" That's who I have to do this scene with on Monday! Some of the kids burst out laughing just to hear his name. And Karko took off his baseball cap and made a great big phony bow and farted at the same time!

I would rather die than go through with this. If only I could get really sick, and have to go to the hospital or something. Last year Tiffany DiAngelo had mono and she was away for two solid months. I wonder what the symptoms of mono are. It would be wonderful to just lie around in a hospital bed for awhile and have nurses bring me my meals and not have to think about anything or do anything.

This is the kind of thing that happens to me all the time. Someone like my sister would never draw Kreepy Karko's name out of a hat, no matter how many pieces of paper she threw back. Sometimes I feel like a cartoon character, always walking around with a black cloud over my head and little raindrops and forks of lightning coming out of it. I should have LOSER stamped on my forehead.

Mom and Dad just keep talking out there, blah blah blah. I can smell pizza. It practically makes me *gag*. We've had that every night this week, because Mom gets the leftovers for free.

That's all we ever have, stuff that nobody else wants. Even this diary — last week Dad found all these hardcover accounting journals on Wellesley Street with a bunch of other stuff somebody'd thrown out. So now I have to take hand-me-down things not only from Mom and Becky but from total strangers. But Dad said they're as good as new, they've never even been written in, so it's just as if he bought them in a store. He thought I'd like to have them because I used to write stories when I was in Grade One. I don't even remember that. But Mom said yes, that's what I used to do. She even used to save the stories, but they must have got lost one of the times we moved.

If only I could get out of here! I'm so sick and tired of it all!

The day after the draw I asked Majeska if I could have a different partner for our scenes. I knew it was totally futile, but I had to try. Nope, no way, she said. I told her it wasn't fair, why should I be the one to get stuck with Karko? I said, "He's so weird and creepy, nobody wants to work with him!"

Majeska said, "Well, how do you think that makes him feel?"

Who cares? I've got problems of my own. I didn't say that, though. You can't say stuff like that to a teacher. Instead I said, "It's his own fault, Miss Majeska! He acts so obnoxious he turns people totally off!"

She said, "We're all human beings and we all have more than one side. That's something you have to learn in drama."

Yeah. Right.

I said, "I know I can't do a good job with Karko and I'll probably flunk and it just doesn't seem fair, that's all!"

She said, "You have to make it work, Cory. That's part of the exercise."

Well, thanks a lot. What a BITCH! I hate her. Why did I ever, ever sign up for drama? A couple of kids told me that Majeska was really great and her class was a blast. Why did I listen?

The next afternoon Kreepy came up to me in the hall. Yuck! He was so revolting I could hardly look at him. He was in the same T-shirt he'd been wearing since January 2. He said, "So I've been thinking. How about if we do *The X-Files*?"

I just gave him a stare. "*What?*" I said.

"You can be Scully and I'll be Mulder. Say we're on our way to an investigation and then our car breaks down on the Extraterrestrial Highway — it actually exists, you know — and we're stranded in the desert, and we find this alien city that's been built out there in secret. Have you ever heard about Area 51? It's this top secret place in Nevada where —"

I couldn't believe my ears. "What are you talking about?" I said. "This is supposed to be a scene from a *play*. We can't do an *X-Files* episode!"

He looked at me, totally not understanding. I don't think he even knew the difference between a play and a TV show. I felt like turning around and walking away. But what was I supposed to do? I had to talk to him, Majeska forced it on me.

I said, "My mother's friend is a professional actor and he said we should do a scene from *The Glass Menagerie*."

He wrinkled up his nose as if he smelled something putrid. "The glass what?"

"Menagerie," I said. "My mother's friend says it's a great play."

"Never heard of it," Kreepy said. "What's it about?"

I wasn't too clear on that myself. They didn't have it in the library and I didn't even know where I could get a copy of it. But I wanted to sound as if I knew what I was talking about so I tried to remember what Jimmie'd told Mom. "There's this girl who's really shy, and her mother makes her brother invite one of his friends over for dinner."

Karko burst out laughing. "That's it?" he said. "Bo-ring."

What an asshole! I said, "Well, it's not as boring as *The X-Files*! And I have to go to algebra now!" And then I did walk off. And I felt like walking right out of the school and right out of the city and hitchhiking to Orlando. That's where Enrique was, he was giving a free show that week because he wanted to say thanks to all his fans who helped him get to where he is today.

Of course Majeska thought *The Glass Menagerie* was a wonderful choice. She practically went into ecstasies. She said it was a beautiful play. She had a copy of it, naturally. She brought it to school for us. She said she had a part in it at university or something, and playing that part was one of the high points of her life. God, our teachers are all so pathetic.

So Karko came over here to read the play. I felt like I should fumigate the room after he left. He sat on Becky's bed (thank God she wasn't around or she would have choked). He burped, he farted, he ate a whole jumbo bag of chips without offering me one. Plus he was still wearing the same T-shirt. When he saw my poster of Enrique Iglesias he put his finger down his throat and pretended to gag. I hated him so much, I just could have killed him.

We read through our scene and it was totally awful. Every five seconds he had to grunt or laugh or roll his eyes. After we were finished he said, "It sucks."

"Well, Majeska loves it so we have to do it," I said.

Karko said, "I still think we should do *The X-Files*."

Then he opened his backpack and got out a pile of crumpled up papers. He'd already written an *X-Files* scene, and he wanted me to read it. The pages had food stains on them and I didn't even want to touch them. But he wouldn't take no for an answer. He kept staring at me the whole time I was reading, it made me so nervous I could hardly concentrate. But really, it was terrible. I don't like *The X-Files* very much but I watch it because we don't have cable and Sunday night it's the only thing that's on. So I knew all the things he had wrong. I mean, he asked for it, so I told him.

I said, "Scully would never act like this, she's supposed to be really smart and tough. She'd never scream and faint. That's really bogus."

"But they're trapped in this alien city and she's shaken up!" he said.

I said, "I know — you could have them find an amulet or something like that, and it has strange properties that make them act completely different from their usual selves. So she goes all helpless and weak and girlie, and Mulder goes really macho."

I thought he'd probably just burp or fart or something, so I could hardly believe it when he said, "Hey, yeah! That's good!"

It was just something that came into my head. It wasn't that great. I was surprised that he seemed so impressed. He even got out a pen and started writing it down.

"But we still can't do *The X-Files* in class," I told him. "It has to be *The Glass Menagerie* or Majeska will have a seizure."

He said, "Okay, okay."

So I won. But while I was arguing I forgot that winning meant I'd have to dance with Kreepy Karko in front of the whole class and pretend to think he was hot! I'd like to see even Majeska the Drama Queen carry that off! I'm such an idiot! I wish I was dead!

On Friday — I could hardly believe it — he actually knew most of his lines. He only messed up a couple of times. He even said that he didn't mind Jim, his character. He said Jim's okay because he knows how to talk to people and make himself liked. In his opinion Laura is a dud, though. That really made me mad, I don't know why. I don't know why I even cared. I said, "She is *not* a dud, she's just really sensitive and shy!"

He said, "Yeah, but she doesn't even try to get over it, she just acts like a two-year-old, playing with little glass animals and all that!"

I said, "She does try but it's really hard for her. And she's not playing with them, she just likes to collect them and look at them!"

He said, "Well, it's really weird."

I said, "What's so weird about it? Haven't you ever collected anything?"

He said, yes, once he collected Superman comics, but that was normal, it wasn't something dumb and weird like little glass animals.

After that I stopped arguing with him. I mean, what would be the *point*?

Oh God, I just remembered how I showed Brandi Shemar some dumb family photo albums tonight. The more I think about it the more ill I feel. I must have been totally *insane*. And that stuff I said — it's embarrassing enough when Mom talks about it, but for me to go blabbing all that crap to somebody who isn't even related to us, I must have really lost it. Brandi'll tell everybody at school and they'll kill themselves laughing. What came over me? "When she first saw him it was like being hit by lightning." Oh God, I can't believe I actually came out with that! I should just crawl into a hole and die right now!

LOVE

JESSE

Bite into my heart, baby,
Watch me start to bleed,
Touch me up and down, baby,
Give me what I need.

Been a loner all my life
Never found my way,
Sang the blues from town to town
Up until that day.

Nothing ever got to me,
Everything was fake,
Till that day you came along
My first lucky break.

— "BITE MY HEART," BY JESSE MASARYK, 1979

MONA   I was a wild one. My mother thought so, anyway. She thought people who tried to get what they wanted were going to burn in hell. You were just supposed to sit in your living room watching Oral Roberts on TV until you died and went to heaven. I said, "Mom, I can't wait, I want some heaven now." And then I'd put on lipstick and blue eyeshadow and my tightest jeans and my platform shoes and out I'd go. She couldn't stop me. I was nineteen years old and for two years, ever since my father died, I'd been holding down two jobs, checkout clerk at the Co-op store during the day and usher at the downtown movie theatre three nights a week. I was buying lots of groceries and she depended on that. So all she could do was shake her head and mutter.

I always had boyfriends, plenty of them. That was another reason people thought I was wild, because I never stayed long with just one guy. But I was young, I thought I was hot, and there were so many guys around. I think I was always looking for somebody who'd get to me the way certain movie actors did. I liked the rebellious ones, the dangerous ones: Al Pacino in *Panic in Needle Park* and *Dog Day Afternoon*, Jack Nicholson in *Five Easy Pieces* or *One Flew Over the Cuckoo's Nest*. None of the men I met measured up to that. I remember one named Greg. We were sitting in his car when I broke up with him and he bent his head down on the steering wheel and cried. I was amazed by such a burst of emotion because I'd never felt anything like that myself, except when I was standing in the back of the Starlite Theatre watching a movie. It impressed me so much that I changed my mind — for a while at least. A couple of months later, when we broke up again, he didn't take it so hard. Maybe he'd met somebody he liked better. As for me, I was always staring past his shoulder, waiting for something new, something big, something real. I'd lie awake at night, listening to the crickets through my open window, so itchy and restless that I felt like climbing up on the sill and jumping, just for a change.

Remembering that summer now, I think of colours: yellow for the fields of wheat, blue for the sky, red for the fiery sunsets, black velvet for the night, hot pink and lime green for the lights of the fair. Walbrook wasn't a big place and for five nights that July you could hear the carnival music all the way to the other end of town, all the way to our ramshackle house on South Hill. Or could you? That's how I remember it anyway. I was sitting on the back step staring at the dusty yard and over the sound of the television in the living room I heard the music from the fair and decided I wanted to go after all. In those days I moved fast. I made up my mind and two seconds later I was upstairs in the bathroom putting on makeup and spraying myself with perfume and in another second I was standing beside the TV saying see you later. Mom didn't even ask where I was going, she'd given up on that. She just waved her hand in front of her face as if my smell was making her wheeze, and gave me a look that said it all: your jeans are too tight, you're wearing too much makeup, your top is cut too low, your hair isn't combed properly, you look like a tramp. That was how she saw it. But when I glanced at myself in the mirror on my way out, I was happy. Yeah, you're gorgeous! I thought.

What if I hadn't gone that night? Where would I be now? I was bored with everything in town that year and especially the fair — the same old thing every summer, the tacky little midway and the fat farmers' wives and the barkers coaxing the hicks into girlie shows. No, thanks, I'd told my friend Bonnie Harper just a couple of hours before. But it's like there are currents in the atmosphere, and they take hold of you and move you in a certain direction in spite of yourself. So on that summer night in 1979, I ended up walking through the hot dark streets, heading toward the noise and light. My lungs burned as though I was breathing steam. I couldn't go fast enough, it was as if I already knew what was coming. A Buick screeched past with a guy hanging out the passenger window, reaching for me with both arms, moaning and wiggling his tongue. I laughed and wiggled my tongue back. That's what I was like then: nothing fazed me, whatever happened I was ready for it. If it had been a movie you'd have seen me strutting along in time to the carnival music, high-heeled sandals clicking in rhythm, the red glow from the fairground glittering in my earrings and firing up the chrome in the lines of cars parked in the side streets. You'd have seen me stop, and the camera would have zeroed in on what I'd spotted: a five dollar bill lying there in the gutter, neat and whole, almost new, as though somebody'd put it there just for me.

Finding money means something good is about to happen, Mom always said. She believed in God but she believed in luck too, in crazy chance, in the universe suddenly opening up, smiling on you or hitting you with a thunderbolt. Maybe that was just her idea of how God operated. Except she'd never have imagined that God would drop a five dollar bill in front of someone like me. No, only the devil was going to smile on a girl in such tight jeans.

I thought I'd look for Bonnie and my other friends — make a circuit of the midway and probably run into them before long. But I never found them. I never even tried. Because as I was walking past the grandstand toward the Ferris wheel something made me turn my head. I saw the ember of a cigarette in the shadows. And there he was. A vest covered with silver coins and boots with shiny steel toes. Sleek bare arms, long legs, thick yellow hair cut short so that it stood up on top of his head. He saw me staring. "Hi, beautiful," he said.

It really was like lightning. A brilliant flash, a shock of heat and light that puts everything in sharp relief and leaves you sizzling. It was like his image was seared into me in one second, that's all it took, one second for every cell in my body to recognize him as the one I wanted, one second to go limp with thirst and hunger that only he could relieve, one second to think, I'll do anything, I'll die if I can't have him.

"Hi," I said.

That old grandstand had been there a hundred years. Coming into town on Highway 35 you always saw it across a field, a faded white box with a drooping roof. Up close the paint was peeling, the wood was warped, it looked like it was ready to crumble into a heap of rotten boards. Who'd have thought it could seem so marvellous, pale as a dream, floating like a giant silvery pale boat under the navy blue sky, with this lean blond guy leaning against its back wall?

"Looking for your boyfriend?" he asked.

"No," I said. Usually with guys I cracked jokes, put on attitudes, talked tough or skeptical. But with him there was no time to waste. I wanted to clear every obstacle from his path so he could get to me fast.

"Don't tell me you're all alone?" He put a flattering note of disbelief into his voice.

"Yeah."

He had a sweet, slow grin that broke across his face like a beam of light. His voice was low. "Well," he said. "This must be my lucky night."

I felt the hot gravel through the soles of my shoes, every thread in my blouse, the hard seam in the crotch of my jeans, the air rippling over my skin like a delicate fire that burned without hurting. The smell of popcorn and fried onions had a kick. Behind me the Tilt-a-Whirl started up again, hitting my back with a gust of hot wind and a blast of its theme music, "Stairway to Heaven." Oh, yeah, exactly.

I don't know how long we stood there. We must have talked, because somehow I learned things about him, even though I was so excited I could hardly pay attention. All I remember hearing was Led Zeppelin, but somehow I found out that he was a musician in the grandstand show, he was on a break, he was from Edmonton originally, he'd been traveling around all summer with this band, from fair to fair. Yes, yes? I kept encouraging him, and because he didn't move I went to him, taking a step with each yes, closer and closer till I was standing next to him, till the smoke from his cigarette was drifting around me, wrapping me in a soft veil. He took a drag, the ash went red. I imagined his mouth drawing on me, making me flame up the same way. Yes, go on? The band was called Loose Change and they were pretty lame, he was thinking of leaving them. They were the second band he'd been with and he was getting fed up. Maybe it was time to start up a band of his own. Yes? He had one more show to do that night. Yes, and? If I wanted to wait for him, maybe we could go for a drive after. His eyes held me like magnets. When he blinked I imagined his eyelashes tickling my throat. The riders on the Tilt-a-Whirl screamed, long and loud, whipping past. Oh sure, I said, a drive, sure, that sounds just great.

I climbed to the top of the grandstand. The only seats left were right under the roof. On the highway cars streamed past in the blue distance, headlights gleaming and then dying away. The sky was big as an ocean and the stage seemed to float in it, a little magical platform of lights and shifting colours. You could hear a thin metallic vibration in the air, like a current going through wires.

He wasn't the lead singer, that was a big bald guy with a chain-link belt and a voice that had nothing going for it except loudness. I hardly even glanced at him. All I cared about was the one just behind him, out of the spotlight, his vest glittering with silver coins, his silver-toed boots flashing, his long arms glistening with sweat, his fingers moving over the guitar strings.

He wasn't as good then as he got later, but he was good enough. Behind the noisy vocals I heard his chords, fast then slow, fierce then quiet, hard then light, making the wood quiver beneath me, making the hairs stand up on the back of my neck, beating inside my body, giving me the feeling that I was alone in the middle of the prairie, surrounded by sound. Except there were people all around, and even though the music seemed to be all mine, it was like a part of the night too, all the smells and sounds and colours in it. It seemed to rise out of the crowd, out of the breathing and stirring, the rapt attention, the speechless desire for speed and rhythm, movement and pleasure and freedom.

"Jesse Maverick, ladies and gentlemen!"

He took a half-step forward, dipped his head just slightly, still playing, too absorbed in the music and way too cool to be aroused by applause. Jesse Maverick, Jesse Maverick, Jesse Maverick, I said to myself. Even the name was like a crazy guitar chord vibrating under my diaphragm.

I waited for him by the concession stand just outside the grandstand gates. I thought, he won't come, he's forgotten about me already. But he hadn't. The crowd parted around him as he walked toward me, smiling. I thought, God if you never give me anything else in my life, I won't complain.

He threw his arm around me as if we'd known each other for a long time. "Let's get out of here," he said.

We drove out onto the highway. We drove above the speed limit. He had an old rattletrap car and the radio was crackly but he sang and beat out the time on the steering wheel. He told me, "I got this jalop in L.A. and I don't know how much longer it's going to last." L.A., he said so casually. I couldn't believe that I was sitting beside someone who'd actually been to L.A.

In a town called Alden we stopped and had beers. Sitting at

a wobbly table in the half-light, I noticed a tattoo on his upper arm. It wasn't a thunderbolt, a tiger, a big-breasted woman, or anything else you might have expected. It was a small butterfly in royal blue, very detailed and precise, with rose-pink highlights and yellow wing tips. "Do you like it?" he wanted to know.

Any excuse to touch him was welcome. As soon as my fingers came into contact with his arm all the saliva in my mouth dried up. "Wow, I never knew a tattoo could be so beautiful," I squeaked.

"Yeah?" He turned his head to give it a closer look. I felt his breath on the back of my hand. I didn't trust myself to look up. Instead I kept staring at the fine blue markings on his skin.

"I got it in Vancouver," he said. "There was this old Chinese guy in a hole in the wall just off Station Street. My buddies told me I was nuts. They thought my arm'd swell up and drop off. But I wasn't worried, what the hell. It took that old guy just one hour to do it. Didn't hurt a bit. Man, he was an artist."

"I'd like to get one," I said.

"I know a guy in Regina who's pretty good," he told me. "It'd look nice right here." With his forefinger he traced a spot on my chest right above the top of my blouse. "Or here," he said, with a very slight pressure just beside my navel. So I knew he wanted to touch me too. I felt as if I was leaning over a hot stove. I had to take a long swig of beer to cool myself off.

After awhile we left that place and drove on. Finally around 2 A.M. we turned down a dusty side road and he took the key out of the ignition. In the sudden stillness I heard my own shaky sigh. He turned to me. At last, I thought. At last we're here.

They said I was wild, but I'd never done it with someone I'd only known for three hours. I'd never done it outside, in a field, with the smell of manure in my nostrils. I'd never had cold grass and sharp twigs pressing into my bare back, and thought it was wonderful. I'd never been so helpless and ready to give in; I'd never gone red hot and ice cold in the same moment; I'd never cared so little about how I looked or whether I made a fool of myself. His mouth scorched me; wherever he touched me he set off sparks. His arms trembled; his face above me seemed to fill the world. In the middle of everything he gasped, "Oh, Christ, I love this!" I thought he was talking about me and what we were doing, but he pushed himself up and leaned inside the car to turn up the radio. It was Eric Clapton doing "Layla." The high volume made the car rock; notes and drumbeats ran across the grass and pounded in the dirt under my body. I heard the blood rushing through my veins, flooding my heart, making it throb like a trip-hammer. The sound grabbed you, shook you up, took you higher and higher. Then, just when you thought you'd escaped gravity, along came the mellow, slower section, the settling down.

"Oh, no," I said. "Why can't the wild part just go on?"

He leaned back to look into my face. He seemed surprised. "Yeah," he said.

∽

That's what it was like. Days passed and I went through them barely thinking. I didn't consider that the fair had to end, that he'd leave. It was as if the present was an endless time. At the Co-op I made mistakes and got called into the manager's office. At the movie theatre I watched the clock. For once even the movies seemed dull compared to what was happening in real life. I'd stand in the back with my flashlight, staring at the screen without even seeing it, daydreaming about eleven o'clock when the last show let out. I'd walk onto Main Street, always with a spasm of fear, thinking this time he wouldn't be there, but he always was. The sight of his '74 Chevy in front of the municipal park was enough to make me dizzy with excitement. I'd run, I couldn't help myself, I'd jump into the front seat, "Hi!" I'd gasp, and my shortness of breath wouldn't be from hurrying. "Hi," he'd say, with a catch in his voice. He felt it too. Who'd have believed that all the things I did to make myself sexy — the shiny wet-looking lipstick, the tousled hair, the dangling earrings, the halter top — would actually work on a guy who'd been to L.A.? And who'd have believed that the deserted Main Street of Walbrook, Saskatchewan could shine with yellow light, that even the World War I cenotaph could be unbearably sharp-edged, as though it were charged with electricity? I'd have to lean back against the car seat because I was trembling too much to sit erect, I'd close my eyes for a second and see little red flames under my eyelids. It was like I was always a bit drunk. In truth, we did drink a lot and we drove miles of highway and we danced to juke boxes in dozens of small towns, fast dances, slow dances, and then we drove again. He seemed happiest and most relaxed when he was moving. I remember the cool air blowing through the car, the fresh dark smell of it, the gleaming dashboard lights, the way his hands expertly controlled the wheel, the hum of our tires on the road. I remember the country stillness and the singing of crickets when we stopped far from anywhere. On those country roads the car motor would die away and immediately he'd turn to me but his movements would be slow, as if even before he actually touched me he was already caught up in a sort of trance. And I was the same. We moved toward each other as if we were dreaming and there was no question about what to do. He touched me with his mouth and hands, rubbed his face against my throat, our bodies fit together sweetly and perfectly in the dark. His skin smelled of clover, cool water and smoke.

We used to lie in the shadow of the car, listening to songs on the radio, our arms and legs twisted together. A breeze would come up and blow the feathery grass across my breast. I remember how white our skin looked in the moonlight and how black the butterfly tattoo looked below his shoulder. You could always see Highway 35 across a field. It was one of those never-ending western roads, it started way up north in the bush, came down through hills and valleys, through places like White Fox and Nipawin and Tisdale and Wadena and Fort Qu'Appelle, crossed long stretches of windy prairie, and finally hit Walbrook, streaking past the fairground, up South Hill near my mother's house, and out of town again, along the cemetery wall, heading south.

Sometimes we heard the roar of a motor, always far away. No one came near us. We were in our own place.

He told me about all his great experiences. "In Montana I met an old piano man named Blind John Tate. He played with Louis Armstrong for three months once. Somebody had to lead him to the keyboard and sit him down, but as soon as his fingers started moving, oh man, he didn't need any help. I jammed with him one night. People kept buying us beers and we just kept on playing. He said to me, 'Stick with it, son, you're goin' places.' Man, what a night that was . . .

"In northern B.C. me and this band I was with then did a show near a logging camp, and some of the guys liked the music so much that afterwards they took us on canoes and rowed us across the lake in the moonlight, and they made a fire and passed around a bottle and talked till dawn. They couldn't stop talking, they had so many stories to tell us. It was like we'd touched them in their souls and they wanted to give us something in return . . .

"I was still learning to play guitar when I got my first gig. This guitar player I knew couldn't make it so he asked me to fill in for him. It was in this beer hall outside of town. I got a ride with the drummer, a total lunatic, he was already stoned and he kept going off the road into the ditch and then back up again, without even batting an eye, like that was the normal way to drive. The hall was full of bikers and they kept yelling requests for stuff I'd never heard of, 'Hey, how about *"Blood on the Road"*? Hey, do *"Killer's Back in Town"*!' I wasn't used to playing for so long, by the end of the fourth song my fingers were bleeding. Then a fight broke out in the crowd, one guy threw another one right out a window, there was this explosion of glass like you wouldn't believe, and chicks screaming, guys swearing, and somebody even pulled out a gun and fired it into the ceiling, but we just kept on playing, we were afraid to stop, man! There was supposed to be a second show but the manager cancelled it so we only got, like, ten bucks each. Then the drummer's car wouldn't start, so we ended up having to lock up our equipment and hitchhike home. The other guys were completely pissed off, but I felt fantastic. I said to myself, oh man, this is great. This is the life for me."

He'd travelled all over, he'd met so many different people, he had such big ideas. He wasn't even embarrassed to come out with something like, "We touched them in their souls." You felt as if you could be bold and blurt out extravagant remarks too.

"I want to be an actress in movies," I told him. "All you need is one break. Do you think I could do it?"

"Sure," he said. "You're just as good-looking as any of the women I saw in Hollywood."

A flush of happiness went over me from my forehead to my toes, so intense that tears would have come into my eyes, if I'd let them. Instead I laughed. He laughed too.

"Or maybe I'll be a fashion designer," I said. "I haven't decided yet."

"We can do whatever we want," he said. "Nobody's gonna stop us."

It didn't seem hard to believe at all.

REBECCA   Men chase me all the time. I'm lucky enough to have a certain kind of look, so let's face it, that's going to happen. I have to be careful how I respond, that's all. If I let myself get bowled over by every half-attractive guy who makes eye contact, I'm going end up wasting a lot of time and energy. I always have to remind myself to focus on what's important and forget everything else.

For example, with Wayne. The first time he came into Artemis I saw at one glance that he was worth some special notice. He looked to be in his mid-thirties, someone mature who'd been around long enough to establish himself. He was wearing a custom-tailored suit and even though it was mid-February he had a beautiful golden-brown tan. That tells you something, doesn't it? I knew right away he was a substantial man, somebody with things to offer. So when he stared at me and made jokes, I stared back and laughed. His girlfriend didn't like it of course, that he was paying more attention to me than to the clothes she was trying on. She started to glare at me and turn on the sarcasm. But I can't help it that he liked my looks. I suppose I did play on it a bit, holding up dresses in front of myself and that sort of thing. But can you blame me? I don't get so many perfect opportunities that I could afford to let one go by. Yes, it's true I was born with some assets, but even so, I can't just sit back and relax, I have to work hard to make the most of what I've got. I do aerobics three times a week, and every day I drink eight glasses of water so that my appetite doesn't get out of hand. For breakfast I have half a cup of bran cereal with no sugar and a quarter cup of milk. For lunch I have one slice of whole wheat bread with an ounce of low-fat cheese and tomato, some carrot sticks, and an apple. For dinner I have three ounces of protein, a vegetable, and one carbohydrate, either bread or half a cup of pasta. I've trained myself not to like sweets, so I never have dessert unless it's fresh fruit. I'm very firm with myself. People look at someone like me and think, oh, she's lucky, she's got it easy. They don't realize how hard I work and the sacrifices I make.

When Wayne and his girlfriend left the store that day, I went to the window to watch them. They crossed the street and got into a beautiful almost-new Porsche. So I knew I'd been right to make an effort. Just as he was about to slide behind the wheel he looked around, and I knew why. He was hoping for one more glimpse of me. That's why I was standing there, to give it to him. More or less an invitation. From the expression on his face, I knew he'd be back.

It turned out he had a beautiful condo on Harbourfront, with a balcony overlooking the lake. He had both the Porsche and a Land Rover. He had a cottage on Georgian Bay. He had a sailboat. When I was with him I was treated like a queen, and I never had to worry about a thing. Doors were opened, waiters pulled out my chair, ushers hurried to show us to our seats. We didn't have to wait in line or count out change or ask humbly for favours. That's the way I wanted to live.

So if a taxi driver or gas station attendant or waiter flirted with me, was I supposed to take it seriously? I knew Jimmie Glenn had a thing for me; I wasn't blind. Every time I went near the pizza joint he'd be there with his mouth open, staring as if he'd been on an island for ten years and hadn't seen a woman the whole time. When gawking didn't work, he tried theatrical anecdotes, imitations of movie stars, foreign accents, poetical-sounding speeches he claimed to be rehearsing. Mona always looked at me to check if I was being appreciative enough. In her opinion he was wonderful. I could always count on her to go for the phonies and deadbeats. She should have wanted something better for her daughter, but no, she seemed to think Jimmie Glenn was the answer to any girl's prayer.

"He's gorgeous," she said. "And charming, and interesting, and fun . . ."

Well, I couldn't see it. He wasn't very tall and his wardrobe consisted entirely of T-shirts and jeans — except for his Pizza the Action uniform, of course. His hair was always rumpled, as if he couldn't be bothered to comb it. I admit his eyes were quite striking — such an intense shade of blue-green is very rare, especially in someone so dark. But who cares if a pizza waiter has beautiful eyes?

"I didn't know you were such a snob!" Mona said. "And anyway, he's not a pizza waiter, he's an actor!"

Really. I wondered how much money he'd made in the last year from acting. But I didn't say that; there was no point in arguing with her. She just didn't have a clue.

He gave us tickets to one of his plays last September. Mona came home with them, all excited, as if they were for box seats to a musical at the Princess of Wales. No chance, coming from Jimmie Glenn. It was some dreary Canadian thing with only two characters, set in the Maritimes, written by a friend of

Jimmie's, and they were staging it in an old firehall near Queen and Parliament. Please. I'm *not* interested, I said.

"You could at least give it a chance," Mona told me. "God, you're so stodgy. Sometimes I think you're older than me."

Yeah, sometimes I think so too.

As it turned out, Wayne had to take care of his kids that night. He didn't want me to meet his kids yet, he was afraid it would upset them. I must have been really desperate, because I agreed to go to the play after all. Jesse stayed home, naturally; he never wanted to do anything except sit in the kitchen drinking beer. But Cory, Mona and I made a major effort; took a bus, then a streetcar, then walked four blocks in the rain. And of course it was just as bad as I knew it would be. We sat on wooden benches in front of a bare stage and watched Jimmie and another guy pretend to be fishermen for two hours. I thought I was going to pass out cold. I practically needed toothpicks to prop my eyelids open. When Jimmie's character finally died, after talking non-stop for fifteen minutes, I felt like cheering.

But there are always people who like that kind of thing — or pretend they do. During the curtain call Mona was snuffling and making a big production out of blowing her nose, and a couple of people even stood up and yelled, "Bravo!" Probably the playwright's relatives. Cory said it was "okay." She says that whether she likes something or hates it. That's all you're going to get out of her.

Of course we had to go backstage, too; Mona would have died of disappointment if we hadn't. Jimmie and the other actor shared a dressing room, if you could call it that. Actually it was like a closet, and there seemed to be more people in it than there'd been in the audience. Jimmie saw us as soon as we crossed the threshold, though. He jumped up and waved. He had a towel around his shoulders and bits of cold cream in his hair.

"Thanks for coming! What did you think?" He looked at Mona, but I knew that she wasn't the reason his face was so red.

"Oh, it was great!" Mona said. "You had me crying in the last scene. Oh, it was so sad. You were terrific. You were just . . ." And on she went, like he'd just won an Oscar. It was embarrassing. Jimmie didn't seem embarrassed though; he was more than happy to stand there and listen. But finally he couldn't restrain himself anymore, he had to turn to me. He wasn't wearing shoes and he seemed even shorter than usual. Our eyes were almost on the same level. I looked into his and it was like looking at a blue-green lake with shadows on it. Standing so close it's impossible not to notice someone's eyes. It doesn't mean anything.

"I thought you were doing something else tonight," he said.

"No, it turned out I was free after all."

"I'm glad." He was an actor; he knew how to put a certain soft tone in his voice, a certain meaningful expression on his face. I wasn't going to get weak-kneed over it. "Did you like the play?" he wanted to know.

"Well, I didn't cry," I said.

He wasn't so pleased with that answer; I saw a flash like lightning across the blue-green. "No? What would make you cry, I wonder," he said, fast and hard.

There was a second of tension; it made Mona and Cory and some of the other people near us uneasy, hearing an exchange that wasn't complimentary and gushing. I didn't care, I just smiled and shrugged. In another minute everybody was chattering again and it was all forgotten. But Jimmie didn't forget it. He wouldn't say anything more to me and kept his face turned away as if I wasn't even there. Oh, he made a big fuss over Mona and Cory though, putting his arms around their shoulders, drinking in Mona's long-winded comments about the play, giving Cory advice about scenes she could do for her dopey drama class. But me he had to cold-shoulder, just because I was honest. As if it was a terrible punishment to be ignored by him. As if I cared. I was quite content to stand there in silence. Besides, I knew that all it would take was one smiling word of praise and he'd be eating out of my hand again. I just couldn't be bothered.

When we were leaving I looked around, and sure enough, even though a redhead with big boobs was hanging all over him, he was staring after me with that hungry expression men get if they're really far gone. He wanted me whether I hurt his feelings or not. Poor little dope. I never showed the slightest interest, I never gave him one second of encouragement, but he had it bad anyway, he couldn't help himself. I'll admit I felt a little pleased, a little proud of the power I had. But Wayne was still the guy for me. Even Erika was jealous of me for having Wayne. When that beautiful silvery Porsche pulled up in front of Artemis her eyes popped out. He'd lean over to push the door open for me and I'd walk across the sidewalk, a slim girl with long legs and blonde hair blowing in the breeze, like a picture in a magazine, and everybody turned to look. I could almost see the caption: "You've Got What It Takes."

At Wayne's condo I'd stand on the balcony looking at the lake and the lights on the Islands, holding a glass of wine in my hand, feeling clean, happy, safe, as if I'd finally found the place I should be. When he ran his finger down my arm I'd shiver with this sort of longing; to be honest I'm not sure what it was for, whether it was for sex or something else. We'd go into his bedroom, which was bigger than our whole smelly apartment on the Danforth. He had a huge circular bed with dozens of pillows; there was enough room for an orgy on that bed. As a matter of fact, he asked me once if I knew another girl we could "have fun with." Don't get me wrong, I wasn't offended or upset. I'm not naïve, I know lots of men go for that sort of thing. It doesn't mean they aren't in love. I wasn't afraid to just tell him no, I'd rather not. He didn't try to pressure me. Didn't that show he really cared?

That's not to say he never made me mad. He could be really insensitive and dumb sometimes. I didn't think it would be such a terrible thing if I met his kids, but he acted as if the very sight of me would traumatize the little darlings so badly they might want to commit suicide. How was I supposed to feel about that?

The worst thing was last October, though. His parents were coming to town for the weekend and I was pleased at the prospect. I thought if I could make them like me it would be a step in the right direction. As soon as he told me about the visit a whole scenario flashed through my mind: what I'd wear, how I'd do my hair, what I'd say. I'm usually quite good with older people. But gradually it dawned on me from the way he was talking that he wasn't even planning to introduce me to them. He said something about not seeing me till Tuesday, after they'd left. I said, "What do you mean? Can't we all do some things together?"

He said, "Oh, you wouldn't want to. You'd be bored to tears."

"No, I wouldn't," I said. "I'd really like to meet them."

"Trust me," he said. "They're my parents so I have to see them, but I don't want to inflict them on you."

I can always tell when a man isn't being honest. His eyes won't focus, he laughs a lot, he taps his fingers on the tabletop, he tries to change the subject. We were in Vivace, Wayne's favourite place for lunch. He glanced around as if he wanted to order more drinks. But our glasses were still full.

"So you don't want me to meet them?" I said.

"Sweetheart, believe me, I'm doing you a huge favour." He glanced around again. "Are you sure you don't want more than a salad? Why don't you have something else?"

I just looked at him. Finally he couldn't ignore the fact that I was staring and not saying a word.

"What?" he said, with a nervous laugh. I didn't answer, but he wouldn't give in, he had to keep pretending that he didn't know what was going on. "What's the matter? Did I say something wrong?" Like that.

Well, I wasn't going to help him wriggle off the hook. After a while he had to face the music and make an attempt to justify himself. He said, "Oh, sweetie, really, it would be just misery for everybody. You don't know what assholes my parents are. They're so pretentious and they're never going to understand why I'm with someone like you." He must have realized how that sounded because right away he fell all over himself trying to explain. "I mean, someone so young. And so different from my ex-wife. They loved her, they want me to find somebody else just like her. A ball-breaker in a power suit pulling in a hundred thou a year, that's my father's idea of the perfect woman. In five minutes he'd be grilling you, where you work and where you've gone to school and what books you've read, looking down his nose the whole time. Why should we put ourselves through that shit? They only come down from Montreal twice a year and the faster it's over the better I like it."

I took a sip of wine. It was hard to swallow. I had to look down at the table. It's ridiculous, I don't know why I let it get to me so much. It's just that I'd been seeing myself in a certain way, desirable I guess, special, the kind of girl guys would brag about and feel proud to be with. But it was obvious he wasn't so proud. He thought his parents would look at me and see a pathetic little nobody, young, stupid, with a Grade Twelve education, working as a clerk in a dress shop, going nowhere. I hated him for thinking that about me. I hated him so much, I felt so bad, that I couldn't sit there. I got up. The glasses tinkled and some of my wine slopped out onto the white tablecloth.

"What are you doing?" he said.

"Well, if I'm such a zero, maybe you'd rather not sit across from me," I said.

"Oh, come on. For God's sake. Don't be so childish. Sweetie. Just a minute. What is it that you —"

I didn't wait to hear the end of the question. I walked out. I thought he might run after me. Not that it would have helped, but when he didn't I felt even worse.

It was bright and sunny on the street, one of those fall days when the colours remind you of a box of crayola crayons — magenta, teal blue, burnt sienna. But if I feel lousy I don't want the day to be beautiful, I want rain and thunder and wind. I get kind of hysterical sometimes. People wouldn't know it from the surface; they'd see me and think, oh, look at that cool blonde walking down the street. But inside I'd be saying all these hysterical things to myself. Like, he doesn't give a shit about me! He thinks of me as a fling, he thinks that just because I'm young and don't have a university degree he doesn't have to take me seriously! I'll show him! He'll be sorry! Why am I so stupid and ugly, why am I such a mess, what's going to happen to me? When he's ready for someone more important he'll dump me, and then what will I do? What will I do? What will I do?

I was supposed to be back at the shop by one-thirty so that

Erika could go for her lunch. I thought of phoning and telling her I was sick. But she didn't pay me when I was sick. So I went back. All afternoon I kept thinking the phone behind the counter would ring, because when we'd had a fight Wayne usually called right away trying to mollify me. But he didn't call.

This is it! He's through with me! I'll never ride in the Porsche again! I'll never go up in the elevator to the fifteenth floor and walk through the double doors onto that thick carpet, I'll never stand on the terrace anymore drinking expensive wine, I'll never stretch out on that circular bed! I'll always be poor and ugly and pathetic! What was I born for, I might as well be dead!

That's what was going through my mind. Meanwhile I was smiling, saying, "Oh, that's a great colour on you."

It must have been a Monday because I remember we closed at six. All afternoon I was longing for six o'clock to come, but after I'd said good night to Erika and watched her walk away, I realized that I had nothing to do but go home. The thought of going back to that grungy apartment and sitting there all night caged up with Jesse and Cory, waiting for Mona to come home with a greasy bag of leftover pizza, made my stomach turn over. I started to walk. I didn't know where I was going, just putting one foot in front of the other. After a couple of minutes I noticed a bookstore — not a Chapters either, one of those little places without a coffee bar or anything special, just racks of books. Usually I wouldn't dream of going into a place like that; those shelves on all sides make me feel claustrophobic. Besides, I don't read books, I'm too busy for that kind of thing. But for some reason, that night I decided it would be a good idea to go into this joint called Pages. Who knows why? I guess I thought I could look at some of the fashion magazines. When I'm feeling awful they cheer me up, because everybody is dressed in beautiful clothes and jewellery, and they're dabbing perfume on their arms, stepping out of expensive cars, drinking liqueurs, climbing sweeping staircases, sitting on stone terraces beside the ocean. I flip through the pages and my heart starts to lift because at least I can think that there are places in the world where everything is all right.

So I was standing in the magazine section, holding a copy of *Elle*, gazing at a photo of Elizabeth Hurley on a street in Paris, and suddenly a voice beside me said, "Hi!"

I turned around, and it was Jimmie Glenn.

The first thing I noticed was that his face was flushed. Seeing me always did that to him. Then I noticed his ratty old jeans and his sweatshirt with the logo all faded, saying "On the Fringe." I knew it had something to do with a theatre festival that happened every summer, but I thought, exactly. And you always will be.

He was holding a bunch of books. Not the kind of books normal people read for fun; they were all by writers with first names like Konstantin and Uta and they had titles like *Building a Character*. Give me a break. I thought, if you used your money to buy some decent clothes instead, you might be a little more successful.

But this is the most annoying part — I actually felt slightly embarrassed to be caught holding *Elle*. As if he'd see it and think, oh, a fashion magazine, how shallow and brainless. Can you imagine that? I mean, to care for one second about the opinion of a scruffy pizza jockey from Nova Scotia? Ridiculous.

"What are you doing here?" he asked. "I couldn't believe my eyes!" He'd already decided I wasn't the type to hang around a bookstore. Of course, he was right, but it irritated me just the same.

"I come here all the time," I told him.

"You're kidding. Me, too," he said. "I live just around the corner."

"I work just down the street."

"You're kidding." Everything I said made him laugh. He was nervous, or happy, or both. I wasn't nervous at all. Or happy. I didn't feel anything. No, that's not true. Something about his laugh, that colour in his face, that intense blue-green stare, made me feel short of breath. Maybe it was excitement because he was so hot for me. I'd been feeling completely lousy and lost, but standing there with him by the magazines, strength came back into my body, I was like myself again.

After awhile, without actually agreeing on it, we moved toward the door. Out on the street it was still light but the sun was low behind the buildings, leaving the top stories dark but making a golden glow on the sidewalk.

"Where are you going now?" he asked.

I shrugged.

"No special plans?"

"Not really," I said.

"Me, either," he said. And he gave another laugh. I felt the sunlight on my shoulders and the back of my head. Maybe I looked a bit like Elizabeth Hurley standing on the Champs Élysées with her hair all shining. He was staring at me as if he didn't want to blink for fear I'd vanish. Again I felt short of breath. The people and traffic around us were just a blur, a roar.

"Do you want to come to my place and have some tea?"

Tea. At his place. That was the best he could do. Any other time I would have said no. I don't know why I didn't that night. Maybe it was because I wanted to keep on feeling like Elizabeth Hurley a little while longer. I heard myself say, "All right."

But Elizabeth Hurley wouldn't have been caught dead going into the house where he lived. There was a new condo development right across the street with a gold and blue sign giving the price range for the different units: $188,999 to $600,000. What a contrast. His place looked as though no one had remembered to tear it down when the neighbourhood started changing. The porch was sagging and beside the door was an old wreck of a couch, piled high with magazines. I wanted to turn around right then and there, just say forget it.

"I'm in the basement," he told me. He didn't even seem ashamed that he was living in such a dump. It was almost insulting. I thought he couldn't like me so much after all, or he'd have cared more about the impression he was making. But Mom had brought him to our place a couple of times and maybe he figured his was no worse, so why would it bother me? He didn't even have the whole basement to himself, just one room jammed with cheap stuff — a hot plate, a tiny refrigerator, a sink full of dishes, a wobbly card table, a narrow bed not even made.

I looked at those dishes stained with old tomato sauce and a sick feeling rolled over me like a tidal wave, I actually thought I might choke or burst into tears. I always told myself, I'm going to get away, I'm going to do better, and then over and over again I seemed to come up against the same things, the ugly little rooms, the smell of other people's cooking, the shabby furniture, the dirty windows looking out on weedy yards and garbage cans, and I couldn't help wondering if there was any escape, or if I was chained there till my dying day.

"Sorry about the mess," he said with a laugh. "Maid's day off." He took a dishtowel, shook it out like a magician, and covered the dirty dishes. "There," he said. "Now we don't have to look at them." Then he knocked some magazines off his bed and pulled the blanket smooth. "Have a seat. Now all I have to do is find some teabags."

What choice did I have? I sat down on the edge of the bed.

I didn't want the tea when he finally brought it. I didn't want to drink out of the mug he gave me because I wasn't sure it was clean. I just sat there holding it in my hands. I wouldn't have been surprised to spot a rat in a corner of the room.

"You haven't dropped by the restaurant for weeks." He cocked his head and smiled. "I missed you."

God. It's unbelievable how someone like him operates — drags a girl back to his miserable little hole, hands her a chipped mug with tea in it, and then stands over her like a king, thinking he's seductive.

"I've been busy," I said. "How long have you lived here?"

"Here? I have to think. Almost a year, I guess."

Almost a year. And he had to think about it before he could be sure.

He started looking through a stack of CDs. Guys like him can always afford hundreds of CDs and books, even though they're living in a cellar. "How about some music?" he said.

"Well, actually, I should be going pretty soon." We both remembered that on the street I'd said I had no special plans. I wondered if he'd get mad and point that out. But he just turned his eyes on me, those soft blue-green eyes, and said, "Oh, come on, stay a while."

And you know, this is the incredible part: I actually fell for it a bit, I mean in spite of everything I felt a little spasm of something in my body when he looked at me that way and spoke in that coaxing voice. I should have laughed out loud, set down the cracked mug with the tea untouched, and walked out the door. But no, I kept sitting there on the lumpy bed. I even took a sip of tea. It wasn't so bad; it had a slight taste of cinnamon.

"How do you like this?" It sounded like a guitar, nothing special. "It's a lute," he told me. Leave it to him to have a CD of lute music.

"It's a recording of Elizabethan serenades," he said. "I've got a small part in *Twelfth Night* at the Downtown Theatre Collective. I play the clown. It's typecasting."

He thought he was kidding. So I smiled. "How much do they pay you?"

He shrugged. Not important, of course. "It's for the exposure, more than anything else. And the chance to play Shakespeare. What a challenge. I can't wait to say some of the lines in front of an audience. Sometimes you just get sort of drunk on the poetry. Man, it's a glorious feeling!"

"Is it going to be another one without scenery or costumes?"

"Does that bother you? They're not really necessary, you know. What the audience imagines is usually better than sticking a few tacky trees and a cardboard wall on the stage. All you need is a little lighting." He switched on a small lamp at the head of the bed and switched off the overhead light. "And maybe some sound effects. A fountain." He turned on the faucet at the sink. Water ran through the dishcloth with a hiss. "Now imagine you're in a garden in Illyria."

"Oh, sure," I said. He thought that just turning off the light would make me forget about the dirty dishes, the clutter, the clothes hanging on bare metal hooks, the stains on the wall, the uncurtained window, the whole squalid mess we were sitting in.

"No, really." Right in front of my feet was a patch of light from the street, with shadows of leaves moving in it. "Look at that. Lilac bushes. Why not? You're Olivia, you're sitting on a stone bench in your garden, smelling the lilacs. You'd make a great Olivia. 'O, when mine eyes did see Olivia first, / Me thought she purged the air of pestilence!' That sounds like you."

I've been given a hot stare before. I've been paid compliments, not in words from Shakespeare, it's true, but in lots of ways and in lots of better places. I wasn't going to fall apart. But the dim light did help; it softened all the harsh edges, hid the dinginess, glistened on his black hair, made a soft shadow on the side of his face.

"You're in your garden and you hear me." He started to sing in a faint voice, as though he were far away.

O mistress mine, where are you roaming?
O, stay and hear; your true love's coming,
That can sing both high and low.

I'm not a big Shakespeare fan; I always think that people who claim to love him are just putting on an act to make themselves seem cultured. But with music it sounded kind of nice and wasn't as hard to understand as I'd thought. Besides, he was a good singer, it's undeniable. Every word came out so clearly, with such a nice, full tone that it seemed to chime in my head. Later I looked up *Twelfth Night* in a drama book of Cory's. That's why these particular lines have stuck in my mind, I guess. It's not that I know anything about it.

He pretended to be walking slowly along, playing air guitar. Or maybe I should say, air lute. "I'm not surprised to see you," he said. "I knew you were here, I was singing to you all along." He stopped short, with a passionate gaze that was teasing on the surface, and had something else underneath.

What is love? 'tis not hereafter;
Present mirth hath present laughter;
What's to come is still unsure;
In delay there lies no plenty;
Then come kiss me, sweet and twenty,
Youth's a stuff will not endure.

Halfway through the verse he dropped to his knees in front of me and after he'd finished singing he stayed there, his hands out, his chest rising and falling. Behind him in the dark, water was running softly; I could almost believe there really was a fountain. He was so close that if I'd moved my leg half an inch it would have pressed against him, I would have felt his fast breathing and his heart beating against my knee.

I thought, what if I do it?

See, he got me at a weak moment. I'd been feeling so desperate and depressed, so confused, so weary. I thought, what if I just lie back and let it happen? Wouldn't it be easy? Shut my eyes, lie back, let this fantasy take over, pretend to be in an unreal place where I can do whatever I want and there aren't any consequences. It seemed to me that I'd been fighting a long time, I was exhausted, and I just longed to let go, to give in, to feel that lumpy mattress under my spine.

I was still holding the mug of tea. I pressed my thumb into the place where the rim was chipped.

"I have to go," I said. He was almost on top of me, but somehow I managed to stand up and get past him. He made some kind of a sound, like "Oh no," or "Why," but I didn't turn around.

"I'm meeting Wayne. I'm already late." I heard him getting to his feet but I kept my eyes fixed on the exit. The doorknob felt greasy under my hand. You're right, I told myself. Don't stop, get out of here fast.

He stood at the bottom of the stairs. "Wait," he said, and then, "Shit!" I pretended not to hear.

I don't even remember walking to the corner. All I remember is feeling burning hot, breathless, hardly able to hear or see because of the roaring of my heart. And then I was back on Queen Street, and the traffic was streaming past. The sidewalk was still dry but rain was coming, I could smell it in the air, a trace of damp freshness that for some reason made me think of Saskatchewan, made me ache with homesickness, made me remember nights when I was around eight years old and used to run home from school, just because I was a good runner and loved to go fast. One night the sky got dark, a storm was coming, but I ran faster than the storm, one block after another whirling past, the fresh air rushing through my lungs, and I got to our porch just before the thunder cracked and the rain started to fall.

I don't know why a simple thing like that sticks in your mind. You'd think the good part would be arriving home, being safe inside when the storm breaks. But all the joy of the memory seemed to be concentrated in the part where I was still running, with the smell of rain in my nostrils, and nothing in my way.

That was a long time ago.

Near McCaul a woman was sleeping in a streetcar shelter. She had a dirty old blanket and she was using a pair of filthy shoes for a pillow. That's what can happen to a person who stops thinking, who lets herself go. And nobody'll help, or give a shit. They'll walk past without a second glance.

People who say other things are more important than money are either hypocrites or idiots. What's love worth if there's nowhere to sleep but the sidewalk? Who respects a person who's carrying everything she has in a plastic bag and walking through the snow in rotten sneakers? Art and music — all that crap — what does it mean if the hallway outside the door stinks of urine and old cigarettes, but still the rent's too high so that by the end of the month there isn't enough left for a lousy cup of coffee? No, money is number one, and everything else comes after. People with money can moon over books and paintings. They can worry about what will make them happy. They can have sex with whoever they want. They can fall madly in love with some zero who sings Shakespearean verses and has beautiful blue-green eyes. People without money have to be smart.

I went into the Queen Mother Café. Usually I march right past the dessert display and just order coffee. But that night I stopped and looked. There was a chocolate and peanut butter pie, about nine inches thick. I've trained myself not to like either chocolate or peanut butter because they're both crammed with fat and calories. But that night I thought, I'm going to have a piece of pie. A voice in my head said, eight hundred calories, maybe more. I thought, I don't care, I don't care! Someone opened the door and I got another sweet-smelling breath of rain.

I sat at a table by the window. I don't think I'd touched chocolate or peanut butter for more than three years. The first bite was so intense that it made me shiver; it was as though I tasted it all over my body, as though I felt the pleasure in my scalp and all the way down to my toes. The silky texture of the filling, the rich curls of chocolate, the buttery flakes of pastry almost brought tears to my eyes. When I'd eaten the whole thing I thought, I want another piece. The same stern voice reminded me, sixteen hundred calories. Eight bucks in total. I don't care, I thought again. I deserve this at least! For some

Mom asked me if I wanted to invite anybody over to eat birth-day cake and I told her, "No, I have no friends." Mom never likes to hear stuff like that. She won't believe it.

That was the day I first met Brandi. She was a new girl and we started walking the same direction after school. I found out she was from Jamaica. She'd never seen snow before and she thought it was neat. I showed her how to make a snow angel. She wasn't satisfied to just make one, so we made a whole bunch of them in the empty lot beside the Stafford Arms. The snow looked blue after the sun went down so there were all these dozens of blue angels all over the place when we were finished and we both had our backs covered with snow. It was childish but kind of fun.

Then after supper, Mom brought out this cake all covered with candles, and everybody sang happy birthday to me. Even Becky sang. It was weird — just before I blew out my candles I saw all three of their faces, leaning forward in the candlelight, as if they were all making a wish.

Dear Enrique,
Last night I waited for you on the fire escape. I could
hear the music from the Paradise Dance Hall and see
the pink and blue lights reflected in the puddles. The
dancers' silhouettes flashed across the windows. I saw
a couple kissing in the doorway, pressing together
until their bodies became one shadow, and I hoped
that soon that would be you and me. I thought I
heard your footsteps and my heart was on fire. You
could have any girl you want but for some crazy rea-
son you want only me. And I want only you, mi amor.
I knew you were coming, you were walking fast,

*Broadview, then Chester, Logan, Carlaw, Pape, then
Jones Avenue, then Donlands. The neon signs were
blinking, making embers in your eyes. I couldn't
move, I heard your footsteps, pounding like thunder. I
was so terribly lonely till you came. And then all of a
sudden*

MONA "I knew it," he said. "I just had this feeling. I didn't
go to the 7-11 on Saturday. I was walking past the drugstore on
the corner, not even thinking about it. Then I saw the lotto sign
and something made me go in. I almost asked for a quick-pick,
but something stopped me. I thought, no, it has to be all odd
numbers. And I just filled them in, bam bam bam bam, just like
that. I told you, didn't I? Remember, everybody was predicting
disasters, but I told you I had a feeling the year 2000 was going
to be lucky for us?"

"You check it," I said. My hands were shaking so much that
I could hardly push the ticket toward him. "Maybe I made a
mistake."

He just kept staring at me, his eyes glowing like light bulbs.
"It's weird, you know," he said. "When I was putting it in my
wallet I thought, this is the one. No shit, that's exactly what I
thought."

"Check it," I begged him. "Maybe I'm reading it wrong. You
have to check it too before we can be sure."

He grabbed the newspaper. "Put on your glasses," I told him.

"Where am I supposed to be looking?"

"There, right there!" My finger left a damp smudge on the
newsprint. I couldn't sit still, I had to get up and walk around.
The ceiling light seemed to be pulsing, giving off waves of hot
electricity. He leaned over the paper, his glasses perched on the

end of his nose. His shadow quivered on the wall; it looked like the shadow of a strange, angular bird with a big beak. I tried to swallow and couldn't; I thought maybe I was going to be sick.

"Well?" I said when I couldn't stand it one second longer.

He raised his head. He was smiling. I couldn't take the smile at face value though. "Yeah? Well?" I said again.

He nodded. "Yep," he said.

"Yep," I repeated in a sort of daze.

You think it'll never happen to you. But in another part of your mind you were always sure that someday it would.

You dream about it often. You warn yourself, don't be an idiot, it's just a dream. But you keep on dreaming anyway.

You know the odds are against you. But you always think there might be a day when you finally beat the odds.

"I can't believe it," I said.

"I almost didn't go in," he said. "But something made me turn my head and see that sign. You know, ever since —" He paused and then went quickly on. "I mean, well, for the last ten years, anyway, it's like we've been under a jinx, everything we did went wrong. But now we've finally shaken it, it's over. Now we're gonna have good times again!"

It made me nervous to hear him sounding like that. I opened a cupboard and looked inside. I don't know what I was looking for. Then I closed it again. "What shall we do?" I said. "I don't know what you're supposed to do."

"Calm down."

"I'm calm," I told him. "I'm just as calm as you."

"We don't need to do anything right away," he said. "We should sit on it for a couple of days until we decide what we want."

"I read about a guy who won five million and went on a

huge spree, and got so plastered that he passed out in an alley and drowned in a puddle of water."

Jesse laughed. "We're not going to drown," he said.

"And wasn't there somebody — yeah, I read this too — this couple collected their million dollar cheque and then two days later the guy had a heart attack and died. And there was this guy who won the jackpot but before he had a chance to spend a dime he found out he had cancer."

He laughed again. "You know what? There are people who win and don't die! There are people who buy a yacht and sail around the fuckin' world!"

He was standing up. I hadn't seen his face look like that for a long time. For years, actually. He was like his old self, cocky, grinning, full of fire and confidence, ready to wail, the old Jesse Maverick. Electric light blazed on top of his head, made his hair look bright again, bright yellow like the sun at noon.

"Shall we tell the kids?" I said.

"No, not yet," he said. "Let's wait a little while, let it sink in. They're asleep anyway."

I pictured them lying in their beds — beautiful Becky with her long lashes making shadows on her cheeks, little Cory turning restlessly, talking in her sleep — neither of them knowing that everything had changed. All of a sudden I thought, they'll be able to go to university. They'll be able to go to France and Italy. And then I thought, I'll be able to go to France and Italy.

"What are you crying for?" he said. He reached out and took hold of my hand. He hadn't done that for a long time either.

"I'm not," I said. I laughed.

"We've got lots to think about," he said. "We have to make lots of plans."

You feel as if you've been locked up in a cage. You've been

in that cage for years. You're always sweating and struggling but you can't escape, you've almost given up. Then all of a sudden the door just opens. You can walk out. You can run. You can breathe deep. You can sing. You can dance.

I went to the window and opened it wide. Warm air came pouring in. On the way home from work I'd thought the air seemed really sultry, heavy, oppressive. Not anymore. It felt light and smelled sweet, it touched my face like someone's gentle fingertips. I leaned over the window sill. The sky was a beautiful deep violet-blue with sparkles in it. People were laughing on the street and the neon signs looked like Christmas lights. It felt as though he must be right, happiness was coming back, turning the corner like an old friend you've missed and longed to see. The bad times were over.

LOSS

JESSE

I thought I knew all the answers,
I thought I'd keep playing the game.
But now you're gone and you won't come back.
Am I to blame?

Everything was fine one day,
The next was all misery and pain.
Can't believe that you're gone and you won't come
    back.
Am I to blame?

Am I to blame, didn't love you enough?
But I loved you as much as I could.
Am I to blame, didn't take enough care?
But I cared more than I ever said.

I thought that I had time ahead
So it hurts just hearing your name.
'Cause you're gone away and you'll never come back
And I know that I'm to blame.

— "AM I TO BLAME?" BY JESSE MASARYK, 1990

MONA   I have to come at it slowly, otherwise I can't handle
it. I have to be very gradual and careful, and lead up to it.

I always thought three was a lucky number for me. Jesse and
I got married on October 3. On September 3 I found out I was

75

pregnant with Becky. Cory was christened on February 3. My little boy was born on July 3. His birthday fell right between Canada Day and the American Fourth of July, so it always seemed as if the celebrations, the picnics, the fireworks, the parades, were partly in his honour. I remember standing in a field outside town on a hot summer night, my stomach twice its usual size, my ankles swollen, holding Cory in my arms, Mom sitting sideways on the front seat of the car, her arm resting on the open door, and Becky racing through the grass, blonde hair flowing behind her in the dusk like a wave of silver. Jesse wasn't there of course; the band was playing somewhere that night. But I knew that long after midnight I'd be lying half asleep and I'd hear the car radio in the street outside our house and that would mean he was home.

I can still picture how the fireworks burst across the sky. Becky stopped tearing around and stood with her face turned upward, like an angel in one of those Renaissance paintings. She inhaled sharply and then let the air out in a sigh of amazement. "Oh-h-h-h!"

I said, "Look, Cory, look up at the sky, can you see the colours?" I saw flecks of red and gold and green floating in her eyes. She clapped her pudgy little hands.

Even Mom said, "Oh, that was a nice one." Her emphysema was worse by then; she always sounded out of breath, as if she'd been running hard. But even she was happy that night.

And two nights later my little boy was born. All my kids were beautiful, but I really think he was the most beautiful of all. Right from the beginning he had lots of curly, fair hair and dimples in his cheeks, and even though he was too young to smile, he looked as if he wanted to. Sometimes I still see his face in dreams.

No, this is too fast. I've got to slow down, I'm not ready yet. Let me think of happy things for a while longer.

The day we got married was as warm as August, a beautiful Indian summer day, the kind of afternoon you only have in fall, when everything seems to be touched with gold, and the leaves drift down like confetti through the soft, smoky air. Jesse wore jeans, a tight black T-shirt with LET'S ROCK emblazoned on it, and his silvery vest that clinked when he walked. He was IT as far as I was concerned. I would have picked him above kings, movie stars, sports heroes — above all the other men in the world.

The minister who married us didn't like the whole set-up, that was obvious. Didn't like Jesse's outfit, didn't like mine — short skirt, loose silk top with no bra underneath, bare legs, clunky sandals, red toenails — didn't like Jesse's new bandmate, Ben, with his yellow alligator boots and dark glasses, or my friend Bonnie who kept chewing gum and giggling. It made me happy to be disapproved of; I felt young, unbelievably young and sexy and free. We didn't care about all the old, tired things that mattered to old, tired people. We were going to live at top speed, running after what we wanted. We weren't going to be afraid of anybody or anything. The more the minister frowned the more my nipples swelled and pressed against the inside of my thin silk blouse.

He was reading the marriage service out of an ancient book. It was full of old-fashioned phrases like "to thee I plight my troth." I had no idea what that meant, it seemed like a foreign language. But I was supposed to repeat it. I stumbled over the word "troth," and Jesse, who'd already got through his part without any mistakes, thought he should help me. "*Troth*," he whispered. That struck me as funny. All of a sudden the whole thing struck me as funny — the two of us standing there so solemnly, going through that antiquated ceremony, obediently mouthing all the words as if we believed in them. I couldn't help myself, I snickered. Jesse grinned. Ben snorted. And Bonnie, who'd already gotten a giggle from words like "yes" and "I do" gave an all-out, piercing shriek. The minister's lips went tight and his voice got stern, like a high school teacher telling off a rowdy class. "This is not a laughing matter," he said.

Oh no, no, we know that, we're sorry, we didn't mean anything — all of us, even Ben, rushed to apologize. But later, crossing the lawn toward Jesse's car, we were hysterical. "Did you see his face?" "I thought the poor fucker was going to choke!" "This is not a laughing matter!" "To thee I plight my *what?*"

I wasn't the one who'd suggested getting married, believe it or not. And I wasn't pregnant, either. The summer we met we'd been just driving those country roads, in the afternoon or at night, watching the highway disappear under the car, seeing the lights of the little towns spring up across the horizon. The car radio always seemed to be playing one song, Pat Benatar doing "We Live for Love." When you're nineteen you think the summer's twelve months long and Christmas won't come for twenty years. I watched him on dozens of stages, in dozens of dim bars or grandstands or hockey arenas, and it felt as if I could go on that way forever. He'd take a break between sets and we'd go outside. Sometimes we'd just stand against a wall and neck for a few breathless minutes, but other times we'd hurry to the van, fall across the tarps in the back and make fast, hard love, as if we were about to be shot and had to come one more time before we died. Then we'd go back inside and he'd climb onto the platform and start playing his guitar, moving its shiny body with his pelvis, caressing the strings with his long, lazy fingers, while I stood on the dark dance floor, swaying, entranced, half-asleep, half-dreaming.

Then one day, sitting at the A&W in Walbrook, eating burgers and fries, he said casually, "We could get married."

I was stunned. I swear it had never even occurred to me. That sort of thing seemed to have nothing to do with him and me. I said, "You're not serious."

He looked at me with his sweet, lazy smile. "Sure," he said. "Why not?"

That was his favourite phrase. Unless you could think of a good reason against it, you should just go ahead and do whatever came into your mind.

Mom said, "I knew it. Are you in trouble?"

I'd expected that to be her first reaction, but I pretended to be indignant anyway. "No! We love each other and we want to get married, that's all!"

She wouldn't turn her eyes away from the TV set. "Where do you think you're going to live?" she asked, staring at *Three's Company*.

That was the hard part. I rushed it out before it could stick in my throat. "Well, I was kind of thinking we could live here. Just for a while."

She didn't say a word. The only sound was the TV audience laughing uproariously at some unfunny joke.

"There's lots of room," I said. "And of course I'll keep helping with the expenses."

Nothing.

"Jesse's new band isn't too well known yet, so they're not making a lot of money right now," I said. "Once they build a following it'll be different. We're going to save up and eventually we're going to Vancouver and then maybe L.A. One of the guys in the band, Ben, has some contacts in the recording industry. They're going to make a demo tape and send it out, and they might be able to swing a record contract." I knew she wouldn't go for anything too grandiose, so I was trying really hard to sound practical and rational. I didn't even mention my ambition to be an actress or a dress designer. Even so, she turned to look at me with an ironic smile.

"Oh, Mona," she said. "Grow up."

She thought growing up meant accepting the fact that you'd never do anything exciting or wonderful as long as you lived. And she'd always been like that, as far as I could recall. Even in old photographs she always looked kind of grim, wouldn't smile for the camera, as if that were too childish and silly to be considered. Only one photo was different. She looked about fourteen or fifteen and she was with a bunch of other girls the same age, all dressed in middy blouses and shorts. She had her arm around one girl's neck, her head was back, her eyes were closed and her mouth was wide open in such a huge laugh that you could almost see her tonsils. That picture always seemed unreal to me, because even though I could see the facial resemblance I couldn't believe that girl could have turned into my mother, a woman whose strongest reaction to anything was a dry smile or a shake of her head.

Even the day my father died, she didn't gasp or shriek or burst into tears. He'd come downstairs that morning with his face so pale it looked almost yellow. I still remember how his fingers shook as he sat at the table. He said he'd had a terrible dream. He wouldn't tell us what the dream was about, but he was sure something bad was going to happen to him if he went to work. I don't think I'll go, he said, I think I'll stay at home. Mom treated it like complete nonsense, she wouldn't hear of it.

"Don't be ridiculous, Joe, anybody would think you were ten years old, trembling in your boots because of a dream! Grow up, be a man!" Now I realize that she might have been scared. Just five months before she'd had to leave her job in the Union Hospital cafeteria because of her emphysema, and his wages were all they had to survive on. That didn't occur to me at the time. I just thought that she was cruel and unfair. He listened to her, got dressed and went out the door. I can still see his expression, sick and scared, but he smiled at me and shrugged as if to say, what are you going to do? He was working for a farmer just north of town, helping to repair an old barn. He told the farmer about his dream and the farmer was more sympathetic than Mom. "Sure, Joe, take it easy today. Stay here by the shed and mix paint; don't go up on the roof with the other guys." I guess Dad was relieved; mixing paint on the ground wasn't much of a dangerous job, what could happen to you doing that? He saw a good-sized mixing pail sitting over by the side of the barn and went to get it. Just then one of the guys up on the roof dropped a iron bar. It rolled to the edge of the roof and fell off into the air, hurtled down, down, down, just as Dad was bending over to pick up the pail, and hit him in the back of the head. I don't know what his last moment was like. Did everything just go black, or did he have a second to be conscious of what was happening, a second when he understood that he'd been right, that sometimes you're right to be frightened by a dream?

Mom's face didn't move when they told her. After a minute or so, she just nodded and started tapping her fingers on the arborite tabletop. Her breathing got very harsh and raspy but she didn't say a word. Then I could hardly see her anymore for tears. She turned into a fuzzy shape sitting stiffly upright while

I yelled, "He told you he didn't want to go but you made him!" And someone, I don't remember who, started patting my shoulder, murmuring comforting words. Mom just kept sitting there, breathing like someone underwater.

Later we found out that Dad's accident wasn't even covered by workmen's compensation. Farm labour fell into the optional category and this particular farmer hadn't signed up for it. No private insurance either. He said he'd been farming for thirty years without a single problem, so he never thought anything like that was necessary. He felt bad and wrote us a cheque to "help out." Or maybe it was just to keep us from trying to sue. We used it to pay down the mortgage on the house. After that we were on our own.

If Mom ever felt guilty about insisting that Dad go to work that day, she kept it hidden. But when I told her I wanted to name Joey after him she said, "I'm not sure that's such a good idea, is it? Your father was never a lucky man."

I thought, how dare she? It was all her fault anyway! I remembered Dad's soft eyes, his smile, his big brown arms, his voice saying, "How's my girl?" I remembered the way he looked at Stuey Ferguson's wedding, sitting at a table in white shirtsleeves, laughing. I wanted my son to have his name. But maybe I should have listened to Mom after all.

Anyway, she didn't try to stop Jesse from moving in. She pretended not to like him, but I knew better. He always knew how to get to women; even my tough old mother wasn't impervious. He played his guitar for her, different types of music, not just rock but old-time blues, folk songs, even a few hymns. "What do you say, Blanche, any requests?" He always called her by her first name. He always complimented her on the meals she cooked. He always thanked her for everything. After a month or so, she stopped mentioning his haircut and his weird clothes and his tattoo.

I wonder what she thought some nights lying in the dark on the other side of the wall. She must have heard us. She must have known what we were doing when we went upstairs in the middle of the day "to take a nap." She never made a comment, never asked a question, never smirked or frowned or raised an eyebrow. It was as if she'd never heard of sex. God knows I'd never heard her and Dad make a sound.

That little bedroom, the one I'd slept in all my life, turned into something entirely new. I could smell his cologne on the sheets. He'd take off his rings and leave them on the bedside table, they'd glitter in the light from the window. His spangled vest would lie in a heap on the rug. He'd come home in the middle of the night, the door would open and his shadow would ripple across my legs; I could feel it as well as see it, as though even his shadow had heat. *Hi. How was it tonight? Great. Oh, I was really wailing, man. It was like I was riding a rocket. I wish you'd been there. Me, too.* Whispering because we didn't want to wake Mom up. Or maybe because we just felt like whispering. He'd lean over me. His hair would touch my breast. *Oh, that tickles. Yeah? Let me tickle you here too. How about here? And here? Oh yeah, yeah, yeah.* Beyond the window the snowy prairie rolled away toward the black horizon, the mercury dropped to thirty below. But in my room it was another long, hot summer night.

The band started to get more gigs, but we still couldn't seem to save any money. There were so many things to spend it on: meals in cafés, beers, clothes, studio rentals, $500 for a guy to design an album cover, $2000 for plating, pressing and packaging a thousand LPs with the band's best tunes, gas for the car, repairs to the van, presents for each other, airplane tickets to go to Winnipeg for a two-night stand that a friend of Ben's had set up, one thing after another. But we were young, we didn't worry, we had all the time in the world. Money was going to be falling into our laps before long. The band would get a recording contract and their first professional album would go platinum. I'd get parts in movies, or design clothes, or be a photographer like Linda McCartney. We'd be famous and rich. And in the meantime there were always rooms where we could go and shut the door. As long as we had that nothing else seemed very important.

In our second summer together I went with the band on tour. Full Fathom Five they called themselves that year, after a poem that Danny, the literary one, remembered from school. No one could explain what it meant but it sounded impressive, and the name looked good on the black and white album cover we'd had designed: *Full Fathom Five Rocks Tonight.* I could imagine future albums, blazing with colour because they'd be paid for by a big record company that could afford it: *Full Fathom Five: Live in New York City, Full Fathom Five's Greatest Hits.*

They were planning to play fifteen towns in Alberta and Saskatchewan, and come back semi-stars. I was the only wife or girlfriend who went along on that tour because the van would only hold one extra person, and it was my turn. I'd sit in the back seat with a magazine in my lap, taking an occasional gulp of warm beer, nodding in time to the car radio, watching the landscape roll by like an endless road movie, cinemascope and stereophonic sound, fields so yellow and skies so blue and clouds so white that they all seemed artificial. I had no doubt that every day was going to turn out sunny; every night would be clear and warm.

We pulled into the first town, a place called Cardinal, at four in the afternoon. It looked like a nothing place, even smaller and deader than Walbrook. But Jesse had it all figured out. "Radio station's CFTL. Afternoon deejay's name is Mike Tessiuk," he told us after consulting a little notebook he was carrying around in his breast pocket. We watched him as he crossed the street toward a pay phone in front of the post office. Everything he did in those days seemed to be full of confidence and style, his fluid straight-ahead walk, the way he flipped back the door of the phone booth, leaned against the glass and crossed his ankles, the way he slipped the notebook back into his pocket. I felt as if I could be happy doing nothing all day and night but watching him. He dropped his coin in the slot, spoke for a couple of minutes and came back. It all happened so quickly that we didn't think he could have had much luck. He kept a poker face, sliding in behind the steering wheel without a word.

"No dice?" Ben asked.

He turned his head, looked at us solemnly through his dark glasses, gave a heavy sigh and repeated the dialogue. "'Full Fathom Five? You guys playing tonight at the Diamond?' . . . 'Yeah, and we've got a record and we'd sure appreciate some airplay —'" He paused and we all waited. "'Sure, man, drop it off and I'll try to get it on before seven.'"

"Well — all right then!"

"Yeah!" Jesse said with a laugh.

This is how I remember the Diamond: a little place on the edge of town with a blue neon sign in one window, blinking toward the highway and an empty field. A chalkboard just inside the door with some writing on it: "Hamburger Deluxe special: $3.99. Live band: starting 10:00 P.M." Ben turning to look at the rest of us: "Wonder what time the dead band starts." Farmers sitting around in the dim interior, wearing baseball caps turned backward. Smells of cigarette smoke, beer, aftershave, and a whiff of disinfectant every time the washroom door swung open and closed. Bursts of music from the old juke box in the corner. The guys are at the back setting up and I'm alone at the bar, staring at a wall covered with autographed photos of other bands who once played the Diamond, feeling a little shaken because they are so many of them and some of them are so old that the edges are yellow. Dozens of guys and the occasional girl, standing with their instruments and drums, smiling eagerly or trying to look cool: The Boppers, Red Dawn, Mace, The Dark Knights, Howling Wolf, Bobby and the Rockets. I'd never heard of any of them and I can't help thinking that they must have been just like us, driving into town in a van packed with instruments and boxes of records they'd paid for themselves, ready to rock, thinking this was just the beginning of a wild ride to the top of the mountain, and what happened to them in the end? Wally, the owner of the Diamond, leans across the bar and says, "Do you guys have a picture I can put up?" Even though we have a whole box of autographed pictures in the back of the van I say no, because I don't want to see Full Fathom Five up there on that wall with all the other faded faces. But my second rye and ginger erases tremors and sad thoughts, I feel a buzz in my head, a tingling in my fingertips; I'm excited, I've been excited for hours, for days, and now the excitement has reached such a pitch of intensity that it's hard to sit still, my blood is beating, my knee is jerking in time to some weird internal rhythm, it's as though I'm about to perform myself. A new, younger crowd comes in, guys and girls, someone's cool sweaty arm brushes against mine as they pass and it feels like an electrical charge. Wally reaches out and strokes my shoulder. "It must be tough on you, sitting around waiting," he says. He thinks I'm cute, he's been giving me the eye since we first walked in. He's a short, overweight guy with thinning hair, but he excites me too. Everything excites me. "Another shot?" he says. "It's on the house." I smile at him. "Okay, thanks," I say in a throaty murmur. Then there's a loud guitar chord, a drum rattle, light comes up on the wooden platform and there they are, Ben holding the microphone, Titch with a cigarette behind his ear, twirling his drumsticks, Danny crouching down to check an amplifier, Steve taking a last swallow of beer, and Jesse with his head lowered, still tuning his guitar.

"Hi, everybody, great to be here tonight in the great town of Cardinal in the great province of Saskatchewan!" The kids in front give a cheer, pound the tables with their glasses. The farmers just stare.

"We're gonna start out with a song written by a member of the band, Jesse Maverick, right here!" Jesse raises his head, nods, flashes his sweet, lazy grin. And they launch into "Wild Road," the one I helped him with. I thought of one line, "Too lucky to die," and he said that one line gave him the shape of the whole song. Ben throws his head back to belt it out, Jesse moves back and forth across the stage, stopping occasionally to lean in to the microphone and provide harmony or to play a few bars on a harmonica. His vest flaps against his bare chest, his skin glistens under the ruby red overhead light, he's the sexiest man alive, and a couple of the girls at the front think so too, they're standing up and dancing in front of the stage, giving him seductive looks. One of them is pretty gorgeous, long streaked hair, tight jeans, gold bangles on her arms. But I don't feel worried, not for a second; I like it that these other women want him, it turns me on. Go ahead girls, flirt all you want, because he belongs to me. And how do I know? I just do. Because every few minutes he looks to the back of the bar where I'm sitting, hey Mona are you watching, do you like my moves, how about that little riff, do you think I'm good, do you want me, do you love me? All night his eyes seek me out in the shadows beyond the stage. I'm the one, I'm the only one.

That was the Diamond.

The next day we were all sitting in a roadside diner over plates smeared with leftover egg and hash brown potatoes, all of us a bit subdued, half asleep. I had a hangover — from too many rye and gingers, from the hot prairie wind, from his voice whispering come here, come here, come here, from his hands all over my body, from the swirling dark and the twisted sheets, from the roar of cars on the highway, their headlights making flowing waves of light across the ceiling of the motel room.

"So what's the next town?" Titch asked, staring into his coffee cup. He'd already asked that question twice before.

Jesse looked at the rest of us with a smirk.

"Green Lake," Ben said. "Shit, man, why don't you write it down?"

Titch set his cup down and rubbed his eyes. "Why should I?" he said. "I'm not driving, am I? Just wake me up when we get there."

While we were waiting for Steve to pay the tab, Ben turned around and said, "That bastard never did play our record, did he?"

"Didn't he?" Jesse said. "How do you know? We weren't listening to the radio every second."

"Well, I never heard him play it. Nobody I asked heard it. I don't think he played it. Shit, we drive all the way over there, tramp up two flights of stairs, then the bastard can't even bother to slap it onto the turntable."

Jesse shrugged. "That's the way it goes."

We were heading out the door. There was a pay phone on the outside wall. "Let me try," I said. "What's the number?"

Jesse handed me his notebook. The guys all stood there while I dialed. It was a really small radio station and they put me through to the deejay in a minute flat.

"Hi, Mike," I said. "This is Mona and I was wondering if you take requests? . . . You don't? Oh no. Oh, gee . . . Well, because I wanted to ask if you could play something by Full Fathom Five. My girlfriends and I saw them at the Diamond last night and we thought they were absolutely great. Especially the lead guitar, Jesse Maverick, he was red-hot, Mike, you wouldn't believe it!" The other guys snickered and rolled their eyes. Jesse smiled at them and shrugged modestly.

"They're doing another show at the El Rancho in Green Lake tonight and my brother's going to drive us over there so we can see them again. But we really wanted to hear something by them right now. They said they dropped off a record with you yesterday and, oh, Mike, if you could just play something from it, me and my girlfriends'll love you forever!"

Five minutes later, driving down Cardinal's Main Street, we heard the deejay's drawling voice say, "Well, we don't normally take requests until after ten P.M. —" Everybody yelled out loud and then Jesse shushed them — "but I just got a call from Mona, and she and her friends are real anxious to hear something by a new band called Full Fathom Five. They played the Diamond last night and tonight they're going to be at the El Rancho in Green Lake, so if you feel like a drive maybe you better head over there and check 'em out. So okay, Mona, this is for you and your friends, from F F Five."

"Wild Road" came pouring through the airwaves, out from under our dashboard, out of radios all over Cardinal, out of radios for miles around, Jesse's guitar chords, Ben's voice, Titch's drumbeat. It sounded just as good as it had in the basement of Mom's house when we first popped the record onto the stereo. No, even better. We were all laughing and cheering; Jesse had to pull the van over to the curb because we were in danger of crashing it. Too crazy to stop, too hot to slow down, too lucky to die! Ben's voice belted, as loud and confident as Mick Jagger's, Bruce Springsteen's, Robert Plant's. Titch leaned through the back window of the van, leaned so far he almost lost his balance and we had to hold on to the back of his jeans to keep him from falling out.

"Hey!" he yelled at all the passing cars and trucks, "Hey, listen to your radio!" And somebody turned up his volume and, sure enough, "Wild Road" pounded back to us across the pavement, as though it was coming from every corner of the town, from every door and window, and everything was moving to its beat.

In the middle of all the commotion Jesse looked at me in the rearview mirror, that kind of look you can only get from someone you're wild about, the kind that starts pulses of heat all over your skin, makes your breath stick in your throat, dries up your saliva so you can hardly swallow, makes your scalp tingle, makes it hard to smile because your face is trembling.

A few minutes later we were driving out of town, past the Diamond with its unlit sign, looking dusty and deserted in the daylight. All of a sudden I had an impulse.

"Hey, you know what?" I said, "Stop for a minute. I promised the owner one of these." I grabbed an autographed glossy of Full Fathom Five from the box in the back and took it inside. It didn't seem scary anymore to have that picture up on the wall with all the others. I wanted it to be there.

This is something else I remember from that tour. One of our last stops on the way home was an old dance hall in the middle of the prairie, halfway between Walbrook and the town of Forget, called Club 13. It looked completely deserted when we first drove up, as if it hadn't been used for twenty years. But there was a poster on the front door advertising a dance, "featuring Full Fathom Five." Sure enough, just as the band were setting up, the first cars started to arrive. I was standing at the open door, hearing the guitar chords and the hum of amplifiers behind me, and silvery streaks of chrome started flashing through the twilight, coming down the highway, along the side roads, one by one. A full moon rose over the wheatfields. Club 13 had windows that opened; you could stand on the dance floor, look up, and see that big old moon floating in the sky like a shiny silver dime. More and more people kept arriving, pouring through the doors, saying, "We could hear the music all the way to Forget!" They danced, they cheered, they went out for a smoke, they came back and shouted, "More! More!" When the music was quiet they were quiet, when it was loud they sang out the words. Jesse improvised a guitar solo and they chanted, "Jesse, Jesse." I could see his face, completely alive, completely free, his eyes shining so bright you'd have thought they were full of tears, except that he was laughing. He didn't want to stop playing; the show was supposed to end at one A.M. but every time the crowd yelled for more he and the band came back. It must have been almost three when they finally called it quits, and crossing the parking lot we saw that lots of people hadn't wanted to leave, they'd just fallen asleep in their cars. That was the greatest night we ever had.

Then I found out I was pregnant with Becky. That didn't fit in with any of our plans and I was really upset. I thought Jesse would be upset too. I thought he might want me to have an abortion, and I was ready to do it. I said to him, "I don't know how this could have happened! I've been taking the pill and I don't think I missed a single day. One or two at the most!"

He had a faraway look on his face and his lips were moving without making a sound. He was writing a song. The melodies just came to him, while he was driving or walking down the street or sitting in a bar. Sometimes he'd wake up in the morning with a particular tune going through his mind. He'd started to improvise on stage a lot more and the rest of the band had to play along. They didn't like it, but he said it took him places he'd never been before. Once in a while he'd snort a little coke afterwards to keep the feeling going. Once in a while I did too.

As soon as he heard the word "pregnant" he snapped to attention. "Great," he said. "It'll be fun to have a kid, why not?"

Maybe I should have been relieved or glad, but I wasn't. I felt a hard jolt of irritation. I think that was the first time I ever felt irritated with him — the first time I ever felt anything negative. I'd never thought of us as the mom and dad type, I'd thought he shared my opinion that we were way too hip and nonconformist for that kind of boring, provincial stuff. It seemed as if he'd responded too fast, without even thinking. He was so impractical, he thought life was easy and simple and he was wrong! But I was still at the stage where you don't want to accept that the guy you love has any flaws at all. You'd rather find fault with yourself. No, no, he's right. I'm being too uptight and cautious. We won't be typical parents. It *will* be fun!

He turned out to be a really warm and affectionate father. Sometimes when I was in a bad mood I told myself it was because he didn't really care enough, didn't feel any particular responsibility, left that all up to me. But maybe I was being unfair. The kids adored him. He was away a lot so when he came home it was an event. It's Dad! Dad's here! Doors banging, feet pounding down the stairs, screaming and shouting. He'd stagger through the back door with all three of them hanging on him, everybody laughing hysterically. His eyes would meet mine above Cory's head. With kids it wasn't so easy for me to go on the road with him anymore and I missed it, all of it, the van, the beers, the diners, the greasy french fries, the music, the snorts of coke, the intoxicated sex in anonymous motel rooms. My body would be twitchy and hot from nights of abstinence. His look would still make my mouth go dry, my heart throb. I'd try to find a sign in his face that he'd been with some other woman. I remembered them hanging around in front of the stage, smiling, moistening their lips, bending forward to show the tops of their breasts, I imagined their soft voices saying, "Hi, Jesse, I loved your music, Jesse." What did he do if I wasn't there watching? I wasn't so sure anymore; I had doubts. But when he came home he still looked at me as if I were the only woman he'd been thinking about.

One afternoon we were all in the kitchen. Becky was about six, Cory was a toddler and Joey was still struggling to stand up in his playpen. Becky was already so beautiful that strangers would stop me on the street to comment on it, and one eccentric woman even insisted on snapping her picture. I'd seen a cute outfit — powder blue shorts and a white top with little blue leaves on it — in the window of the Chic Shoppe downtown and brought it home for her to try on. Nothing pleased Becky more than new clothes, and blue was her favourite colour. She was standing on a chair to get the full impact of her appearance in the mirror on the back of the kitchen door when we heard a car in the driveway. Jesse had a couple of gigs out of town and wasn't due back until the next day. But Becky said, "Dad!" Sure enough, when I looked out the window above the sink I saw him coming up the path toward the house. Becky jumped off the chair and ran to the back door to fling it open. "Hi, Dad!" Cory tried to run too but lost her balance and fell flat. Even Joey started bouncing up and down, shaking the bars of the playpen. In came Jesse, carrying a boom box. "Hi, Dad, look at my new outfit!" Becky cried.

He looked at me. "The last gig fell through," he said. I couldn't help feeling a sharp twinge of disappointment, even exasperation, because that meant at least seventy-five bucks less in the kitty. Later on he'd need cash and I'd have to find it somewhere.

Becky wasn't concerned about any of that, of course, she hardly heard it. "Dad, Dad," she kept insisting, jumping up and down, "you're not looking! See, I've got a new outfit!"

He looked. He opened his eyes wide, clutched his heart, pretended to swoon. "Wow," he said. "Wow, Beck, you're a heartbreaker!" She laughed happily, a delicate pink blush spread up her neck into her cheeks. At that moment Bob Seger burst onto the boom box, singing "Betty Lou's Gettin' Out Tonight."

"Hey!" Jesse cried, turning up the volume. "Becky Lou!"

Becky laughed again, shyly, breathlessly. He grabbed her hand and spun her around. Cory gurgled with delight and tried to spin too. Joey squealed and clung shakily to the playpen railing. The music was so loud it made the window panes rattle, and Mom appeared in the kitchen doorway, her mouth open to tell us to quiet DOWN, for heaven's sake! But when she saw Jesse and Becky jiving, she couldn't say a word, she couldn't help but stand there smiling. Becky wasn't a good dancer, she was a bit stiff and tight, but Jesse moved her around with such speed and energy that it seemed to loosen her up, and every time Bob Seger sang "Betty Lou" Jesse sang "Becky Lou" on top of it. "Becky Lou!" he yelled joyfully. "Becky Lou!" Becky's little feet in white socks and white sneakers flashed across the worn linoleum, trying to keep up with the lightning-fast piano chorus, her long blonde braid whirling around her head like a rope of gold.

I wonder if Becky ever remembers that afternoon.

We have an old Instamatic photo, Jesse and the kids on the living room sofa. I never look at it, it hurts too much. But if I close my eyes I can see it so clearly it might as well be right in front of me. His shirt and shoes are off, his guitar is lying across his lap, and Becky and Cory are sitting on either side of him, pressed against him, looking up, because he's lifting Joey high in the air. He used to do that all the time, hold Joey in one hand and raise his arm; Joey would perch there on his dad's palm, smiling, not the least bit afraid because he was so absolutely sure his daddy would never let him fall.

No. Think of something else happy.

This is just a fragment — I never remember all the details, only that it's after sunset, and we're taking a drive. It's summer, you can smell cut grass. Becky and Cory are in the back seat; Joey is sitting on my lap, his feathery hair tickling my chin. Let's stop for ice cream, somebody says, so we pull into Dizzy Dee's, a little shack just off the highway where you can get the best ice cream on the face of the earth. I order a cone with two scoops of lemon-vanilla, my favourite, and the sweet, tart, creamy flavour melts into my tongue. Joey gets ice cream all over his face, even a little wisp on the tip of his nose. All of us are shadowy in my memory (because it's so long ago, because it's dusk?) but I can hear our murmuring voices, I can see the soft yellow glow of the ice cream, and the fields rolling away under the dark, velvety sky. On Highway 35 a solitary car passes, going fast, its headlights beaming. We won't be here forever, we'll be moving in another minute, soon we'll be speeding down the highway too. We haven't failed at anything yet, we haven't disappointed each other; our dreams are still so close, we still believe they'll all come true. And we're all together, eating ice cream. How could you help but be happy?

I don't know when I first realized that things were going to be a lot more complicated. I had to leave my job at the Starlite Theatre because working the evening shift at the Walbrook Inn paid better and we needed the money. All of a sudden I wasn't a teenager anymore, I'd somehow turned into a grown-up woman who filed an income tax return and listed grocery clerk and waitress (part-time) as her occupations. And maybe one day I understood that a grown-up woman with three kids was going to find it pretty tough to pack her bags, hit the road, have a new life. Maybe I faced the fact that even in Vancouver or L.A. it took more than daydreaming about movies to make you an actress, more than sewing your own dresses on a little machine to make you a fashion designer, more than snapping cute shots for the family album to make you a photographer. Maybe there was a day when I looked in the mirror, frozen with fear, and thought for the first time, I'll never be anything but this.

❧

"Look, you've got one solo and we're doing four of the songs you wrote, what more do you want?" Alan yelled one afternoon. Jesse was in a different band by then, the fifth one since I'd known him. They called themselves The Midnight Express. They were all sitting around at Mom's kitchen table. Titch Austin was the only other survivor from Full Fathom Five. The other guy, Mack, kept his eyes down. Jesse just stared, as if he wanted to burn a hole in Alan's skull.

"What do you think people come for?" Alan said. "A good beat, some fun, some dancing, a singer doing some songs they know! They don't come to sit through a dozen endless fucking guitar solos!"

Jesse said, "We're never going to get anywhere doing other people's material. We have to have our own sound and our own style, otherwise what's the fucking point? Does anybody want to record a group who just does covers of old Rolling Stones tunes?"

Alan gave a sarcastic laugh. "Does anybody want to record that shit of yours? How many places did we send that last demo tape, and not one answer, not one. Correct me if I'm wrong. There were seven people in the audience last night, and before long three of 'em had left! What's the fucking point of that? Is that joint ever going to have us back?"

"So you figure we should just cover the Stones and the Beatles to make sure we get our money, huh?"

"You're fucking right. What are we in this for, so we can all go into a trance listening to you jerk off? Who do you think you are, Jimi fucking Hendrix?" He looked at Titch and Mack. "Help me out here, will ya?"

Titch tried to be loyal. "Lots of people really go for Jesse's music," he said. "It's what they remember most."

"Oh yeah, they remember it all right," Alan said sarcastically. "Well, what about you, Mack, are you going to just sit there with your finger up your ass, or are you going to express an opinion?"

Mack cleared his throat. "Well, um, Jesse, you know I really get off on some of your stuff, but hey, let's face it, sometimes the paying customers aren't too cool, right? I mean . . ."

Jesse slumped way down in his chair, put on some earphones, closed his eyes, and nodded his head in time to some music only he could hear. When Alan started handing out shares of the minuscule take from the night before, he didn't even bother to open his eyes, just held out his hand. Alan slapped the money onto his upturned palm and he stuffed it in his shirt pocket without counting it, without even looking at it.

My flashes of irritation were coming more frequently by then, and I didn't try to argue myself out of them anymore. It's not that I didn't understand the way he felt; I was bored with the subject of money too. I didn't want to waste any time thinking about it but I wished we had more of it, just the same. We were still living with my mother, I was still holding down two jobs and, even though he was away working four nights out of every seven, he was always asking me if I had any extra cash. I was sick of having to be the practical one. I wanted to be crazy and reckless and temperamental sometimes too.

After the guys had gone, he said, "I'm getting fed up with these assholes. Maybe it's time for me to start looking around for a new band."

Hearing that made me feel so tired that I just wanted to rest my head on the table and cry.

"Alan doesn't give a shit about the music," he said. "Typical front man. All they can think about is attention and chicks and money. But the music is the only thing that really matters."

He looked at me, waiting for me to agree. Finally I nodded. Then he put the earphones back on and closed his eyes.

"Da-da," was the first word Joey said. The second was, "Boom." When he heard music from the stereo speakers he rushed over and put his ear against the mesh. When he was only two he could shake some maracas and dance around with what actually looked like rhythm. "That's my kid for sure," Jesse laughed.

They're so innocent. They run to you, their faces all lit up, so happy to see you. They think you're a giant, a hero, there's nothing you can't do. Sometimes I can still feel his little hands against the back of my neck. Sometimes I can still hear his little voice. "Look, Mommy! Watch me!"

If I hadn't had a party that day. If I hadn't let myself get all frazzled because Mom criticized the decorations in the living room. If I hadn't had those two rye and gingers to settle my nerves. If I'd watched him more closely. If I'd taught him better. If I'd served the cake a little earlier or a little later, if I'd kept the kids in the backyard, if I'd made sure they were playing a game, if I'd been better organized, if I hadn't been so careless, if I hadn't been so thoughtless, if I hadn't been so stupid. You keep thinking that way till you drive yourself crazy.

Okay. This is what happened. Jesse was late. Joey kept coming into the kitchen to say, "Where's Daddy?" I said, "He'll be here soon." If I'd just said, come here a minute, Joey, sit in Mommy's lap. If I'd held onto him for just a few minutes. But I didn't. I turned away; I heard his footsteps clattering down the hall. Oh, Joey, don't go, come back.

I decided not to wait any longer to serve the cake. I told Becky to put the candles on it. I started getting the plates and forks out of the cupboard. In the meantime Alan was dropping Jesse off. He parked across the street and Jesse got out of the car. They'd been arguing about something, as usual, and Jesse kept standing there. Joey must have heard his voice. He ran out onto the front step and said, "Daddy! Look what I got!" He was holding one of his birthday presents, a kind of metal figure that you could take apart and rebuild in different shapes. Jesse looked around, nodded, waved, but kept standing there arguing with Alan. Joey was excited, he wanted his daddy to see his marvellous new toy, he couldn't wait. We'd told him so many times about the danger, cars turning off the highway so fast. Don't forget, always look both ways, Joey! But he didn't that day, I suppose all he saw was his daddy standing so close. He ran into the street.

I heard Cory scream. I forget what she said, maybe it was No! or Stop! or just Joey! And after that a sort of thud, very faint, like a shot glass splintering. You wouldn't have thought it could be very important. But I knew. It's always your nightmare with kids, that you'll make a mistake, that you'll look away for one second, let your mind wander, and then it will happen.

I don't remember running. I don't remember what I did to get there, just that I was in the street, and Mom was standing at the curb, shaking and wheezing, holding Cory's face against her belly and trying to keep Cory's eyes covered, and there were a lot of other people too, and a woman was crying, saying, "He ran right in front of me, I didn't see him till it was too late, I slammed on the brakes but it all happened too fast, I'm sorry, I'm sorry, I'm sorry." Becky must have come running too, because I remember her standing there with her hand over her mouth, still holding the box of blue birthday candles. Jesse was on his knees, I saw his face, white as newsprint, his shoulders heaving and his chest going up and down, as though he were sobbing, except that his eyes were dry. Broken pieces of the metal toy were scattered on the road. My little boy saw me. He was terrified, I saw the awful terror and pain in his eyes. He tried to hold out his arms. He whimpered, "Mommy." He wanted me to pick him up, he thought that I'd be able to help him, that I'd take the pain away and make everything all right again.

You can't pull time backward. You can't take the clock hands and wrench them around, there's nothing you can do except crouch there on the blazing concrete, your head throbbing, the poisonous taste of rye in your mouth, thinking, oh please God, let it be two minutes ago, let me have another chance. But God doesn't hear you.

It's not fair. He never hurt anyone or anything, he was always so happy and laughing, he just wanted to be loved. Tell me why such a thing has to happen. Bad luck? Bad, bad luck? But you don't want to accept that, you can't believe it was just some kind of fluke, as if he was nothing, as if he was just a pebble that got knocked out of the way accidentally. That's impossible. I knew we must have done something terribly wrong. I knew what it was, too. We were too careless. We didn't pay enough attention, we thought of ourselves first. We were everything to him, but he wasn't everything to us. We always had other things on our minds. We had to be punished for it. But he was punished the most, that's the part that's so cruel. I hope that someday I'll be able to wipe it out of my mind, his little face that afternoon.

That's the only thing I want to forget though. I want to remember everything else, every minute of every day he lived.

LEAVING

JESSE

It's a long long road
Can't see the end
But I'm stayin' on it
Goodbye my friend

Breakin' out of this box
Nothin to hold onto me
Hundred twenty miles an hour
Only way to be free

No more bosses
No more fools
No more time clock
No more rules

On Highway 35

No more yes-men
No more cops
No more liars
No more props

On Highway 35

No more memory
No more pain

No more losses
No more gain

Just get on Highway 35

No more questions
No more fears
No more loving
No more tears

Just keep on going, keep on driving,
Don't stop, ignore the signs

On Highway 35
— "HIGHWAY 35," BY JESSE MASARYK, 1990

MONA   I didn't know what was going on in his mind. Later he wrote that song, "Am I to Blame?" I never had a clue that a thought like that had even occurred to him. If he'd asked me, I would have said yes, yes, you are to blame, and so am I for choosing someone like you. All of a sudden all the things I'd loved about him made me sick: the charm, the intensity about his music, the tattoo, the hair, the eyes, the body. They all seemed to signal his lack of weight. When he came into the room I couldn't look at him, when he said something I could hardly bring myself to answer. I was relieved when he left the house, hoped he'd stay away for hours.

At the same time I felt so lonely, it was worse than dying. I'd lie in bed at night with an ache all through my body, and even though I couldn't see out the window from where I was, I knew that past the thin curtains was a field of grass, and beyond that was the highway, and beyond that was Green Hill Cemetery where my little boy was in a box underground. I thought of his curly hair, his long eyelashes, his plump little hands, all still and in the dark. If it rained I imagined the rain falling on the grass on top of him; if it was windy I imagined the leaves blowing over his grave; if the night was warm and peaceful I imagined the warmth and peace penetrating down through the earth and comforting him. I wished I could believe in God and heaven so that I could imagine he was somewhere up in the clouds, happy, waiting for me. But I couldn't believe in that. I knew I'd never, never see him again in all eternity.

Then the bedroom door would open and I'd turn my face to the wall and pretend to be asleep. I'd lie there with my eyes shut tight, listening to Jesse undress, saying to myself, he's forgotten already, he never thinks of it, he's so stupid and shallow he doesn't even realize that nothing will ever be the same. So self-absorbed that he had to be late even on his son's birthday. So busy arguing about some unnecessary, unimportant thing that he couldn't even turn around and say, "Wait there, Joey! I'll be right over!" When the bed sagged under his weight I felt all my muscles contract in rejection. Selfish, I thought. Bastard. Disgusting. He let out a sigh. I hate you, I thought. How dare you sigh. After awhile he seemed to be asleep. How nice to just fall asleep, I thought. How nice to have no feelings, to put everything behind you. You don't have any idea, you don't know what love means. I'd move as close to the edge of the bed as possible. Then tears would come into my eyes and trickle silently onto the pillowcase. And on and on it went, the freight train whistle, the awful, long, drawn-out sound echoing across the desolate prairie, like a human voice wailing through a sort of emptiness that had no peace in it, no hope, no mercy.

He'd sit in the basement for hours. We'd hear the guitar, and his voice humming or singing. You can still sing, I thought. You can still play. The smell of dope would come drifting through the crack under the basement door. I'd be thankful that Mom was up in her room lying down. As soon as I heard him coming upstairs I'd grab Cory's hand, go out into the yard and shut the door behind me. Becky took her cue from me, I guess. In a matter of moments she'd be out there too, sitting on the swing. One day Cory said, "Mommy, are you mad at Daddy?" and Becky answered, "It's all *his* fault what happened to Joey!" Cory turned to me. "Is it?" she said.

I should have said, "No, it wasn't anyone's fault. It was just a terrible accident." But I didn't really think that, so I couldn't force the words out. The only answer I could give was to shrug my shoulders. Then I looked around and saw Jesse inside, watching us through the kitchen window. He wouldn't have been able to hear what we were talking about, but I suppose he felt what we were doing, we three on the outside of the house, looking at him without smiling, turning our faces away.

One afternoon he brought home a bag of long johns. "Look what I've got, Blanche," he said, waving it in the air. Mom didn't seem angry toward him like the rest of us, but something had gone out of her, some kind of energy and will. She spent a lot more of her time lying down. She gave him a half-smile and shook her head. "I don't have much of an appetite for sweets these days," she said.

He looked startled. He wasn't used to having his gifts rejected. We don't want your lousy doughnuts, I thought. Go to hell. The greasy bag sat on the kitchen counter all day and all night, untouched.

He stayed away longer, he came home later. Fuck every

woman you see, I thought. Go ahead. It's the only thing you're good at anyway.

I had a dream that I walked into the backyard and Joey was there, playing with his trucks. My heart almost stopped from joy. I said, "Oh Joey, oh sweetie, it was so terrible, I thought you were dead!" He turned his head and laughed, his loud gurgling laugh with the high note at the end. I opened my eyes in the dark, still trembling with happiness, and then I smelled the cold stillness of the house and thought, oh God, it was only a dream, he is dead, he is dead. At that moment the bedroom door creaked and Jesse came in, reeking of stale tobacco, booze and sweat. I turned on my side, fast.

"Are you awake?" he whispered.

I didn't answer.

 ❧

It was a Sunday afternoon. He stood in the kitchen and told me he was going to Alan's to talk over some things. I was making sandwiches.

"You don't want lunch then," I said with as little expression as possible.

"No. Thanks, but we'll likely just grab something downtown." He kept standing there, as if he expected me to ask questions or make some sort of comment. Finally I had to look around. I saw with one glance that he'd taken something, maybe downers to calm himself after getting high the night before. I turned away without a word. Just go, I thought. Get out. I heard the screen door click. Through the window above the sink, I saw him unlock the Chevy with one easy twist of his wrist, I saw him swing his body into place behind the wheel. I remembered when I first knew him, when I was so dazzled that every movement he made cut into my heart. You fool, I told myself. You stupid slut. He made you cream your jeans, and you thought that was all you'd ever want. Now here you are. He plays the guitar, he writes songs like thousands of others, big deal. He's over thirty and not going anywhere. What a miserable failure. But he's so full of himself he can't even see it. And now he's killed your little boy.

I don't know why, I can't explain it, heaping abuse on both him and myself gave me some kind of relief. It was like I had to beat both of us with the heaviest, roughest club I could find, for Joey's sake. Somebody had to pay and we were the logical ones. The more brutal the insults the better I liked it, the more right it felt.

The car, the old red Chevy, pulled out of the driveway, metal glinting in the pale autumn sun. It was four months to the day after Joey died.

A little later Becky came in. Cory, Mom and I were sitting at the kitchen table, eating our tuna fish sandwiches. Becky flung herself into a chair, took a sandwich and looked at it with distaste. Then she said, "Where'd *he* go?" She'd started referring to Jesse that way.

"To Alan's," I said.

She gave a snort, put her sandwich down untouched and started to kick the table legs with both feet.

"Do you have to do that?" I asked. She stopped kicking and folded her arms across her chest. Her eyes looked pure blue in the light from the window, the exact shade of Jesse's but cooler, clearer.

A lot of people in town knew the old red Chevy. Later several people said they'd seen it that afternoon; on the road to

English Lake, in front of the Regis Hotel, on the highway near Green Hill Cemetery. A guy named Irwin who worked in the 7-11 at Four Corners said Jesse stopped by about 5:00 and bought a bag of grapes. That was the last time anybody in Walbrook laid eyes on him.

I was furious at first, but not worried. He'd stayed away for days before. I kept expecting the phone to ring, I was prepared to slam the receiver down in the middle of his explanations and excuses, I was almost looking forward to it. But he didn't phone. A week passed. In all our years together he'd never gone that long without getting in touch with me. You creep, I said to him in my mind, now you're forcing me to call Alan, and you know I hate talking to Alan. This is the last straw.

"You're kidding," Alan said. "You haven't heard from him?" I heard a booming stereo in the background, and lots of loud voices as though a party was going on, even though it was the middle of the afternoon.

"No, I haven't, Alan, that's why I'm calling you. He hasn't been home since he got together with you last week. What happened?"

"Look, just the usual bullshit, okay? I told him we had a great offer from this club in North Dakota and he pissed all over it and walked out. Right? Anything else you want to know?"

"He didn't say anything about leaving town?"

"He said he was tired of playing 'It's Only Rock 'n Roll.' That's our fucking signature tune. Nope. Tired of it. The North Dakota guy wants us to do lots of oldies, he's having an oldies week. He's paying fifteen hundred bucks for a three-night week-end, so hey, I'll do oldies, right? It's only one fucking weekend.

But nope, not Masaryk. No oldies. He'd rather clean toilets than do oldies, he says. Fuck. Where does he get off, huh? I'm telling you, I'm fed up with this self-righteous bullshit and so are the other guys. If you do anything to make a few bucks you're selling out. If you try to give people what they want you're selling out. The only thing that isn't selling out is sitting in a basement somewhere playing weird shit that no one else wants to hear. Well, you tell him that we're taking the gig in North Dakota and we're going to play oldies, and if he wants to go, fine, and if he doesn't that's fine too. Okay?"

After he'd hung up on me, I sat in the gloomy kitchen, listening to the dial tone. For the first time I felt a prickle of fear. Then I heard someone in the doorway and turned my head. Becky was standing there, her pale hair all windblown, spraying out over the shoulders of her purple velvet coat.

"I hope he never comes back!" she said. She sounded as if she meant it, but her eyes looked so hard and bright that I thought she might be trying to hold back tears. Before I could answer she whirled around and ran up the stairs.

Those words — "never comes back" — repeated in my brain. Once he told me about how he left Edmonton. He was driving home after a party and took a wrong turn. He'd gone the same way a million times, but that night he wasn't thinking and made a mistake. He had his guitar in the back seat. He had a jacket and his wallet. That was all. He drove to the edge of the city, then out onto the highway. It was long after midnight; there were no other cars on the road, it stretched out ahead of him, free and clear. He thought, why don't I keep going for a while? By 8 A.M. he was five hundred miles away. "And I never went back," he told me. Wow, I thought, how thrilling, how romantic.

The kitchen was quiet. I could hear the hum of the electric clock. It was late fall and every day the dark came earlier.

He couldn't leave me that way, I said to myself. He couldn't do that to me.

Three weeks passed, then four. The days seemed agonizingly long. I'd come home from work and lie on the sofa, watching TV with Mom. That was the only thing I had enough energy for. Every time the phone rang blood rushed to my heart until it felt ready to explode. But the person calling was never Jesse.

At night I lay on my back with his empty place beside me, listening to the freight train whistle. Never coming back. Never coming back. That's what I thought it said.

You get so angry you can't sit still. *So this is what you're really like*, you say to this absent person who's betrayed you. *So this is you. You can walk away and not look back. You can leave three children — yes, three, because he's still here, even though you killed him. Why should you care though, just hit the road. You couldn't even say goodbye, you coward. Well, go to hell then. I'll forget you, see if I don't. I'll find someone better than you, so much better than you. I'll forget you so completely that even your name will be wiped out of my mind. We'll do fine without you, it's better this way, in fact I'm glad you're gone. Singing, dancing, having a great time. So glad!*

Then something happens — you hear a song on the radio, or see an old photograph in a drawer, or find a pair of silver-toed boots in the back of the closet — and the pain hits you by surprise, like a punch that you didn't see coming. You can't get your breath, you can't swallow, all your nerve endings hurt, your eyes burn as though they've got bits of glass in them. You ask yourself, how can I go on living?

You wake up from a restless sleep, you think you heard a

footstep on the stairs. You think, he's back! You think, oh, thank God!

But it's only old boards settling, it's only wind under the door.

You speak to him again, not so angry this time, injured instead, incredulous. *How could you do it? And not even say a word? Did you stop loving me? How could that be possible? Where are you? Can you walk along a street in some other city, can you make a joke, can you eat a burger, and never think about me, how I feel, what I'm doing? Can you close your eyes at night and not ask yourself if Becky misses you, or if Cory cries herself to sleep? Doesn't your body still want me, don't you remember all those crazy nights, don't you remember that once you said, "You're killing me and I'm dying happy?"*

But you remind yourself that you hadn't made love with him for months, not since the day Joey died. And that last afternoon when he stood in the kitchen, you hardly looked at him, you hardly said a word. It's your fault he left; that's obvious. So you try something new in these conversations that you carry on in your head. *I didn't mean it,* you tell him, *not a single thing. I'm sorry, please forgive me, please give me a chance to explain. Please phone me, please come home, please, please, please.*

But still the phone doesn't ring, and every day the silence seeps through your pores, taking up more space, crowding out everything else.

⁓

I had to work on Christmas Eve. Talk about depressing. There were three people in the café, two old men and one old woman, all sitting at separate tables. One of the old men was quiet, barely raising his head from his plate, but the other man and the woman were both eager to talk, catching desperately at every pleasantry I made, ready to discuss the weather or politics or any other subject for as long as they could stretch it out. Beyond the plate glass windows the parking lot was full of swirling snow.

Will I get old here? I asked myself. Will I spend my whole life looking out at this parking lot? When I'm sixty will I still be standing here, holding a coffee pot, wearing a pink uniform with a tag saying, Hi! I'm Mona?

I was always talking to Jesse in my head, arguing, explaining, pleading. *We were supposed to go together*, I said to him. *It's not fair. I wasn't supposed to be left here all alone.*

At eleven o'clock I had to close up. The old woman was the only one in the place by then. "Merry Christmas!" she said bravely as she went ahead of me out the door. I saw her picking her way down the icy sidewalk, probably on her way back to some tiny apartment, to a little Christmas tree on a stand and an old movie on TV, one with a happy ending.

Everybody was in bed when I got home. Our Christmas tree was unplugged. The whole house was quiet and dark. Of course I thought of the Christmas before, of course it made me want to cry. Jesse had played a rock version of "Silent Night," thumping on the body of his guitar with his hand, and Joey had tried to play along on his favourite gift, a bright red toy piano. "That's right, Joey!" everybody encouraged him. "Good boy, Joey!" The memory of all that sound and gaiety was so strong it almost made an echo in the dim hallway.

There was writing on the notepad beside the phone. I walked over with a flutter in my stomach. I thought that, since it was Christmas Eve, Jesse might finally have phoned. But the message was from Mom. "Don't forget to turn down the thermostat." That was all.

&

So then you tell yourself, okay. It's over. That's life. People leave people all the time, do you think you're the only one? Pull yourself together. Get on with it.

The days get longer, the air gets milder. The first leaves start to show on the trees. There's a new guy who keeps coming into the café, he always talks to you, tells you you're looking good, you think, well, well, I'm not dead yet. Another waitress tells you that this same guy owns a used-car dealership in Alden. So he'd have a few bucks. You think what it would be like to have a few bucks for once.

❧

One afternoon in June I was sitting on a bench in the municipal park, eating my lunch, eating it fast because the Co-op only gave me a half-hour lunch break. I saw a battered green car pull up to the curb and out of it stepped Titch Austin, Jesse's old bandmate. I hadn't laid eyes on him for months, but he looked like exactly the same comically sad, sadly comical little guy. He started to walk straight toward me, and I knew he wasn't just coming to say hello. He had some news. I put down my sandwich. My hand was shaking. It seemed to take him a long time to cross the lawn.

"Hi, Mona," he said.

"Hi, Titch," I said.

"I wanted to tell you, I saw Jesse."

So there it was. He wasn't dead, he hadn't disappeared from the earth, he could be seen, he could be talked to. I wanted to ask questions, but my mouth didn't feel ready to form the words. I just looked up at Titch, squinting in the sun.

"He's in Toronto," Titch said.

"Toronto," I repeated. My voice sounded like it belonged to

someone else, someone dry and unconcerned. I waited for him to go on. I tried to prepare myself for the unspeakable pain of hearing that Jesse looked great, that he had a girlfriend and a recording contract, that he was driving around in a flashy new convertible with the top down, happy as a king in the big city, doing all the things we dreamed we'd do.

"He's in bad shape," Titch said. "I think he's on something."

"What? You mean, like coke? Not smack?"

"A combo maybe," Titch said. "He seemed really out of it. He could hardly talk straight."

I just sat there, staring up into the bright sunlight around Titch's head.

"I said, man, what are you doing here?" Titch told me. "He said he didn't know. He kind of laughed. He said, this is where I ran out of gas money. I said, fuck, man, what's the matter with you? He just kind of shrugged his shoulders. I said, are you playing anywhere? Nope, not at the moment. Hocked his guitar. I said, well, geez, man, what are you going to do next? He said, have another beer I guess. I said, what about Mona, don't you think you should at least give her a call? He said, actually I think they're better off without me. Really, it didn't look good at all. I thought I should tell ya."

He'd written down an address. *Garden Hotel, Queen Street East.* He wasn't sure if Jesse would still be there, but it was something anyway, maybe it would help me track him down, if I wanted to. I said, "Thank you, Titch."

He hesitated, shifting from one foot to the other. "I'm sorry I didn't do more," he said. "I told him he should get some help to kick, but you know what he's like."

"That's okay, Titch," I said. "Don't worry about it. Take care."

I put the piece of paper in my pocket. Then I went back to

work. At six o'clock I went home and had supper with Mom and Becky and Cory, as usual. I didn't tell them anything. After we'd done the dishes, I said I was tired and was going upstairs to lie down. They looked at me oddly, because that wasn't something I'd normally have done.

I lay on the bed, looking through the top window pane. There was still light in the sky. It was almost summer. I must have fallen asleep. It seemed to me I was sitting on the front step, and it was twilight, summer twilight, and I could hear music from the fair, and I felt sad because it reminded me of Jesse. But then, in the distance, there was a clinking sound, a faint tinkling like wind chimes, or like sequins rippling in a warm breeze, and down at the corner, at the end of the street, I saw someone walking and then pausing in the shadow of the poplar tree. He had spiky yellow hair, and he was wearing a black vest covered with silver coins. He just stood there; he didn't come any farther. Oh, baby, I thought, I knew it was you, I knew you couldn't really leave me.

I woke up in darkness. The window was open, the smell of cut grass drifted over the window sill. I heard voices in the next room. It had to be quite late, and Becky and Cory should have been asleep. I got up without even thinking; I was going to ask them what they thought they were trying to pull.

They were talking so softly it was hard to tell their voices apart.

"Gee, is it ever quiet. What's that?"

"Just a car out on the highway."

"How come we can hear it so plain, Becky?"

"Because at night you can hear things from far away. That's what I'd like to be doing right now. I'd like to be driving down the road in the dark, really fast, just going, going, going."

"Maybe that's how *he* felt."

"Oh, who cares? I'm closing my eyes now."

"Good night, Irene, good night, Irene . . ."

"Shut up and go to sleep, Cory."

". . . I'll see you in my dreams."

I stood in the hall for awhile but they didn't say anything more. And then I knew what I was going to do.

Mom was against me, of course. I wanted to leave Becky and Cory with her, just for a little while.

"Just until I find him and get settled," I told her. "Then I'll send for them."

But she wouldn't bend one inch. "You think you can go on like a teenager forever, but you can't," she told me. "You have to grow up someday. You have to learn. You've got two kids and they should come first."

I said, "They do come first. I'm doing this so they can be with their father."

"Don't you have any pride?" Mom asked. "He walked out on you. And now you want to go running after him, cap in hand. I wouldn't do it, let me tell you."

"I know you wouldn't," I said. "Look, Mom, I helped out after Dad died, I quit school and went to work full-time. I did-n't mind doing it, I wanted to. But now you're okay, you've got your pension and everything, and now I need your help. It's not that much to ask. If Becky and Cory could just stay here with you for a couple of months, until I —"

"No," Mom said. "I'd help you with something sensible, but not this. It's up to you to look after your kids. You're their mother. Either take them with you or stay here."

"All right," I said. "Thank you, Mom. Thank you very much for all your support. Thank you very much for always under-standing."

When she heard the news Becky jumped off the sofa and screamed, "Forget it!" at the top of her voice.

"Look," I said, "this is what we're going to do, so get used to it."

"I'd rather kill myself!" Becky shrieked. Cory stared at both of us and burst into tears.

The next day I went downtown and bought a second-hand car for five hundred dollars. That was half my savings right there. So I had five hundred dollars left to drive all the way to Toronto with two kids, buy food, find a place to stay, all that. But the more trouble everybody gave me, the more determined I felt. Nothing in the world was going to make me back down. "I'll get a job as soon as we get there," I told them all. "I've never had any trouble getting a job."

Becky wouldn't pack. I went into her room and packed things for her. She sat on the bed with her arms folded. She said, "It doesn't matter, I won't go."

I tried to appeal to her. "Oh Becky, come on. Your dad needs us. Don't you want to see him?"

"No," she said. "You do whatever you want, but I'm staying here."

"Where?" I said. "Grandma doesn't want you." I shouldn't have put it so bluntly, but she really made me furious.

"I'll sleep in the park!" she said. "I'll get clothes from the Salvation Army! I'll go to the Co-op store and ask for scraps! Anything would be better than going with you!"

"Don't be such a brat," I said. "Do you think this is easy for me? This is really hard and you're making it worse." I heard a quaver in my voice. But Becky wasn't moved. She was just as tough as Mom.

"I'm not going and you can't make me," she said.

"You'll do what I tell you," I said. The same thing Mom always used to say to me, the thing I vowed I'd never say.

The day we left, Becky locked herself in the bathroom and wouldn't come out. No threats or pleas would work. Finally I had to get a neighbour guy to take the lock apart. It was a muggy day; there was thunder in the air. Or maybe I only think there was thunder because everybody was so angry. Mom wouldn't come out of the house. She didn't even stand at the window to see us drive away. Becky sat in the back seat with her arms folded, breathing hard, her face scarlet, her pale hair all dishevelled because I'd had to drag her down the stairs and literally shove her into the car. Cory chose the last moment to pee her pants and I had to open three different boxes to find her some clean blue jeans.

But finally we were ready and I stuck the key into the ignition. Then on impulse I leaned out the window and yelled at the top of my voice. "So long, Walbrook! Goodbye, Mom!" I screeched the tires pulling out of the driveway. We were off.

So I did it. Even though everybody fought me, even though no one understood, even though I had no idea what would happen, I loaded up that old car and set out. When I look back now at that person I was then, I can hardly even believe it was me, but I feel kind of touched, kind of impressed and proud. That person didn't just sit there, she didn't stay in the same safe hole all her life. She took a chance. She walked out of the house she'd lived in for thirty years, got into her rattletrap car and drove out onto Highway 35. She always said she'd leave, and one day she finally did. Rain had started to fall but that didn't stop her. Her two kids were confused and upset but she felt sure it would work out all right in the end. She drove past the cemetery and for a second it was as if she could see right through the trees, all the way to the back fence where the little grave was with its little marker. But she thought, he isn't really there. He's coming with us too. And she stepped on the gas. She had a lot of ground to cover that day. She refused to grow up, she refused to say, this is all I can get. She was going after the man she loved because he was the one she wanted, no one else would do. She was going to shoot out into the world and do amazing things after all. God, she was like a character in a movie!

It didn't rain very long. In about ten minutes the sun came out, and the puddles on the road shone like gold all the way to the horizon.

II

ARRIVING

JESSE

This is a good day
Someone's been watching over me
Picked me up right off the ground
Told me I was free

So I ain't got a headache
Ain't got bad breath
Ain't got a hangover
Ain't scared to death

This is a real good day
Sun came out after weeks of rain
Gonna lie on the beach this afternoon
And tomorrow I might go to Spain

— "GOOD DAY," BY JESSE MASARYK, 2000

MONA   I woke up out of a sound sleep. It was still early. The sun was shining. "Shall I phone and tell them I'm not coming today?" I asked Jesse.

He laughed. "Well, what do you think?"

"But didn't you want to sit on it for a few days?"

"So? You don't have to go into details. Just tell them you're sick."

"But I used up all my sick days in February when I had the flu."

He looked at me. "Who cares?"

Then it struck me, what it was going to be like. Who cares? I didn't have to worry whether Dominic would be mad, or dock my pay, or even fire me. I didn't have to worry about anything Dominic said or did, ever again. Dominic could go piss up a rope!

There was a pigeon sitting on the fire escape railing, right outside the window. Its feathers gleamed, the colour of amethysts, of emeralds. The sun was already hot. But that didn't matter either, because we could buy an air conditioner. Air conditioner, hah! We could buy a whole new house, with a swimming pool! We could buy airline tickets and fly to the north pole if we felt like a breath of cool air! We could do any crazy thing that came into our heads!

"This is really happening, right?" I said. "I didn't just dream it."

"We should lock the ticket up somewhere," Jesse said. "Only you and I should know where it is."

"Oh my God, I think I just left it on the kitchen table last night!" I threw back the sheet and started to get up, but he grabbed my arm.

"Don't worry, I've got it right here." He'd laid it on the bedside table under his wallet. I saw all those precious numbers, circled in pencil. Such a little scrap of paper it was, to mean so much, to change everything! I was scared to see how fragile it looked. It could catch fire and burn to ashes, it could be stolen, a gust of wind could blow it out the window and into someone else's hands.

"Maybe we should cash it in right now," I said. "Right this morning, before something happens to it."

"No, no, I think that's a lousy idea. I was always so dumb about this kind of thing before. This time I want to be smart.

You have to be prepared. You can't just walk in there and collect a cheque for six million dollars and then walk out onto the street again. You have to know exactly what you're going to do and have everything planned in advance."

He was very brisk, business-like, sure of himself. I hadn't seen him like that for years. In fact, I'd never seen him like that. It almost seemed as if he'd won the lottery before, as if he was used to handling large sums of money.

"Well, where should we put it then, to be sure it's safe?"

"I've been thinking about that," he said. "Maybe we should take it to the bank and put it in a safety deposit box."

I saw us going down the rickety stairs and out onto the street, with the ticket in his frayed wallet or in the compartment in my purse, the one with the broken zipper. I pictured us turning over that fragile bit of paper to someone at the neighbourhood bank, then walking away, leaving it behind. I thought, no, we shouldn't do it that way, that would be completely disastrous. It wasn't logical; it was one of those gut feelings you get sometimes, those feelings that are so powerful no sensible argument can shake them.

"No," I said. "Not a safety deposit box."

"Why not?"

"You know what? I don't want to take it anywhere. I won't feel secure if it's out of our hands. I think we should keep it with us until we're ready to claim the money."

"Here in the apartment? That's kind of risky, isn't it?"

"We'll hide it somewhere safe. As long as we're the only ones who know where it is, it'll be all right. Won't it?"

"Okay. And I've been thinking, maybe we should wait a while longer before we tell Becky and Cory. You know what kids are like, they don't mean to blab, but they can't resist, they have to spill it to somebody. Let's just keep it between us till we get everything sorted out. A couple of days anyway. Maybe on Friday we'll claim the money."

We were both sitting up in bed by that time, facing each other, like two kids conspiring. "Friday," I repeated. "Friday we'll claim the money."

The lunatic who lived below us let out a yowl. He did it so often that neither of us reacted. But suddenly I thought, soon we won't have to listen to him, not for the rest of our lives.

"Okay, where should we hide it?" I asked.

He shrugged. "I don't know. You think of somewhere."

I tried to remember movies I'd seen, the places people hid money, jewellery, treasures. Beneath the floorboards? Behind a secret panel in the wall? In a shoebox? Under the mattress? Scarlett O'Hara hid money in a baby's diaper when the Yankees were coming. But we didn't have a baby in diapers.

All of a sudden I knew what to do. "Come on," I said.

It was as if Joey could be part of it somehow. His little face smiled at me from the cheap metal frame. He was standing on the back step of Mom's house in Walbrook, squinting in the sunlight, his hair blowing in the breeze like yellow feathers, my sweet little boy. Through the years I'd sometimes had this fantasy that he was nearby watching over us, feeling bad if we were in trouble, trying to send good things our way. It occurred to me that maybe he'd sent us the lottery ticket. I know that sounds dumb. But it just seemed right — absolutely ideal — to put the ticket in the picture frame, hidden between the backing and the photo. I felt as if he'd protect it and keep it safe for us.

"There," I said to Jesse. "Perfect."

Becky came out of the bedroom. I put the picture back on the shelf. She was rubbing her eyes, still half asleep. She saw us in the living room. I guess it probably looked a bit strange, both us standing there all bright and alert at nine o'clock on a Sunday morning.

"What's with you two?" she asked. Morning wasn't her best time, she was always grumpy and disgusted with everything.

It was really hard to keep quiet. Really hard not to run over to her, grab her by the shoulders, scream the news out loud. But I controlled myself. I thought Jesse was right, we shouldn't get them excited until everything was confirmed.

"Nothing," I said. "Why?"

She stared at us. Probably we were both grinning like idiots. No wonder she was suspicious. "What's going on?"

Jesse shrugged and again I said, "Nothing." But I couldn't keep a sort of giddy laugh out of my voice. "No, really. Nothing."

She stared for another moment, not smiling, stone faced. The words rushed into my mouth, ready to spill out, Becky, Becky, you'll never guess, something wonderful's happened! But it was too soon. She shook her head and turned away with a sharp twist of her shoulders. "Fine," she said. "What do I care?"

REBECCA   Artemis has pink walls and very pale pink shades on the lights. That's because most people look better with a little added colour. When a customer is trying something on and sees her reflection all soft-edged and rosy, she thinks, wow, I look great in this. And out comes her credit card.

But that day I was in a bad mood and sick of being tactful. One woman annoyed me with her attitude, very superior and bossy, bring me that, take this away, I said *green*, not *blue*. That type. Usually I have myself under control but that afternoon it got to me. She put on a dress I really loved, and she looked like a cow in it. It was too good for her. She was forty-five or fifty and heavy, with big tacky rings on her fat fingers. It made me sick to see her preening, turning to look at herself from different angles. That was my cue, I was supposed to say, oh it really suits you, or, oh it looks very elegant or, oh it's a perfect fit. Instead I said, I think maybe it's a little young for you.

Which it was.

She was outraged, of course. She told Erika that I was a snotty bitch and she didn't plan to shop in Artemis ever again. Then she flounced out onto Queen Street and huffed away. Erika was a bit peeved and asked me if I had my period. No, I didn't. It wasn't that. Maybe it was because Wayne still hadn't phoned me to apologize for the night before, so it was obvious he didn't care how I felt, he wasn't even going to consider the idea of us moving in together. Maybe it was because I was asking myself how much longer I'd have to go on the same way, waiting on jerks, doing their bidding and taking their abuse like a slave, working, working, always working, even on a beautiful Sunday afternoon when most people were sitting in sidewalk cafés enjoying the sunlight. Maybe it was because that morning as I was leaving I heard Mona phone in sick, even though she obviously wasn't sick, even though I knew she had no sick time left. Completely irresponsible; forty years old but who'd ever guess it from the way she behaved sometimes. And Jesse obviously had no intention of going to work either, even though he'd just got a call back at the Putnam Warehouse and was actually supposed to be bringing in some money for a change. Maybe it was because of how both of them were acting, so cute and giggly and secretive, obviously cooking up one of their schemes, obviously forgetting that their schemes always turned sour. Maybe it was because I was asking myself why I always got the bad breaks, starting with parents like them for example.

I'd stopped calling them Mom and Dad long ago; they didn't deserve it. They were more like a really annoying older brother and sister, constantly doing stupid things, getting into trouble and having to be bailed out. I was sick of it.

I put the dress back on the rack. The fabric was soft as a feather. I would have liked to wear it with nothing underneath. I thought how it would feel, so light and smooth against my skin that it would be like walking naked through summer air, on a beach somewhere in the south.

It cost five hundred dollars. Two weeks' salary. Two and a half weeks with tax.

CORY   JUNE 11, 2000, EVENING I'm in the bathroom, sitting on the floor and using the toilet seat as a desk. This is the only room we have with a lock on the door.

I can't believe what happened today. I'm still not sure I didn't dream it. It keeps going through my mind and I can't sleep.

Tomorrow is our scene for drama, so Karko was supposed to come over here to rehearse it. We had to figure out the dancing and all that. It was vitally important. Mom and Dad even promised to leave for a couple of hours so we could have some space. But they were acting really *weird* all day. They kept bursting out laughing for no reason. And right after lunch Dad got out a bottle of champagne that somebody gave him, like, three years ago. He always claimed he was saving it for a really special occasion, not even New Year's Eve at the beginning of a new century was good enough. Then, all of a sudden out it comes and he wants to drink it on a totally ordinary Sunday afternoon. I thought Mom would stop him from opening it, but no, she just laughed and got out some glasses.

"Do you want a taste, Cory?" she asked me.

I said, "No, are you kidding? I have to rehearse that scene this afternoon and I have to be totally alert! And besides, when are you guys *leaving*? You promised you'd go out. We need lots of space to practice the dancing."

"Hey, your Dad's a great dancer," Mom said. "Maybe he could give you some pointers."

"Sure," Dad said. "Do you want to start now?" And he actually tried to grab me and swing me around. I couldn't believe it. I haven't seen him so lively for, like, the last hundred years. I said, "No, cut it out! What's the matter with you guys, why do you have to get all weird today? Can't you just *go* somewhere?"

But I knew once they got started on that bottle of champagne it would be practically impossible to get rid of them. And I could just picture the whole grisly scenario, them standing around all tipsy and full of cute suggestions while Karko and I stumbled over each other's feet trying to dance. I started to feel totally sweaty and agitated just thinking about it. So I went over to the sink to get myself a glass of water and that's when the real catastrophe happened. As soon as I turned on the tap the water pipe below the kitchen sink blew open and started spraying smelly, yellowish water all over everything. The rug got soaked in about five seconds and the tiles on the kitchen floor started to curl up and still the water kept coming. I was screaming and swearing but Mom and Dad hardly even seemed upset! It was like they were already drunk, even though they'd only had one sip of champagne each. They just stood there holding their glasses and watching the water pour out. Mom said, "Should I call the super?" and Dad said, "Why bother, he won't be there. Let's just call a plumber." Usually they'd both be moaning and worrying about how they were going to pay a plumber. But not today. I said, "Oh, shit, what am I supposed to do! Where are we supposed to rehearse?" But they didn't care, I don't think they even heard me.

Then right in the middle of the chaos the phone rang and of course it was Karko wondering what time he was supposed to come over, even though I'd already told him two o'clock about a million times. Dad said, "Ask him if he knows anything about fixing pipes." Big joke. I told Karko we were going to have to rehearse at his place because ours was a disaster area.

He said, "Oh no, we can't."

It's been this way all along, he always had to come to my place, I could never go to his. Not that I was dying to go to Kreepy Karko's house, believe me. But it really bugged me that he wouldn't let me, even once. Plus I wanted to hang up so Dad could phone a plumber before the entire place got flooded.

I said, "Look, our scene's tomorrow! This is an emergency!"

He said, "Well, couldn't we meet at McDonald's or something?"

I couldn't believe my ears. I said, "We have to practice the dancing, for God's sake! What are we supposed to do, go spinning around in front of the cash registers?"

Then there was this dead silence at the other end. All I could hear was water still rushing out from under the sink, like a gallon a minute. I just wanted to scream. Why does everything have to be so hard and why does everybody just make it *worse*? Dad was bending over to take a closer look at the pipe — as if he'd be able to fix anything like that in the next millennium!

So I said, "All right, forget it!" and was just about to slam down the receiver when Karko said, "Okay, okay, meet me at the corner of Bloor and Avenue Road! We'll go from there!"

It didn't even make sense, but I yelled, "Okay, whatever!"

and slammed down the receiver. Mom and Dad were just stand-ing there with their champagne glasses, not lifting a finger even though everything was falling apart. I didn't know what was with them. For a minute it crossed my mind that they were *both* on drugs or something, Mom too.

I said, "Well, aren't you going to *do* something?"

Dad said, "Hey, let's see if it all floats away. That'll save us the trouble of throwing it out."

Mom looked at him and laughed. "Yeah," she said.

So I couldn't help it, I started crying. I said, "This isn't funny! I have that fucking drama scene tomorrow and I have to rehearse it or I'm going to get a D, and you promised I could do it here but obviously now I can't and you don't even care! And I guess when I come home I'll have to wade through two feet of water to get to my fucking bed but I guess you don't care about that either!" Mom said, "Hey, I don't want to hear the F-word out of your mouth until you're at least eighteen!" I cried even harder. I said, "Well, I'm fucking *upset*, can you blame me?" Then Dad said, "Look, don't worry, we'll take care of it. You go meet your friend and we'll take care of everything."

Of course I didn't believe him. They didn't look as if they were about to take care of anything at all. But I just wanted to get out of there. I absolutely ran down the stairs, so that even if they did call me back I could pretend I didn't hear. I'd stopped crying by the time my feet touched the pavement. Our place was such a zoo today that even the thought of meeting Kreepy Karko on a street corner seemed *thrilling* in comparison.

Walking from the subway toward Bloor Street, I spotted him right away in the distance, looking even fatter and creepier than usual. It's almost summer but instead of his usual baseball cap he had on a big, stupid, ugly toque. He's got enough problems without wearing a toque like that. It struck me that maybe he was trying to dress like Enrique Iglesias in my poster. Pathetic or what? Enrique is hot in a toque because he's so gorgeous. All it did for Karko was make him look like the biggest loser on the North American continent. The only good thing was that we were in a part of town where nobody we knew would ever see us. For sure Karko didn't live there. Kreepy Karko living within a thousand blocks of Bloor and Avenue Road? NOT. I didn't have a clue what he had on his tiny mind.

I walked straight up to him and said, "I hope you're not going to say we're going to McDonald's because I told you that won't work."

He rolled his eyes, like he'd never even thought of McDonald's. He said no, no, he had a good place, and started walking. So what could I do, I went along with him. And right away he started talking about the *X-Files* screenplay. What a one-track mind. He said that after Mulder and Scully infiltrate the alien city in the desert, just as they're about to discover how it got there, they're exposed as intruders. But he was stuck, he couldn't figure out an ending.

I said, "I know. You could have them lose the amulet. Mulder drops it while they're being chased by alien police. They're running and being shot at with weird alien weapons, and they can't stop. But without the amulet, even while they're running everything starts to change. After a few minutes they realize nobody's chasing them anymore, and then they realize they're in an ordinary city. It's their own city where they started out from. They see the same café where they had coffee at the beginning." All of a sudden I had another idea. "I know! Why don't you say that all the time they were carrying the amulet their cell phones didn't work, but just at the moment they recognize the café, Mulder's cell phone rings, and it's Skinner saying, 'Where have you been? I've been trying to reach you for hours!'"

Karko always looks at me as if *I'm* an alien. "That's *good*," he said. "How did you think of it?"

Well, duh, how do I know? It just came into my mind, that's all. I don't even know why I always get involved in Karko's dumb ideas anyway.

We turned down a side street beside a big new condo complex. There were a bunch of fancy stores on the main floor. We walked by one called La Ville Blanche. It had four windows and in each one was a wedding dress.

About half a block down was a lot full of weeds and in the middle of it an empty house. It was big and quite old-looking and — this is the strangest part — all the windows were bricked shut, as if just nailing boards over them wasn't good enough. Why would anybody do that? They own this house but they don't want to live there and I guess they don't think they'll ever want to live there, but instead of selling it they just leave it and fill the windows with bricks so nobody can see inside or get in. At least I would have thought nobody could get in, but then Karko said, "Come on," and started walking around the side of the house. I was stunned! I said, "What are you doing? Are you nuts?" At the back there was another yard in an even worse mess, weeds and garbage everywhere. Karko showed me one little door with a window in it that wasn't bricked, just had boards nailed over. He pushed at one of the boards and it was loose. He reached his arm in and fiddled around for a minute and then the door clicked open. I couldn't believe it! I said, "Are you out of your mind? I'm not going in there!"

"Why not?" Karko said. "Are you chicken? Nobody's going to know. I come here all the time."

I don't know why, but I ended up going inside. I must be crazier than I thought. One minute I was saying no and the next I was standing inside in pitch-blackness. I couldn't even see Karko, I just knew he was there because I could smell barbecue-flavour potato chips on his breath. Then he switched on a flashlight and shone it on some steps going up. He said, "There's a room just up there. I've got candles."

"This is absolutely insane!" I said. "Are we supposed to rehearse here?"

"It's perfect," Karko told me.

I guess I was curious to see it, so I went up the steps. I thought to myself that I wasn't staying, I was going to leave right away. When I stepped over the threshold into the room it was so dark that at first I didn't know whether I was in a closet or a gymnasium. I said, "I can't see anything!" and I thought my voice sort of echoed, but I wasn't sure if maybe I'd just imagined it. There was a tiny sliver of light close to the ceiling on one wall, where a couple of bricks had come loose. It was like being inside a cave. I felt as if I'd gone blind. Karko struck a match and his face flamed up all red and weird, with that stupid toque perched on top of his head. He had a candle holder, sort of a candelabra, I guess, made out of iron, with spaces for six candles. Once they were all lit I could see that he had a sleeping bag on the floor, and a boom box, and a suitcase. He even had some school books. He said he didn't live there though. He said he just went there sometimes when he's fed up with things at home. I don't know if he was telling the truth or not. I said, "You actually sleep here sometimes? It's so cold and creepy." He said it isn't too bad, he keeps his clothes on and climbs inside the sleeping bag and it's quite cozy. He said he doesn't get along too well with his father and sometimes it's better to just go there.

God, I don't get along too well with my parents either, but I can't imagine sleeping all alone in that cold, dark place. Plus, I couldn't help thinking maybe Karko brought me there because he wanted to do something disgusting to me. Not that he'd ever shown any interest or made a move on me, but guys are so obsessive about sex you can never be sure they're not thinking about it. Also it crossed my mind that maybe he was a homicidal maniac and was going to slit my throat. A homeless girl got murdered in an abandoned house just a couple of winters ago and of course I thought of that right away. So I really wanted to leave. But he said it was a perfect place to rehearse the scene — lots of room, nobody around to bug us. He said, "It's kind of like in the play, they haven't paid their electric bill so all the lights are off and they have to use candles." I was surprised he'd even think of that, he always acts as if he's not at all interested in the play.

I said, "Yeah, their lights are off but it's not supposed to be about ten degrees below zero. They aren't supposed to be waltzing around with their teeth chattering."

"Oh, come on," he said, "it's not that cold."

He put a tape in the boom box. It was Led Zeppelin singing "Stairway to Heaven." It wasn't the right kind of music at all, but actually it worked okay, because the first part is sort of slow and soft like an old-time song. He put his hand on my waist. I had to hold his other hand — *yuck*, but what else could I do? The candles gave a nice glow, and some red light from a restaurant sign next door got in through the crack in the wall and made a little red shimmer on the ceiling. I could pretend it was from the Paradise Dance Hall, like in the play. At first I tried not to see Karko's face. I tried to pretend he was Enrique Iglesias. I tried to look past his shoulder and picture Enrique's dark hair and Enrique's smile. But Karko kept getting in the way. I kept feeling the buttons on the front of his coat and smelling his barbecue-chip breath. And I was pretending so hard to be Laura that he started to seem kind of like Jim. He knew all his speeches. When I said mine he came back with his right away, so it was almost as if we were actually talking to each other. He said some of his lines in such a kind of good way that I felt them inside, as if I really was Laura dancing with Jim. But at the same time I was still myself dancing with Karko and feeling proud of how well we were doing it. It's hard to describe. There was no sound from outside, maybe the bricked-up windows kept it all out. The only sound was the boom box music and our feet on the floorboards. I kept imagining how we'd look to someone watching, two little people moving around together in a circle of candlelight, as though we were on a stage in the middle of a spotlight, and out there in the dark an audience was sitting. But at the same time, nobody was there, we were all alone, a really shy girl and this guy she used to have a major crush on, dancing together in her apartment across the alley from the Paradise Dance Hall. It was the weirdest feeling I've ever had. I even thought a couple of times that I was going to cry, not because I was sad exactly, but just because I felt kind of *emotional*.

And then do you know what that creepoid did? All of a sudden, sure enough, he *kissed* me. He just leaned down and kissed me right on the mouth. It happened so fast I didn't even have a chance to duck or turn my head or anything, all I could do was stand there with his big slobbery lips planted on mine for, like, five seconds. Then I got over the shock and punched him and shoved him away. I mean, I should have known, right? He's a guy, isn't he?

I said, "What do you think you're doing!" I felt like his creepy spit was all over my face. I had to keep wiping my lips to get it off.

He said, "Well, it's part of the scene!"

"No, it is NOT!" I told him.

"Sure, it is, yes, it is, right here, right here on page —" He picked up the book and started turning pages so he could show me.

"That's later!" I told him. "That happens later! We said we were stopping at the part where he breaks the unicorn and all along we've been doing it that way and you know it!" Believe me, I'm not an idiot, I knew exactly where the kissing part came and that's why I made sure we ended our scene a couple of speeches before. The dancing was bad enough, but I wasn't going to kiss Kreepy Karko for any drama class in the world. So what happens? He gets me off in some dark deserted house and tries to sneak it in anyway, like I'm not going to notice! God, it's impossible to trust a guy for one second, they've all got it at the back of their minds, no matter who they are, even the biggest, stupidest, dopiest, creepiest, most clueless ones think they should try it, it's totally unbelievable! And I couldn't help thinking how dark it was in there, and how nobody knew where we were, and how he was a lot bigger than me.

Even in the candlelight I could see his face was all red. "I just thought it was a better ending," he said. "You know, the way it ends now is kind of blah, so I thought, like, if they kiss each other it's kind of like, hey, wow, something's really happening here! Like, in the *X-Files* movie, everybody's waiting for Mulder and Scully to kiss, it's what everybody wants!"

I said, "Just forget it, Karko! If you think I'm going to kiss you in front of the whole drama class you're dreaming!"

He said, "Okay, okay, relax, Masaryk, don't get your drawers in a knot, I'm not so hot to kiss you either!"

Yeah, right, that's why he was slobbering all over me the first chance he got. Anyway, then we just stood there for a few minutes, with our arms folded, neither of us talking. He was pissed off at me and I was double pissed off at him. Plus, even though it was so cold in there, I felt all sort of sweaty and out of breath. I almost walked out, the only thing that stopped me was I didn't want him to think I was scared or anything like that. Finally I decided I'd try to be a little mature. For sure Karko wasn't going to.

I said, "Okay, should we try it again?" He gave a shrug, sulky like a little kid. I said, "And we're going to end where he breaks the unicorn, right?"

He gave me this sarcastic look and kind of snorted, like I was being really childish and paranoid. Yeah, right. Like he didn't give me a reason to be paranoid.

We went over it a few more times and he didn't try anything else. And I have to say, it didn't seem too bad. After he got over his snit Karko thought so too. He said, "You know what, I think we're going to do okay."

I think so too. Knock wood. I'm actually looking forward to tomorrow a little bit now — although I'm still dreading it too. It could still be a complete disaster.

When I was leaving, Karko said he was going to stay. I said, "Overnight? Are you nuts? It's so cold." He said, "Oh, don't be such a wimp, Masaryk. I've stayed here sometimes in the middle of winter. This is nothing." He got out a bunch of grubby papers and a pen. I said, "What are you doing?" He said after I left he was going to write down my *X-Files* idea before he forgot.

He said, "You know, in the desert in Nevada there's this place called Giant Rock, it's, like, seven stories high, the biggest piece of solid stone in the world, it can even be seen from outer space. Apparently there've been lots of UFO sightings around there. It was, like, a sacred place to the Indians too. It's got these strange magnetic properties, it channels energy, like Machu Picchu or Stonehenge or the Pyramids. When people get near it they feel some kind of power coming off it. We should work that in somewhere, don't you think? Maybe that's what Mulder and Scully see first, they spot it from the Extraterrestrial Highway — it could lead them to the alien city, huh?"

He showed me the way back out and held the candle for me so I could see where I was going. I could still feel his spit on my mouth. I kept wanting to wipe it off.

He said, "You know what, maybe when I'm finished the screenplay I'll send it to Chris Carter in Hollywood. They pay, like, fifty thousand dollars for a script, you know. I'll share some of it with you because you've really helped me."

I could hardly keep from laughing. Somebody's going to pay him fifty thousand dollars for that script? Yeah. Right.

Still, I have to admit that, when he was bending over and holding the boards open for me and the candlelight was shining across his face, I did think that with the toque off, and if he lost some weight, maybe he wouldn't be a complete beast.

Guess what I found when I got home? Knowing Mom and Dad, I was expecting there'd still be water on the floor, no sign of any plumbers, no super, the whole place smelling like a public toilet. But no, to my amazement everything was fixed, everything was tidy and neat, and they'd ordered Thai food and saved some for me! And not only that, but they didn't say a word about how much it all cost. It was like they didn't even *care*. Too bad things can't always be like this. I'm pretty sure something weird is going on, because Mom and Dad just seem too happy to be real. But right now I've got too much else on my mind to worry about them.

I can't help thinking that while I'm here in the bathroom writing, Karko is across town in that cold, black room, writing too. Or maybe he's rolled up in his sleeping bag now, with only his face and that stupid toque sticking out, dreaming about the fifty thousand dollars he's going to get. When I picture it I feel like laughing and crying, both at once.

MONA   On Monday we went to see Barney Cherniak, a guy who used to be a drummer in one of Jesse's bands, then stopped performing and made it kind of big producing. He also did some programming and promotional stuff for CITY TV. Sometimes, if you were watching closely and didn't blink, you'd see his name in the credits after some local music show. Jesse thought he'd be a good one to talk to. "He's an asshole about everything else," Jesse said. "But he does know how to handle big bucks."

We didn't phone him beforehand because likely he would have put us off. Instead we took the subway and then a streetcar to the CITY TV building on Queen Street, thinking we could probably track him down there. In the lobby we had to wait while they phoned to check with him, and then they directed us to an upstairs office where he was sitting with his feet on a desk, talking on a cellular phone. He and Jesse had got together for beers a few times but I hadn't laid eyes on him for five years or more and he didn't look like the same human being as the one I used to know. His hair was cut really short and he'd gained about thirty pounds. We stood in the doorway, grinning and waving. From the expression on his face it was obvious he wasn't too thrilled that we'd dropped by. Maybe he thought we'd come to borrow money. But he didn't want to be a complete jerk, so he slapped a smile on his face, waved us over, pointed at some chairs. "I'll get back to you," he told whoever was on the other end of the phone, and then hung up. "Well, shit," he said. "J and M. How the hell have you been?" He always called everybody by their initials. That seemed to be the only thing left of the old Barney, the one who wore sunglasses day and night, the one with the long ponytail, the torn jeans, the cowboy hat pulled down over his eyebrows. But I guess I probably looked different to him too. Maybe he was thinking, my God, what happened to her?

I said, "Is that painting yours? I like it." It was on the wall to his right, a house surrounded by trees, beside a lake. He said, "Yeah, that's my cottage on Georgian Bay. The artist is Kurt Mann. A Toronto guy, an up-and-comer. You know me, I like to support local talent."

Barney was always a show-off.

"Listen, guys," he said. "I really wish I'd known you were coming. I'd love to sit around and shoot the shit for awhile, but the thing is, I've got this meeting in about fifteen minutes and I can't get out of it. I've already put these people off twice and I just can't do it again, you know what I mean?"

"Oh, sure," Jesse said in the same laid-back, breezy tone as Barney. "No big deal, all we wanted was some advice. We might be coming into some money soon. Actually, quite a bit of money. So right away I thought, Cherniak's the guy to see. You were always smart on the money angle. You were the only one who came out of Sonic Boom with a dime. I remember you told us you'd invested in Telstar Electronics or something, and the shares had gone up twenty points. Man, it was like you were talking Chinese! You were the first guy I ever knew who had a clue about that kind of crap."

Barney's attitude changed in a flash. All of a sudden his face cleared, he relaxed, sat back in his chair, looked at us with interest. "So you're getting, like, an inheritance, what?" he said.

"Yeah . . . something like that."

"How much are we talking? High five figures, low six, or . . ."

"Seven," Jesse said.

I almost had to laugh at Barney's expression. He was impressed, but at the same time he couldn't quite believe it. He'd known us at a low point, when Jesse was strung out, I was unemployed and we were living in one room across from the Royal Tavern. I guess it was hard to make such a big shift, to see us as people who could say "seven" and not be bullshitting.

"Seriously?" he said. "Well, great. That's great, guys. Glad to hear it." Sunlight was shining on the window pane behind him; all of a sudden it kind of dazzled my eyes, made them sting. There were balloons on the awning of a store across the street, all colours — blue, red, green, yellow, pink, orange — waving in the breeze. It was so good to be sitting there, to be alive, to see those balloons.

Barney started talking about interest rates, investment counsellors, tax shelters, that sort of thing. I tried to concentrate but I just couldn't. My eyes kept going back to his painting, the tall trees reflected in water so still it was like a mirror, a sliver of beach shining like silver in the sunset. I thought maybe we could have a place like that, walk down to the lake hand in hand, sit on the pier with our feet in the cool water, listening to the breeze whispering in the leaves. No traffic, no TVs, no stereos, no car exhaust, no drills, no telephones, no voices except ours. Maybe we could get Kurt Mann to paint us a landscape too. I imagined myself hanging a painting on a beautiful clean bare wall, standing back to see how it looked. I dreamed of myself floating on a raft looking up at the starry sky. The muscles in the back of my neck relaxed, my lungs opened to take in air. I dreamed of what it would be like not to always have to count the cost; not to have to think, if we have fried chicken tonight we'll have to do without orange juice tomorrow morning. What a life it would be, to have fried chicken *and* orange juice any old time you felt like it.

Barney gave us the name of his lawyer and his financial adviser. He told us they were great people; they'd give us all the help we needed. As we were leaving he said, "Well, good luck, guys, I hope it all works out for you. Keep in touch." He had a funny smile on his face, as if he still wasn't sure we'd been telling the truth. Maybe we'd hopped on public transit and come all the way downtown just to jerk his chain.

Jesse wouldn't wait, he stopped at the first pay phone he saw. While he was making calls I noticed a flower shop across the street. They had bouquets of marigolds, such a brilliant yellow they looked like dozens of tiny suns. I went over. Opening my wallet, I felt like Ivana Trump. Flowers were always such a luxury before, the very last thing you'd consider spending your money on. But now I was rich. I could have a bouquet of marigolds anytime I wanted.

I remembered how my mother always planted marigolds in

front of the house every spring. She'd hardly entered my mind until then except for a vague thought that I'd contact her once we collected the money and had it in the bank. All of a sudden I pictured her sitting in the living room in Saskatchewan, her oxygen tube in her nose, watching TV. The phone would ring and it would be me, telling her the news. She'd gasp, the tube would pop right out of her nostrils and fall into her lap. You see, Mom, I was right all along. Everything I've done must have been right, because look how I've ended up, I'm one in ten million, Mom. I was right and you were wrong! You were wrong about Dad, wrong about Jesse, wrong about me, wrong when you wouldn't help, wrong when you said grow up, wrong about everything, wrong from beginning to end, you silly old woman!

For once in her life she'd have to swallow her criticisms and advice and disapproval. For once in her life she might, just possibly, be speechless! I'd listen to the stunned silence on the other end of the line and I'd laugh out loud.

Jesse came out of the phone booth smiling. "We've got an appointment with the financial adviser at three tomorrow afternoon," he said. "He's at the Toronto Bank Building on Bay Street, twenty-fourth floor, way up in the clouds, I guess. He says, Well, of course I'm delighted to help out any friend of Barney's. Can you feature that? Remember how Cherniak used to check the pay phones to see if there was any loose change? Now he's got fat cats on the twenty-fourth floor sucking his dick. That's gonna be us too, you know. We're seeing the lawyer next week, Monday at 2 P.M. She wanted to make it earlier but I said no, we'd probably want to sleep in."

I don't know why but that struck us as funny. Maybe it was the idea of the two of us meeting with bankers and lawyers.

Maybe it was the idea of their having to adapt their schedules to ours. Jesse took one of the marigolds and tucked it behind my ear.

REBECCA   On Monday morning Wayne finally phoned me. He wanted to have lunch.

I said, "Sorry, I've got other plans."

He laughed. "Oh, come on, sweetie. You're not still mad, are you?"

He didn't seem to believe it was possible that I could have something else to do. As if when he wasn't around all I did was sit in a corner with my hands in my lap, waiting for him to call me. I looked at myself in the mirror across from the counter. I thought, is he blind? I could have anybody. Really, anybody. A man with more money than Wayne, a man who treated me better, who begged to be with me night and day.

"I told you, I'm busy," I said. "Why don't you have lunch with your kids?"

I hung up while he was still trying to answer. It felt good to cut him off in the middle of a word.

At lunchtime I walked west along Queen Street near the CITY TV building. If you're coming east it looks sort of creamy and elegant, like a giant five-tier wedding cake with banners on the top, but going west all you see is one flat wall painted completely black, with a sculpture of a car sticking out halfway up, one tire still spinning as though it's just crashed through the brick in a rush to check out some hot news tip. So clever, right? Toronto wants to be a world-class city, but there's always some genius coming up with a bright idea like that, eager to ruin anything that looks slightly sophisticated. Every time I see that idiotic car I have to shake my head in disgust, and that's what I was doing when all of a sudden I saw Jesse and Mona, or two people who looked a lot like them, going through the front doors under the CHUM-CITY sign. Which didn't make sense, because what would Mona and Jesse have been doing downtown at the CITY TV building?

Of course making sense was never a big thing for either of them. In fact the crazier and stupider an idea was, the more eager they were to go for it. Like the time they wanted to take out a loan to buy a nightclub (Jesse's brainwave), when between them they had about fifty bucks. Or the time they wanted to move to Montreal (Mona came up with that one), even though neither one of them spoke a word of French, just because some dumb friend of theirs told them Montreal was like a European city. So there was no reason why they wouldn't just jump on a streetcar and come down to visit the CITY TV building. It entered my mind that maybe it was all part of whatever they'd been up to the last couple of days — their giddy mood, their laughing and nudging each other and whispering together, their not going to work, all that. They never learned, no matter how many times they made fools of themselves. It wouldn't have surprised me to find out that they'd barged into some TV producer's office to say they wanted a show of their own, with Jesse as the star and Mona as backup. That was exactly the sort of thing they'd do without a moment's hesitation. And they'd be amazed when the producer didn't jump at the idea. Well, whatever they were up to, I didn't want to know. I didn't want to hear about it. I started walking faster, as if they were chasing me and I could escape if I speeded up.

Then I spotted that bookstore, Pages. I hadn't been near the place for ages, but all of a sudden I had the impulse to go inside, don't ask me why. It wasn't that I wanted to see Jimmie Glenn again, believe me. In fact I was praying I wouldn't. The first thing I did was look around to make sure he wasn't in the store. And he wasn't. Then I could relax, and standing beside the magazine rack I forgot everything else and remembered that other evening in the fall — the honey colour of the sunlight and his voice suddenly saying "Hi" beside me and the flush in his face when I turned around. Every detail came back, as though it was a really happy memory, instead of just something stupid and useless that I wanted to put behind me.

The magazines didn't appeal to me, I'd seen them all before. Instead I wandered over to the section marked "Drama." I didn't have anything better to do — I was just killing time — so I thought maybe I'd entertain myself by finding copies of those books he'd been holding that night, *Building a Character* and *An Actor Prepares*, or whatever. I thought it might be interesting to see what was in them, what kind of things a zero like him would find so fascinating. It was even worse than I'd imagined. Paragraphs and pages of little black words, stuff like "emotion memory" and "black hole beyond the footlights" and "through-line of action" and "super objective." I wished the guy who'd written that stuff was standing in front of me so I could say, why don't you get off it? As if it was all so complicated and intellectual to stand up in front of people and pretend to be someone else. I shoved the book back into place and just for something to do I picked up *Twelfth Night* from the Shakespeare section. There were lots of black and white photos of old-time actors playing the parts, a tall faggy-looking guy holding a lute, a small dark-haired woman with too much makeup standing beside a fake stone wall with her hands over her chest. I know this is ridiculous, but just for a second I pictured myself beside that stone wall. I turned a page and one line jumped out at me: "I am the man: if it be so, as 'tis / Poor lady, she were better love a dream." And then, even though I hadn't realized I was even reading it, I remembered something from the phony acting book, something about great emotion being shown by simple, natural movement. And that made me remember how he turned and went down on his knees in front of me. And then it was like I wasn't in Pages anymore, I was behind my grandmother's house in Walbrook, lying on the ground, looking straight up at the stars in the sky, smelling the lilac bush and the dirt it was growing from, I was both a little girl the way I used to be, and myself, a grown woman lying there in the dark, waiting for a lute sound and footsteps in the grass.

"Hi," someone said right beside me. I thought, it's not my fault, this isn't why I came in, I swear, I even checked to make sure he wasn't here. I took a deep breath and looked around.

"What are you doing, sweetie?" Wayne said. "I was on my way to Artemis to try and talk to you and then I saw you through the window." He was staring at *Twelfth Night* as if he couldn't believe his eyes. "I didn't know you liked this kind of thing. Shakespeare?"

I felt like an absolute idiot, my face went as hot as fire. "I don't," I said. "Are you kidding?"

He cocked his head. "How come you're looking at it, then?"

"I don't know," I said.

"You seemed really absorbed."

"No, I wasn't," I said.

"Like you were in another world."

It was irritating the way he wouldn't let it go. "I was not," I said, sticking *Twelfth Night* back on the shelf. "God."

Finally he took the hint and dropped the subject. "Well, come on, you'll let me take you to lunch, won't you?" he coaxed.

"You're not going to keep punishing me. Life's too short. You always have a good time with me, right? That's the important thing."

He was so sure of himself it made me sick. But what was the point of staying mad? At least I'd forced him to come looking for me. "Okay," I said.

"Where should we go? You pick the place."

I deliberately chose the most expensive restaurant I could think of. "Epiphany," I said.

He didn't even blink. "Great," he said.

CORY   JUNE 12, 2000 Well, it's over, thank God. I've been dreading today for an absolute eternity and now I don't have to dread it anymore, It's like this huge weight has been lifted off my shoulders.

I was afraid Mom would make a big deal out of it this morning and say again how she wanted to come and cheer me on and all that. But she didn't even seem to remember. She and Dad were still acting totally weird, joking and laughing as if they'd been hitting the champagne again. Neither one of them went to work and they seemed to have some big plan about going downtown to see somebody or other, but I was too nervous about my own stuff to pay much attention. In a way it was kind of annoying that they didn't even remember I had something quite big going on, after they pretended to be so interested in it. But mainly I was just relieved that they weren't bugging me.

All the way to school I kept going over my lines and thinking about all the disasters that could happen, like we'd get up in front of everybody and my mind would go totally blank or, even more likely, Karko's mind would, and we'd end up just standing there with our mouths frozen open. Or one of us would stumble during the dancing or step on the other's feet. Or everybody would laugh when he put his arm around me. Or he'd throw in that kiss at the end, I wouldn't be able to stop him, and everybody would see me being kissed by Kreepy Karko and my life would be ruined forever! For about the millionth time I said to myself, why did I ever sign up for drama?

On top of everything else, Karko had to be standing outside the school, waiting for me. He was still wearing the toque, but he'd actually changed his T-shirt. What a miracle! Except the new one was no improvement — it was bright yellow and from a distance he looked like a giant Tweety-bird. The sight of him literally made me cringe. That yellow T-shirt made it hard for me to believe I'd actually had one or two halfway nice feelings about him the night before. I would have liked to walk right past and into the school without even talking to him. But oh no, forget that idea.

"Hi!" he said, like we were long lost friends or something. He never seems to get it, that I had to work with him because Majeska made me, not because I wanted to. He acts as if we picked each other on purpose.

"Don't tell me that's what you're wearing," I said.

"Why? What's wrong with it?" he wanted to know.

"Well, only everything," I said. "Jim would never wear stuff like that."

"Why not? He's a fun type of guy, I think he'd dress casual."

"Because it's supposed to be, like, the 1940s! Guys never wore toques and bright yellow T-shirts then!"

"How do you know?" he said.

"Everybody knows that! Haven't you ever seen any of those old movies on TV?"

"Black and white?" Karko said. "I never watch black and

white."

Really intelligent, right? Why do I always waste my breath getting into these dumb arguments with him? At the same time I was noticing people walking by and staring at us, probably thinking what a loser I was to be so involved in a conversation with the biggest outcast at Eastend.

I was about to blow him off and go into the school when all of a sudden he got a weird look on his face, as if he'd seen something behind me. I turned around and there was this old rattletrap car pulling up to the curb. I couldn't see who was driving, just a woman with big hair, but the guy in the passenger seat leaned out the window and said something in another language. He looked kind of like Sting, except a lot bigger and tougher and in worse shape. At first I thought he was talking to me and I said, "Huh?" But he was talking to Karko, and Karko went over to the car fast. The guy kept leaning out, speaking this other language that sounded sort of like Russian. Karko answered in English, so I only understood Karko's side. "Yeah . . . Okay . . . Right . . . Yeah . . . I don't know . . . Yeah . . . Okay." The guy was smiling, his voice was quiet, he looked pretty relaxed and calm. But there was something kind of scary about him, I don't know why. Maybe it was because he seemed as if he might be a little drunk, and you never know what a drunk person is going to do. Or maybe it was because of the way Karko acted, so stiff and nervous, giving short answers to everything and staring straight ahead as if he hardly dared to blink.

In the middle of it all the guy looked past Karko at me and said something I know was gross. He had the same look on his face as those boys who stand in front of the Astoria Café yelling disgusting things at you when you go by. But I've never had a grown man give me a look like that. Karko's face got red as fire.

Even though I didn't understand the words, I felt my face get red too. The guy laughed out loud, he was delighted to see us so embarrassed. Then he said one thing in English: "Okay, now I have to go to get rich, just like everybody else in the West! Is right?" He was still staring at me, and I didn't know if I was supposed to answer or what. I could hardly breathe. Finally the car drove away and it was weird how relieved I felt to see it moving.

I said, "Who was *that*?"

Karko said, "Oh, my old man. I told you, he's an asshole." Very breezy and tough all of a sudden, like he hadn't been shaking in his boots a minute before.

"Was that your mother driving?"

Karko's face got red again. He looked past my head. "*No*," he said with a sort of goofy laugh.

I'd never asked him any questions about his family or his life, I never had any interest. All we ever talked about was our drama scene or *The X-Files*. But all of a sudden lots of questions started rushing into my mind.

"Was that Russian he was speaking?"

Karko snorted and said, "Lithuanian," like I was some kind of an idiot not to know.

I said, "Is that where you're from?"

"He is," Karko said. "I came here when I was four so I'm a Canadian."

"Do you speak Lithuanian too?"

"I can," Karko said. "But I don't want to."

"Why not?"

"Because he speaks it," he said.

After that we went into the school. It was strange but for some reason having a weird, scary father made him seem like a more interesting person to me. Even his creepiness seemed more interesting. We were walking side by side and I kept wanting to take another look at him; even the yellow T-shirt didn't put me off so much.

But there wasn't much time to think about it, because we had drama first period. While we were waiting for our turn I remembered all the things that could go wrong and started to feel *sick*. My stomach was jumping and my knees were weak and I could hardly swallow. Karko said he wasn't nervous, but he kept rolling and unrolling the pages of his notebook and I could see his hands were trembling. When Majeska called on us I had this one second when I thought, I can't do it, I have to run out. But of course I didn't go anywhere. A few kids snickered when we got up and somebody said, "Go, Kreepy!" For once Karko didn't burp or fart or do anything gross, though. While I was waiting for him to say his first speech I closed my eyes for a second and pretended we were back in the empty house, with candles and red light from the café next door. I sort of forgot about the kids watching, but at the same time I noticed they were quiet, not making any cracks or snickering anymore. When Karko said his line about not being made of glass, and held out his hand with a little smile, I actually felt as if I sort of liked him. Neither of us forgot a single word, or stumbled, or did anything else klutzy. We did it exactly the way we'd practiced, and it was *easy*. Some of my speeches rang in my own ears and made me excited in a way, I don't know why.

After we finished, everybody clapped and not one person was laughing at us. Majeska just kept sitting at her desk. At first I thought she was mad or didn't like it, but then I saw she actually had tears in her eyes. I couldn't believe it. Did that ever make me feel strange.

She said, "Well, if you make the teacher cry, you get an A."

I think it's the first time Karko ever got an A in his life. It's maybe the third time for me. Incredible! After class a few kids came over and said it was good. Brandi gave me a hug and said, "You were really super." It made me feel like she's still my friend after all.

I always thought nothing good could ever happen to me in this lousy neighbourhood. But after today I'm not so sure. Who knows? Probably I'm being totally *delusional*, it was only a stupid high school drama class, I mean who cares, really? But I can't help feeling a little different somehow, like something new is in the air, something is changing. When I came home there was even a big jar of yellow flowers on the kitchen table.

Karko kept laughing this afternoon. He's not used to getting compliments. Me either, actually. But even more than the compliments, it feels good to know inside yourself that for once in your life you did something that didn't suck.

Oh Enrique, you should have seen me!

LOSERS

JESSE

It's quiet down here
Real quiet down here
Nowhere else to go, no one else to see
Real quiet down here

Out on the street they're dancing
Out in the alley they're playing horns
Up on the rooftop they're having a party
But it's nice and quiet down here

Don't have to talk
Don't have to smile
Don't have to listen
Don't have to answer
Don't have to be nice
Don't have to be cruel
Don't have to play
Don't have to watch
Don't have to stand in line
Don't have to pay
Don't even
Have to
Move.

Oh so quiet, oh so cool, oh so quiet down here
— "DOWN HERE," BY JESSE MASARYK, 1992

MONA   My first day in Toronto was like a bad dream. There was such a glare in the street that I felt as if I couldn't see properly. Heat rose off the pavement in waves, it had a smell like car exhaust or burning tar. I wanted to ask for directions, but everybody I laid eyes on looked too bizarre or crazy to help me. A man was sitting on the curb, wearing a sign, lines and lines of words in bright red all tilting downward: jesus-willsaveyou, takejesushand, beforeitstoolate, thelastdaysare-comingsoon. A mauve-haired woman, big mouth smeared with lipstick, stuck her head out of a café and yelled, "Fucking bastard!" at no one in particular. Another woman wearing lots of eye makeup turned around and gave me this hard, hostile stare, as if she thought I was ready to take her wallet or her boyfriend. My mouth was dry from heat and fear. I kept think-ing, what if I get lost, what if I can't find my way back to the car, what if someone's already stolen it? I'd been tramping for miles, at least that's how it felt, as if my shoes should be worn through, and there were a thousand streets behind me, all of them the same. Somewhere back there on the fringe of the maze, Becky and Cory were sitting in a shabby motel room, eat-ing Kentucky Fried Chicken and watching TV, with instructions to keep the door locked, not to open it for anybody but me. What if I couldn't get back, how long would they wait before they ventured out, what would happen to them then? The sun was so strong it made my brain sizzle, pushed me to the edge of hysteria, I saw myself fainting right there on the sidewalk, or standing on the corner screaming and babbling, taking my place with all the other crazies.

A skinny man who looked almost sane came sauntering past. "Excuse me!" I said desperately. "Can you tell me where to find the Garden Hotel?"

He stopped and gave me a look, suspicious and kind of leering at the same time. He said, "You're right in front of it," with a smile, and then waited. In a minute I understood why. When I turned I saw a row of pictures beside a grimy doorway, lots of women with big boobs and g-strings, and a red sign promising that one of them was "Desirée Blue" and that she was performing inside, once every hour. No, I thought, this is a mistake, a terrible mistake. But then I saw the letters above the door, so faded you could barely make them out, a "G," a "den," an "el." Even though the interior looked as black as a cave, you could hear a faint, steady beat, the same rhythm as a pounding headache; it made you think of bleak mornings, of waking up with a hangover. Cool air hit me in the face, but it wasn't a pleasant cool, it was chilly, musty, rancid, full of that smell people's bodies have when it's been months since they've taken a bath. God, I didn't want to cross that threshold. A shuddery sensation went though my arms as though cockroaches were running up my sleeves.

The skinny guy kept standing behind me. "That's no place for you," he said.

I didn't like the way he said it. In fact, I didn't like him, period. So maybe it was good that he was standing there, because my spine got stiff, my dislike made me feel stronger and tougher. Creeps are the same everywhere and I knew how to handle them. "Get lost," I told him, without looking around. Then I walked into the pitch-dark hallway. What else was I going to do? I'd come two thousand miles, driving early in the morning and late at night, staring at the line in the middle of the highway until my eyes burned, seeing the prairie turn to forest and the forest turn to rock and the rock turn to meadow and the meadow turn to concrete, while money flew out of my wallet with terrifying speed and Cory talked too much and Becky refused to say a single word. And through it all that was the goal I was heading for, the Garden Hotel on Queen Street East, a pastel vision in my mind, seedy but in an old-fashioned, picturesque way, with rusty iron balconies and a faded lobby full of potted plants.

It wasn't the first time something hadn't turned out the way I'd imagined it. The lobby had no plants, just a desk facing a blank, stained wall. At one side, through another open door, there were a couple of men sitting at tables, staring at something I couldn't see — Desirée Blue I guess, doing her stuff in time to that dull, repetitive beat. The rug had cigarette burns in it. The soles of my feet itched, I was sure bugs were crawling around beneath my sandals.

Apparently Toronto had a good supply of creepy guys, because the desk clerk was another one, the type who thinks it's attractive to comb long strands of greasy hair across his bald head. He was reading the Toronto *Sun*. I was used to the Regina *Leader-Post*, so it kind of stunned me to see a newspaper that filled up its front page with a color photo of a blonde in a bikini, and printed a headline like, "Not a Pedophile, Bishop Says."

"Excuse me?"

The creep just about fell off his chair. But when he turned his face took on the same look as the creep on the street, a sort of smirky smile. For guys like that all you have to do is be a woman and stand in front of them to prove there's something dirty about you.

"I'm looking for Jesse Masaryk," I said. "Somebody told me he was staying here."

The creep just sat there, staring at me with that same stupid smirk. Somewhere down a long dark hallway to my left a door opened, then slammed shut, and I got a brief whiff of fried onions, mixed with something else even less appetizing. A throb of nausea shook the pit of my stomach, and all of a sudden I thought I heard another sound above the monotonous drum-beat, a sound like a guitar chord. I was convinced the creep was going to tell me that Jesse was one of their musicians, that he was playing backup for Desirée Blue. I thought I couldn't stand it, if I heard that I was going to lose control, maybe sob or throw up on the floor.

"Look," I said. "Jesse Masaryk. A tall, blond, good-looking guy. Yes or no? I've come a long way and I'm really tired. I've driven here all the way from Saskatchewan. This is my first time in Toronto. It's a lot bigger than I thought and I'm not even sure where I am. Is this the only Queen Street? Jesse Masaryk, do you know him? Can you help me or what? I don't think he can be here. I think the person who told me made a mistake. Is there another Garden Hotel?" I heard my own voice babbling. I kept telling myself to shut up, but in the meantime more words kept pouring out of my mouth. "Can you talk or are you a mute or something?" I said. I was sure the creep was going to laugh, or snarl, or just keep smirking without saying a word. Instead he folded his paper and stood up. "Saskatchewan, huh?" he said. "Whereabouts? My old man came from Saskatoon."

Wouldn't you know it.

There was a Jesse Maverick in 306, could that be him? "Yeah, I wondered about the Maverick," the creep told me. "Anyway, I think he's up there. I haven't seen him go out today."

The elevator wasn't working, so I climbed the stairs. The boom-boom followed me, gradually getting fainter. In the stair-well the walls were an ugly salmon-pink, and the carpet smelled like a thousand stale cigarettes. He's up here, I thought. In another minute I'll see him and he'll see me. But I couldn't quite believe it. I thought maybe it was going to be another Jesse Maverick, an old hobo, a down-and-outer, because how could my Jesse Maverick be living in such a hole? My Jesse Maverick, who was so fastidious that he'd never wear the same shirt two times in a row, who took a shower twice a day, who always smelled like cologne, who glittered when he walked, whose smile made women stop and stare. That Jesse Maverick hiding away in some dirty little room in a bug-infested skid row hotel? With each step upward the words repeated in my brain. It can't be. It can't be.

306 was written on the door in pencil. I couldn't hear a sound from inside. I thought I heard a skittering noise down at the end of the hall, though, like a mouse or a rat. It was too dark to be sure. I knocked. Nothing. Again. Nothing, except for the skittering noise. I tried the doorknob. Anything was better than standing in that hallway. It wasn't much of a surprise when the door opened. Obviously the Garden Hotel wasn't the kind of place where people concerned themselves about locks or privacy.

The first thing I saw was a greasy window with sunlight pouring through. It took my eyes a couple of seconds to get used to all that fuzzy light. Then I saw a grimy sink with some beer bottles underneath it. Finally I saw a guy lying on a bed. I thought, see? I knew this was all a big mistake. It's some old drunk. It's not him.

But it was. I kept standing there in the doorway, clutching my purse like it was some kind of life raft, and then there was a click in my brain and I recognized him. He'd lost about twenty pounds, he looked like a pile of bones stuffed into some old clothes. His hair was plastered down on his head, as though he'd been sweating, or using a lot of sticky hair gel. He was ugly, he was a mess. I can't tell how I felt. I'd been expecting that he'd look like himself, and maybe he'd be glad to see me, he'd grab me and hug me, we'd make crazy love right in the middle of all the squalor and it would turn into the Four Seasons. Or he'd be mad and I'd get mad too, remembering how he'd turned his back and left without a word, and we'd scream at each other, cry, throw things. Instead he just lay there like a sick old man. His eyes were open and he looked in my direction but he didn't seem to see me or know me. I'd been prepared for trouble; after all Titch had told me he was in bad shape. But I'd never dreamed it would be as bad as that. Horror froze me like ice, I couldn't move from the doorway. Then he raised one hand to rub his forehead. His hand looked the same as always, big and beautiful, shaped like the hand of a Michelangelo statue, with the long, graceful fingers that flashed over guitar strings so fast my eyes couldn't keep up, that touched my body on a thousand dreamy nights, that held our son Joey high up in the air until his hair almost brushed the ceiling.

I walked over to the bed. As I got closer he seemed to be trying to focus on me. I stood above him, looking down. "Hi," I said. My voice sounded hoarse, as though I hadn't talked for a long time.

He frowned and blinked. For so many months I'd longed to see him, hungered for one word, fantasized about a passionate reunion. His face was blank, his eyes were like a blind man's, gazing at nothing. "Hi," I said again. "It's me, it's Mona."

A sort of recognition began to struggle in his face. I saw the moment when he finally understood, when the clouds in his brain parted enough to let him know me. Suddenly his jaw tightened, the glaze on his empty blue eyes faded and left a harsh, pointed light. His eyebrows moved upward, as if he wanted to say something sarcastic. I don't think any actual words came out of his mouth. But it was as if I knew the words he wanted to speak. What the fuck are you doing here? he wanted to know. Did you come all the way across the country just so you could keep blaming me and freezing me out?

During the long trip I'd had lots of opportunity to think about what I might say when I saw him again. That I knew I'd been unfair, punishing him for Joey's death, putting it all on him. That I knew it wasn't his fault. That I knew he'd loved Joey too. That I wanted us to start again. I could have told a long story, all about the farewell to Walbrook, the highway, the cheap motels, the hot turkey sandwiches in roadside diners, the gas station washrooms, the lost sleep, the heartache, the loneliness during all those months while he was gone without a trace. But it was obvious he was too out of it to understand any of that, so I made it simple. I said, "I had to schlep all the way across the country to track you down. I don't know why but I guess I must love you, you stupid asshole." My voice shook.

His dry lips moved but no words came out. After a moment his eyes lost their focus again. I poked his shoulder, roughly. "The car's down the street and I've got a motel room," I said. "Come on. Can you stand up?"

Fumblingly he pushed my hand away. "Nope . . . better here," he said.

"What?"

"Better . . . here. No bad stuff. Don't remember. Not thinking. Or screwing up. Just sleep, good dreams. 'S all I want."

I felt panicky, I wanted to scream or weep. But that wouldn't have done any good. I had to be tough. "Liar!" I said harshly. "That's not all and you know it."

He blinked and made a sound, something like a laugh. "Fuck off," he said.

That's what I came two thousand miles to hear. But almost before I had time to feel any pain, his face puckered like a child's, like Joey's. He turned on his side and put one hand over his eyes. His beautiful fingers were stained yellow from nicotine. "Sorry," he said. "Sorry."

He could never talk about things that were deep down. He always relied on charm to get to people, and music to say all the rest. When the charm stopped working and the music dried up, he was trapped all alone inside his own skin.

I thought of a poem I read once, or maybe I learned it in school. I couldn't remember who wrote it, or what it was called, but one line came into my mind, something like this, that at the heart of love lies a pity beyond all words.

Down below in the alley someone knocked over a garbage can. I sat down on the bed beside him. I put my hand on his head and stroked his flat, sweaty hair. He let me.

∽

The smell of tar always makes me think of that summer, our first summer here. On every second block there seemed to be construction going on, the streets torn up, big oily vats of black tar cooking in the blazing heat. I wasn't used to the humidity, I felt like I was walking through waves of steam. It was hard to seem confident or make a good impression because I was always sort of shaky and damp.

Hi, you have an ad in the paper for a waitress?

Oh, yeah, that's been filled. But we'll probably need someone again soon if you wanna leave your name. Nobody lasts here longer than a month.

Some recommendation. *Well . . . okay, I'll leave my name.*
Hi, you have an ad in the paper for a chambermaid?
Oh, yeah. Fill in this application and we'll let you know.
Hi, you have an ad in the paper for a desk clerk?
Yeah. Have you had any experience?
*Well, no, but I'm sure I could do it. I . . . I like meeting
people, and —*
*Okay, you can fill in this form and maybe we'll call you. But
we've had five other applications already.*

That went on for four days. I left my name or an application
form at twenty-five different places and not one of them called
me back. At night we'd sit in the motel room watching television and after we turned it off we'd lie in the dark listening to
the sound of other television sets from other rooms. Jesse was
already gone, he'd only stayed with us for a day and a half,
hardly speaking, getting more and more jittery and desperate,
until a detox centre halfway across town agreed to take him.

Another family, Vietnamese, were living in a room two doors
from ours. The husband went out every day to work but the
wife stayed behind and took care of her three kids, so I got her
to keep an eye on Becky and Cory while I was out job hunting,
and then when I got home I'd watch her kids while she went out
to do whatever she had to do.

On the fifth day I started to get scared. I'd counted the
money in my wallet, including all the small change down to
the last penny, and I had exactly one hundred and seventy-five
dollars and fifty-seven cents left. The motel was costing us forty
a night. Don't panic, I told myself. You can't afford to panic.
Today is the day you'll find something.

In Walbrook, I'd never have taken a job at Roy's Canadian

Grill. I'd have recognized with one glance that Roy was trouble and I'd have turned around and walked out the door. But in Walbrook I knew the way things worked, and I had my mother's house to live in rent free. In Toronto I was confused and stupid, a hick from the sticks with nowhere to turn, and when we ran out of cash we were going to be on the street. So I ignored Roy's hard stare, and the way he touched the corner of his mouth with his tongue, and the way his eyes kept flickering down to my chest while he told me I could start right away. It was a small café, with a counter and five tables, serving short orders, ham and egg breakfasts, burgers and sand-wiches the rest of the day — a bit grubby but I'd seen worse. It closed at nine every night, and it was only a ten minute drive from the motel. I was so relieved that I kept talking to myself in exclamation points: This is okay! This is going to work out! I don't have to stay forever, just till I get some money together, then I'll find something better! On my way home that night I bought us a deluxe pizza and a Dairy Queen ice cream cake to celebrate.

On my second day Roy grabbed my boob. Right before he did it he said, "I've got a bottle of rum in the back, let's have a drink after closing." Maybe he figured that was enough of an intro.

I thought, I can handle this. I took hold of his wrist and moved his hand firmly away, but I kept smiling at him, like I wasn't offended or mad. "Sorry," I said, "but I'm married with two kids, and I have to get home right after work."

Sometimes that's enough; sometimes they'll just laugh, shrug and back off. But it was obvious Roy wasn't going to be so easy to discourage. He didn't laugh, he just fixed me with his hard, hostile stare, the same one he'd given me when I first walked in, as if I was an enemy soldier and he had to figure out how to disarm me before I caused some serious damage.

But what choice did I have? I needed the money so badly. I'll keep looking, I told myself, I'll just stay here till I find something better.

Payday was supposed to be Saturday. I was counting the days. On Friday afternoon Roy asked me to go into the back and get some more hamburger patties out of the fridge. There was no one in the place, but I wasn't suspicious because soon the supper crowd (consisting of three or four people) would be drifting in.

I'd opened the fridge door and was bending over when I heard a creak, or some sound anyway, but before I could turn my head his hand was up between my legs, two of his fingers were right inside my underpants, as fast as that, no hesitation, as if he had a right. His mouth touched my ear. He said, "Come on, you know what it's all about, let's have a good time."

Somehow I'd managed to clutch a package of frozen hamburgers. I got turned around halfway and then clobbered him with it. I didn't try to hold back; I hit him as hard as I could, I didn't care if I broke his jaw. It was because of how his fingers felt, so rough and relentless and pushing and demanding, they knew where they were going and I had nothing to say about it, I was just supposed to flop backward like a rag doll and lie there with a embroidered smile.

He staggered and grabbed his cheek. "Shit!" he yelled. "Bitch!"

"Pervert!" I yelled back. I wasn't going to let him be the only one to scream abuse.

"Get out of here before I kill you!"

"Oh, gee, you're really scaring me," I said. "Why don't you

go fuck yourself? You'll never find anyone else who wants to!"

I walked through the empty café and out onto the hot, tar-smelling street. I'd gone two blocks before I realized I was still wearing the apron he'd provided, pink with a heart-shaped pocket that had "Roy's" embroidered on it. I yanked the stupid thing off and stuffed it in the nearest garbage can. For another two blocks I was still breathing hard, still feeling the adrenalin, remembering the look on his face when he got the frozen hamburger in his teeth, remembering what I'd said, almost laughing, triumphant, yeah, I guess I told him!

But then it hit me, I'd worked at that joint for four and a half days and now there was no chance I was going to get paid for it anytime soon. Four and a half days' work and nothing to show for it, not one red cent. Plus I was out of a job again and what was I going to do? I stopped walking. I just stood there on the sidewalk. A middle-aged woman was sitting on a cardboard box in the space between two buildings, holding out her hand, saying to passersby, "Spare some change?" Soon that was going to be me.

You want to break down and sob. Suddenly it's too much, your mind goes blank. All you know is you're terrified. You think, I can't do this. And you have no one to tell, no one who's going to be moved by your tears, no one who's going to help you. I wished I was back home, going up the sidewalk to my mother's house. I'd say to her, you were right all along, I never should have left here, I was stupid, stupid, stupid, why didn't I listen to you?

But even if I'd wanted to go back to Walbrook, I didn't have enough money to get there. And what about Jesse, how could I leave him when he was in such a mess? Besides, I asked myself, would Jessica Lange or Susan Sarandon go running back home just because things were tougher than they thought? I knew they wouldn't. The characters they played would stick it out, show some guts, figure out what to do.

There was always welfare. But I had no idea how to go about applying for it, and I didn't know if you could get it right away. The only other alternative was to find another job as fast as possible, that very afternoon, before I went back to the motel. I'll take anything, I told myself, I'll clean toilets, I'll pick up garbage in vacant lots, anything.

I bought a paper. I called four numbers. At the first one, the job was already taken. At the second one, I got an answering machine. At the third one, they told me the manager had gone home, to call back tomorrow. At the fourth one, they said to come over and fill in an application. Their address was on the other side of town. They gave me long, complicated instructions about how to get there. As I was walking down the street, trying to calculate how much gas it would take before I found the right street, the directions started slipping out of my mind.

Across the intersection I saw a "Help Wanted" sign in the window of a place called the Taj Mahal. It didn't look anything like the famous one, it was a box of crumbling pink stucco and beyond the dusty glass you could see a faded red curtain and a droopy fern.

A sulky-looking, very dark teenage girl was sitting at the cash register. When she heard what I wanted she turned and called something out to the back of the restaurant. After a minute a plump Indian woman, wearing what I later learned to call a sari, came out of the shadows. There were no Indians or Pakistanis in Walbrook, all I knew about them came from television and British movies, where they were usually kind of colourful and exotic. I was looking for reasons to be optimistic.

This might be all right, I told myself. Maybe there'll be a whole family of interesting, unusual people, just like in *My Beautiful Laundrette*.

Yes, I told her, I had lots of experience. Yes, I could start right away.

"Five seventy an hour," she said.

My stomach dropped. I tried not to show it on my face. "That's not even minimum wage," I said — but not very assertively, I was too desperate.

"No," she said, assertively enough for both of us. "No, no, no, we're licensed."

The idea is that if liquor is being served you're going to get such big tips that you don't need a normal minimum wage. One look around the Taj Mahal and you knew the customers weren't going to be throwing around any fifty dollar bills. It would be single glasses of draft beer or house wine and if you got a loonie once in a while you'd be lucky.

Five seventy an hour. I tried to work it out in my head. Say, an eight hour shift. A day's work would pay for a night at the motel, with a few bucks left over. Five dollars at least for groceries and other stuff, so you wouldn't be able to save enough to make first and last months' rent on a decent apartment, or pay for any emergencies. You'd hardly be able to get by at all. And who knew how long it would be before Jesse would be able to help?

The woman waited with her arms folded. Big gold earrings with turquoise stones dangled from her earlobes. I stared at the flat blue colour, my nose filling up with the odours of oil and curry. I don't think I'd ever smelled curry before. Later I got to like it, but that afternoon it seemed really strong and strange, it almost made my stomach turn over. I saw that nothing was going to be simple, that everything was going to be far more complicated and arduous than I'd ever imagined.

It doesn't matter, I told myself. I'll take it for now. Just until I find something better.

"Okay," I said.

౸

Jesse wasn't supposed to have visitors for a couple of weeks. He was supposed to be removed from all stresses and bad influences so he could concentrate on his rehab. But finally they phoned to say he was ready for company. I thought I should go by myself the first time, just to make sure things were okay before I brought the kids into it again. I drove over to the rehab centre between shifts at the Taj Mahal. I'd already worked the lunch shift and I had to be back at 5:30 for the dinner shift. I'd been doing that for a week because one of the other waitresses was sick. Sometimes I felt so tired that I was afraid to sit down for fear I wouldn't be able to stand up again. But even so, I could never sleep through the night; I'd wake up and start worrying about a million things: money at the top of the list and, after that, were the kids really okay with Mrs. Thieu while I worked so much, where were we going to live, where were they going to go to school, what was going to happen to us all?

In the parking lot at the centre I sat in the car and sprayed myself with cologne to try to cover the smell of curry. Then I got out some blusher and stretched to look at my face in the rearview mirror while I applied it. My hand was actually trembling, not from excitement at the idea of seeing Jesse, but from sheer exhaustion. And all of a sudden I felt angry, I thought, why am I bothering with this? I threw the blusher back into my purse. For all I knew he was still out of it and wouldn't even notice what I looked like. If he did notice maybe it would do him good to see me pale and worn out, stinking of oil and stale restaurant food. Let him know all about it, let him know what he'd put us through.

I wasn't sure what to expect. He might be lying in bed or slumped in an armchair, staring with glassy eyes at a TV set. A nurse told me he'd gone down to the solarium at the end of the hall. As I walked across the long stretch of gleaming tile, I started to hear guitar chords. He was sitting in front of a tall, curtainless window. Bright sun streamed in all around him. He still looked way too thin and his skin was pasty, but his eyes were clear, his hair was freshly washed and fluffy, he had on a white T-shirt and faded blue jeans. He was starting to resemble his old self.

"Hi, how are you?" I said. It was strange, I felt stiff and awkward, as though he was someone I hardly knew. I even had trouble smiling.

"Not bad," he said. "How about you?" There was something raw, young and slightly uneasy about his expression, as though he'd lost his self-confidence, or at least his ability to fake it.

"Me? Oh, fine. Where'd you get the guitar?"

"It belongs to another guy here. He let me borrow it."

Strange emotions were rushing through me, pleasure to see him looking so much better, relief that he was starting to recover, all tangled up with exhaustion and resentment because he got to sit and play music in a nice, sunny room while I was sweating and struggling, working like a dog, running myself ragged in the hot crazy city, with no one to notice or care. I had to sit down, I dropped into a chair next to him. It was like I'd been on uppers for weeks but all of a sudden their effect wore off and I crashed. Something was making me shake, weariness and some other feeling I couldn't even name. It almost seemed like too much of an effort to talk, too hard to form sentences.

"Go on," I said. "Keep playing." I thought I'll just sit here a little while, I won't think about anything; I just want to sit here without moving. Outside I could see the parking lot, a couple walking arm in arm, my car with a dozen others, baking in the heat. I could hardly believe I was off my feet. The chair cushions felt soft against my back. The air conditioning started to dry the sweat on my face. He kept strumming quietly, his long fingers moving over the guitar strings. He started singing too, which was kind of unusual — singing wasn't really his thing. He had a rasp in his voice but it wasn't an unpleasant sound, there was something bittersweet and real about it. I hardly listened to the words at first, just the guitar and his low, husky tone. My heartbeat slowed, my breath stopped going in and out so fast, for the first time in a month I could almost relax. Even my eyes started to feel heavy, as though I could have fallen asleep.

One line penetrated the soft haze. ". . . finished . . . but then she lifted me." I woke up. What? What did he just say?

"I've been working on it for the last two days," he told me. "I don't even know if it's any good. It's so long since I wrote anything, maybe my judgment's off. What do you think?"

"Can I hear it again?" I said.

He started from the beginning.

Down, down, down,
Thought I was down for good,
Didn't know she was driving all through the night
Till she came and lifted me.

Cold, cold, cold,
Thought I could never get warm
Didn't know how fast she was heading my way
Till she walked in and lifted me.

So many things that I did wrong and things I threw away,
I ran so far to walk this lonely street,
But she loved me anyway.
She put a flower in her hair and an earring in her ear,
She got behind the wheel and drove, didn't stop till she
*   got here.*

Lost, lost, lost,
Thought I was lost for sure.
But she said goodbye to her old home
And pushed the pedal to the floor.

And with her smile she lifted me;
With her eyes she lifted me;
With her heart she lifted me;
With her soul she lifted me.

I thought that I was finished,
But then she lifted me.

His face was just a shimmering blur. I nodded.

He never knew how to respond to tears. He pretended he didn't notice them.

"Do you think the last couple of bars are kind of awkward?" he asked.

I shook my head.

"I just stuck in that part about the flower," he said. "I liked how it sounded."

I nodded again.

There I was, feeling as if everything was lousy, worrying that I'd made the worst mistake of my life, afraid that I'd come so far only to get lost in a dark jungle with no escape. But then I walked into that quiet, radiant place and heard that song. Sunlight kept pouring in, so bright it was almost blinding, and I floated in it, light as air. I was thinking that no matter what happened, I could handle it. I was thinking that nothing in the world could beat me. I was the person in that song.

REBECCA Wayne was my first real boyfriend. I'd been out with lots of guys in high school, but that doesn't count. I had to go out with somebody and I didn't want to stay a virgin forever, but they were all just kids from the same sad neighbourhoods as me. Only the ones who sold drugs had any money. So the dates consisted of cheap movies on Tuesday night, or eating french fries at McDonald's, or sitting in somebody's car drinking beer. Is it any wonder I was never knocked off my feet?

On our first big date Wayne took me to see *Phantom of the Opera* at the Pantages Theatre. He'd been to it before with the little darlings, but he was willing to go again because he thought I'd love it, and he was right. I'd never been in a theatre like that, it was spectacular; the carpet in the lobby was about three inches thick. Most of the other people were dressed beautifully. Of course there are always a few clods who just don't have a clue, who'd wear sweatshirts with ratty jeans and wander around breathing through their mouths even if they were at Buckingham Palace waiting to be introduced to the Queen. But most of the women were in evening gowns or silk pantsuits, and when I looked at myself in all the mirrors, standing there with everybody else, I didn't look so out of place. My clothes were off the rack but I knew how to make the most of what I could afford. Anyone would have thought I belonged with a crowd like that, if they didn't look too closely.

We had the best seats in the house, I sank into mine and it was so soft and velvety I almost felt as if I was floating. There was a big orchestra, all the men in tuxedos and all the women in long black skirts, and their brass instruments looked as if they'd just been polished. When the lights went down I could close my eyes and smell expensive perfume, good aftershave lotion, mint, chocolate. Then the lights came up again and the scenes passed by, all colours, blue and pink and red and white, costumes, singers, dancers, a real chandelier, real water, a real boat. That's what a show is supposed to be, not two people in drab clothes standing on a bare wooden platform droning on and on for two hours. A show should be something beautiful and unusual, something you can't see on any street corner, something worth spending money on.

"What did you think?" Wayne asked me afterwards while we were walking to his car.

If I'd acted too impressed he might have got the idea that I'd never been to a show like that before. Which I hadn't. But I didn't want him to know. So I made sure my voice sounded casual. "Quite good," I said.

He took me to a seafood restaurant called Bellissima for dinner. Up to then my experience with seafood was canned tuna or, as a special treat, fish and chips in a cardboard container from Captain Tom's on the Danforth. But this is something I've learned — or maybe I always knew it — that to keep from looking dumb it's important to stay cool, not show any nerves at all. Two waiters kept hovering over us. The younger one brought a platter with the catch of the day, two big fish with their heads still on and their eyes big and oily. The waiter had big eyes too, and he kept trying to use them on me, smiling, talking with a soft Italian accent, does the signorina like scallops, does the signorina like shrimp, we'll fix something very special for the signorina. He was cute, naturally; that's a rule, all flirty waiters are cute. But the bottom line is: they're waiters. My rule is, don't waste your energy.

One good thing about it, though, was that Wayne noticed how this waiter was fussing over me and my stock went up right away. People always value things more when other people want them too. He reached across the table and squeezed my hand. He said, "Did I tell you how gorgeous you look tonight?" Then he turned to the waiter, still twining his fingers through mine, and said in a breezy way, "Why don't you bring us two champagne cocktails to start?" So many times that night I had to catch myself, to stop myself from acting too excited or pleased. I mean, I didn't want to come across like a gushy teenage girl, falling apart when she hears the words "champagne cocktail." I wanted to act as if I had that kind of thing every day. So I just gave a little smile and nodded, like, hmmm, champagne cocktail, yes, not a bad choice.

That night I had calamari for the first time, and swordfish, and asparagus. For the first time I got to taste the wine and then say, oh yes, that's fine, before they filled our glasses. For the first time I heard classical music in a restaurant. For the first time I had espresso, and real cognac. I didn't have to look at the prices, I didn't have to think about it. I could choose anything on the menu, just because I wanted it, and in a few minutes it was on the table. When the waiter brought the bill Wayne just tossed his credit card down without even looking at the total. This may sound kind of mercenary, but that's when I started to love him. He was so big and smooth, his clothes were so nice, he was smiling as if he enjoyed the sight of me, and he didn't give a damn if he'd spent a hundred, two hundred, three hundred dollars — whatever it was he could cover it. I remember how I felt at that moment, a sort of wonderful relaxation, almost like I'd just taken a tranquilizer. I knew that as long as I was with him, I'd be okay. Whatever happened, he'd be able to take care of it. He'd stand between me and everything lousy. A big tall guy in gold cufflinks and a five hundred dollar suit is as good as a high stone wall.

Afterwards we tried to go to a bar he knew, Ted's Backyard, but there was a lineup outside. "Fuck this," he said. "I don't care how trendy it is. My motto is, never wait in line." Only a guy with a lot of money and self-confidence would say something like that. I started to love him a little more.

A BMW pulled up to the curb and a guy leaned out. "Hey, Wayne, is that you?" Some of the people in the lineup turned to look. It was a brand new BMW, like something out of a car commercial. I had a flash of how we must look standing there, dressed for a party, with that shiny car beside us, one of us bending down to talk, and the other one — a tall blonde, me — standing upright in a silky dress with the wind blowing her hair, while the announcer says, "This is the car for your future."

The guy in the BMW said, "And who's this?" giving me the once-over. He was about the same age as Wayne, but not so attractive. Still, he was in a BMW, so he wasn't a complete zero. I gave him a smile while Wayne introduced us. His name was Ben. His wife Linda was in the driver's seat. A lot of women that age are named Linda. She barely turned her head when I said, "Hi." A lot of women that age don't like women my age, especially when we're going out with their husband's friends.

Ben was impressed with me. Or else he and Linda had just had a fight and he wanted to bug her. Maybe it was a combination of both. He said to me, "You look like what's her name — the movie actress. You know who I mean. Where'd you meet this character? How come he's always so lucky?"

I opened my mouth but Wayne answered for me. "One day I turned around and there she was," he said. "It's because I was a good boy all year."

"Hah!" Ben said. They were both laughing so I pretended to think it was funny too, but it struck me that Wayne had managed to avoid mentioning the fact that he'd first seen me in a dress shop where I was the clerk. Not that I was so eager to have it told. But somehow this whole scenario went through my mind, that some night Wayne and Ben would meet for a drink, just the guys, and then they'd drive down Queen Street in that BMW, right past Artemis, and Wayne wouldn't even turn his head, and Ben wouldn't even know, and I'd be standing inside, my back reflected in the circular mirror, my face behind the glass, shadows from the Artemis sign falling across my dress; I'd be all alone, no customers, standing there in the empty lit up store, looking out into the street just in time to see that BMW glide by.

They worked at the same place, that's how they knew each other. Later I found out that whenever two guys from the bank came together, all they could talk about was the bank and the other people they knew there. But that night I wasn't used to it and it kind of stunned me to hear all the names flying back and forth: Forbes was being sent to Buenos Aires, Silvera'd just come back from California, Klein was going to Japan,

Lorenzo'd been promoted to senior manager, McAllister'd been slapped down to plain manager.

"And he deserved it, too," Ben said. "The guy's a wimp."

"Sloane's got bigger balls than any of 'em," Wayne said. "She's the one who got rid of him. I walk in at 7:30 every morning and she's already in her office on the computer."

"I went home at 8:30 last night and she was still there," Ben said. "She leaves the door open just a crack so she can see who's going by. McAllister never got in till nine and he left at six. That's what killed him."

"She's going on a walking tour in the Andes this summer."

"Yeah, I don't think the Incas have got much to teach her about human sacrifice," Ben said. "Silvera invited us to Costa Rica this year. He has a ranch down there."

"Don't go. I went last year and it was a drag. Drop-dead scenery but there's nothing to do. Some people don't have a clue how to spend their money. Scarlatti's buying a condo in Miami. I told him, oh come on, man, Miami's strictly for the blue hair crowd. Get with the program. Saint Isaac, heard of it? Due south of Key West. Gotta get in on the ground floor, it's gonna be big. But right now nobody knows about it and you can get a great three bedroom with an ocean view for three hundred and fifty. Two thousand square feet, not counting the patio."

"Yeah, Matthews got one, three hundred and ten, right on the beach."

"How big?"

"I'm not sure, but at least fifteen hundred."

"Yeah? Not bad."

I glanced through the windshield at Linda. I thought she'd still be avoiding eye contact, but no, she was looking right at me. I would have smiled then, I think, just to be friendly, but her face was completely cold and blank, as if to say, you're Trash. So I didn't smile. But I wasn't going to be the first one to look away either. I kept staring and not smiling until finally her eyes shifted and she pretended to be suddenly fascinated by something on the other side of the street. Ha, ha.

Afterward we got into Wayne's car and drove. The Porsche wasn't as flashy as the BMW but it was more elegant and sumptuous. I decided I liked it better. Linda was welcome to Ben, Wayne was the one for me. I settled back and breathed in the rich, leathery smell. The lights went by like stage lights, as if the streets were just part of a play so I didn't have to worry, I didn't have to care about any of it, it couldn't hurt me. For some reason I noticed Wayne's hand on the steering wheel, how smooth and well-kept it was, the fingernails all clean and gleaming, as if he'd had a manicure that day, and the gold ring he always wore, with the two small red stones that looked like rubies. I had an impulse to lean forward and kiss his hand, I don't know why. Of course I didn't do it. He would have thought I was completely weird.

Instead I said, "Do you own a summer place?"

He said, "Yeah, I have a little cottage on Georgian Bay. Great boating and fishing. The area's getting more developed too, so if you feel like getting dressed up one evening and having a good meal somewhere, you only have to drive five miles or so and you've got three or four good restaurants to choose from."

"Oh, yes," I said. "That's important."

"We could drive up next weekend, maybe," he said.

For the tenth time that night I had to take a deep breath, I had to tell myself to stay cool, cool, cool. "Hmmmmm, I'm not sure I can, I think I've got something else on Saturday . . . oh well, I could cancel it, I guess."

He winked at me. "Great," he said. "I'm thinking in a couple of years I'll start looking for a place down south too. You need somewhere to get away in the winter. January and February here are like fucking death, don't you think? So you have a condo in the Caribbean say, and you just hop on a plane and in a couple of hours you're on the beach."

"Yes," I said. "Absolutely."

I closed my eyes. I saw myself walking on a vast crescent of sand, with fiery waves lapping over my feet and the sun setting behind palm trees. I was wearing a bikini top and a long wraparound skirt. I looked fabulous. There was a tall tropical drink in my hand. The announcer said, "Don't you deserve to get away?"

The whole world seemed to be opening up for me that night. I was really happy. It felt like the first time in years that I'd been happy. I could have sat in that car all night, just driving and driving, like I was sailing on an ocean liner through all the streets of the city. But then he pulled up to the curb in front of a dingy doorway with a neon sign above it saying "Hot Pink" — except the vowels were dark, so it looked like "H t P nk."

"Have you ever been here?" he said. "Sometimes these places have some interesting stuff going on."

It didn't look like it to me. I felt like I'd fallen out of the sky and hit the ground. To someone in his situation it was fun and colourful and gritty, I guess. But a place like that was no novelty for me. I'd imagined going someplace stylish, with soft lights and a bartender in a white shirt pouring cocktails, and some kind of slow, dreamy, sexy music — jazz or something like that. I never thought we'd go to a grungy beer hall like you'd find in

Scarborough. What a letdown, especially after the rest of the evening had been so beautiful. But I didn't want to come across as a snob. If you say you don't want to go into a place like H t P nk people think you're uptight and not a fun person.

So I said, "Okay, sure, let's check it out," and tried to smile as if I meant it.

He said, "We don't have to stay if we don't like it. We'll just have one drink and move on."

As soon as he opened the door a roar came up the rickety staircase, voices and clinking glasses and laughter, all drowned in a booming rock beat. A tall beefy type with two black eyes signalled us enthusiastically at the bottom of the stairs. "Come on in, good seats in front, people!" Two guys in blue jean jackets were standing on chairs waving and calling to somebody on the other side of the room. The black-eyed character bellowed at them over his shoulder, "Hey, down off the furniture!" and without a pause turned back to us, friendly as could be. "I got a nice table right at the front, close to the band."

"I'd rather not be right at the front," I said. "You can't hear yourself think."

"What?"

"You can't hear yourself think!"

"But who wants to think, right?" the black-eyed guy said, laughing his head off. "Huh? Better not to. Right?"

It was so dark and so cloudy with cigarette smoke that you could hardly see, just shadowy, bobbing forms everywhere you looked, yelling at each other above the noise of the music. We'd only been there about thirty seconds and already I had a headache.

"There's a table right in the corner," Wayne told the man with black eyes. "We can sit there."

"What?"

"Right there in the corner! We're going to sit there! We're not planning to stay very long!"

"Huh?"

"We're not planning to — why am I telling you this? Forget it."

"What? Can't hear you!"

"Forget it!"

The band was awful, three weird guys doing something ancient and corny like "Twist and Shout." They didn't even look as if they belonged together. One of them was old, about forty, with dark glasses and a baseball cap turned around so that the peak went out over one ear. Wow. The second one was in his late twenties, with a big bush of hair that he kept tossing back in a sort of feminine way, as if he was in a snit about something. He was wearing a black undershirt with a Batman logo on the chest. Their drummer looked like a kid, like about eighteen, his chubby face all red and sweaty, bending over his drums, working hard to make as much noise as possible. What a winning combination.

The guy with the black eyes slammed two big, greasy mugs of beer down in front of us. I hate beer. But Wayne seemed to be having a good time. He was grinning, anyway. So when he clinked his mug against mine I forced myself to smile and take a drink. It tasted thin and yeasty. I felt like spitting it out. Some pimply zero staggered against my chair, stared down the front of my dress, and said, "Well, hi!" What am I doing here? I asked myself.

But Wayne was pounding his hands on the table in time to the so-called music, laughing, even singing along on the chorus: "Come on, come on, baby . . . yeah, yeah, yeah . . . uh huh, uh huh!" I have to say, I was disappointed; I'd thought he had better taste. But maybe it was a chance to let loose after a week at the bank.

After a while he got up to go to the washroom. He'd barely turned his back before the pimply zero was back leaning over my shoulder. "Wanna dance?"

"You've got to be kidding," I said.

"What?"

"No, thanks!"

"I can't hear you!"

"N-O! Go away!"

The lead singer, the one with the baseball cap, stepped forward and grasped the microphone. "All right, people, are ya having FUN? Hey, an old friend of ours is here tonight and we're going to ask him up here to do something. Jesse? Come on."

You know those fairy tales where a child gets cursed in the cradle? Sometimes I feel like that. As if there's an evil fairy who's following me around to ruin things, over and over again. As if I'm never going to be free of this bad spell I'm under.

He climbed up on the stage, wearing a leather jacket, jeans, and black boots. When the light hit the top of his head you could see that his hair was going thin on top. There was a little roll of flesh above his belt. His rings flashed as he took the guitar somebody handed him and slipped the strap over his shoulder. He stared at the crowd like a challenge, as if to say, "Take me or leave me, I don't give a damn."

The other so-called musicians were waiting for their cue. He glanced over his shoulder with a nod, and they started to play, first the keyboard, then the drums coming in on the second bar, finally his guitar on the third. Of course he couldn't do any old hits, or anything anyone might recognize. He was above all that. He had to segue right into some weird composition of his own, and the audience was supposed to sit there listening rapturously. Before long the keyboard died away, probably because Batman didn't have a clue what Jesse was doing. That didn't faze Jesse though, he didn't need anybody, he could go on for hours all by himself. He nodded his head to the rhythm, planting one foot forward, the heel of his boot going up and down. He closed his eyes. His fingers moved over the strings in a fast, show-offy way. He made the body of the guitar bounce against his pelvis. God, it was laughable, it was an embarrassment. At first I felt cold, then hot with shame. I was way in the back, of course no one could have known that there was any connection between us. But I felt as though a neon sign must have appeared above my head, with an arrow pointing down, saying (in H t P nk style) "D ght r."

When Mick Jagger and Keith Richards prance around looking like wrecks, you don't mind so much because at least they were something once, they made a fortune, they were famous and successful. But he never did anything worthwhile in his whole sad, stupid life. He never had what it takes, but he couldn't grow up and accept that fact, oh no. He was too immature and weak to face the truth, so he had to get into drugs, fall apart and need to be taken care of, when he was the one who was supposed to be strong, and take care of us. Because of him we had to come to this city and live like bums. Because of him we never had anything beautiful or valuable, because of him we had to move from one ugly hole to another, because of him we never had one decent home. Because of him I never got to go to the Caribbean, or Mexico, or Europe, because of him all I ever got were useless daydreams, lying on my bed, staring at the cracked ceiling, listening to cats on the fire escape and drunks in the alley, smelling the toilet down the hall.

His body kept vibrating, his feet kept pounding on the boards, as though the drumbeat had got inside him. He kept his eyes closed. That was always one of his favourite tricks. Such an artiste, totally absorbed in his own music. I guess lots of people fall for that kind of bullshit, but it makes me puke. Oh, I'm not denying that even I was taken in by him for a while, a long time ago, in Saskatchewan, when I was so young I didn't know any better. I used to wait for him to come home, my heart used to give a jump when I heard his voice in the yard, I used to run to meet him along with everybody else. I used to have this favourite song that I always asked him to play, something he called "Becky's Song" and claimed he'd written just for me. Yeah, I admit that when I was sitting beside him listening to him play that song, I thought the world was almost perfect. He seemed so tall, so fair, so blue-eyed, so broad-shouldered, so slim, so handsome, just the way a man should be in every way. "Dad!" I'd say, just to get him to look at me, "Dad!" and the word was like a caramel candy in my mouth, warm and sweet, melting through me, filling me with pleasure and happiness. But I was only a child. That was before I found out what the world is all about. That was before I found out what he really was: an egotistical, self-pitying phoney, a coward and failure who never cared about anyone but himself. Sometimes he'd lie on the bed for days on end, just staring at the ceiling. Laid off for the hundredth time. We'd have nothing to eat but potato chips and peanut butter out of a jar. Mona'd sit at the table counting all the change in her purse, asking us to check our pockets for dimes or quarters, seeing if we could come up with enough cash to buy a loaf of bread. So it would be off to the food bank, again. He couldn't help. Ever. Just lay there, just stared. I woke up one night and heard his voice from the kitchen. He'd applied for a job and hadn't got it, as usual. "What experience do you have, what education do you have, they want to know," he told Mona, "Like you need a B.A. to be a fucking janitor!" Yeah, he was too good for it, he was made for better things. But what about the rest of us? He never thought of that, did he?

"Wow," Wayne said, sitting down beside me, "this guy's a real old rocker!"

Jesse played on, twitching his left leg in time to the drum beat. He played for so long that I started to think they'd have to open a trap door under his feet to get him off the stage. Then suddenly he stopped, one last chord and his hands dropped, just like that. He didn't nod or bow or say "thank you" either. That would have been too ordinary and normal. He just backed up and stood there listening to the feeble applause as though it was for someone else, resting his hands on the borrowed guitar.

The band climbed down off the platform, taking a break before their last set. Jesse drifted toward the bar, his arm draped over the shoulders of the guy with the baseball cap. One or two women stopped him, congratulating him on his performance, I guess. There are always women who go out of their way to like weird, pretentious stuff, just to prove they're more discerning that anyone else. And there are always women who think any guy with a guitar is hot stuff, even an old never-has-been with a beer belly and thinning hair. He smiled down at them, lapping it up like honey, as if he was still that sexy young hotshot in the vest and silver-toed boots. Pathetic.

"Can we move on?" I said to Wayne. "I'm kind of tired of this place."

"Okay, sure."

I didn't look back as we went up the stairs. What was there to see, after all? A flabby middle-aged man standing at the bar, kidding himself the way he'd done his whole life, refusing to accept the fact that he was never going to be a rock star, or anything at all.

In the car Wayne showed me a little plastic bag with some pills sealed in it. "Look what I scored," he said. "Help yourself."

I'm not a big fan of drugs; I never wanted to follow in *his* footsteps. But if you're always refusing, people think you're afraid or prudish. Besides, I wanted to feel happy and light again, the way I'd felt earlier in the evening, before we hit H t P nk. You get so tired of always being angry. I popped a couple of pills in my mouth. Wayne said, "God, you're unbelievably hot," and bent over me. It was the second time that night he disappointed me. I might as well have been back at Eastend Collegiate, getting pawed in Robbie Canova's 1979 Honda. But if I'd resisted or suggested going back to the condo first he'd have thought I wasn't spontaneous. So I just leaned back into the soft upholstery, and before long the pills started to work. Each tense muscle loosened, one by one each jangling nerve went smooth and still. You could hear the music from H t P nk but soft and faraway, like someone playing a radio turned down low. Past Wayne's shoulder I watched the wires turn from dull black to gleaming silvery-blue, like streaks of Day-Glo across the sky.

CORY   JUNE 13, 2000 Today in English lit class Karko fell asleep and started snoring. Mr. Rodriguez said, "Will somebody wake Karko up, I can't hear myself think." So the girl sitting in front of him turned and gave him a couple of pokes, and finally he came to life and sort of half-sat up and yawned. He had a big red mark across his face from where he'd been lying against the coils on his notebook. He didn't even seem embarrassed. He said, "What? Is it morning?"

I can imagine falling asleep in physics or social studies, but Rodriguez is *hot*. He looks kind of like Michael Jordan and he even used to play football — just the CFL but still, he got paid for it. Who knows what made him come back to this hellhole? We've had three different principals this year alone. I bet Rodriguez won't be here long either. He dresses so great and has such a beautiful smile, you can hardly take your eyes off him. It's like he dropped down here from another, better planet.

He was teaching this poem about a guy who was locked up in a dungeon for twenty years or something. He said it was based on real life. You can visit this prison in Europe and see where the guy's footsteps wore out a path on the floor from pacing back and forth. One of the boys made a joke that jail isn't so bad in modern times, you can play sports and watch TV all day. Everybody laughed. But Rodriguez got a totally serious look on his face. He said, "Your friends say stuff like that cause they think it sounds tough, but you don't see them at night when they're alone and crying. There's nothing nice about jail. You get up when you're told and you go to bed when you're told and you have no control over anything. You get strip-searched, they lock you up in an eight-by-four cell and you're looking at the world through bars and you aren't going anywhere. Does that sound like a good time?"

All of a sudden everybody was really quiet. Nobody had a thing to say.

Then Karko pipes up. "Sounds just like school," he said. If someone else had come out with that, everybody probably would have laughed. But because it was him, everybody just rolled their eyes and groaned.

At lunch he kept hanging around with his notebook and the latest stuff he's written on the *X-Files* screenplay. Brandi said if I really didn't like it I should tell him to get lost. She said she saw him panhandling at Yonge and Bloor on Saturday, and she wouldn't let a loser like that get near her, even if he was good at drama. I said, "Yeah, but he can't help it. His father's a really scary guy and they don't get along, so he's kind of on his own." I guess I can't blame her for being surprised. I was amazed too, hearing myself say something like that, almost defending Karko. Brandi's mouth practically fell open. She said, "You don't *like* him, do you?" I said, "No! Are you kidding?" But she started laughing and saying, "Cory likes Kreepy Karko! Cory likes Kreepy Karko!" until I could have strangled her. She isn't really my friend anymore. She doesn't have a clue about me, I'm so NOT what she thinks.

Plus, she told me today she's tired of Enrique Iglesias now, he's *boring*, she likes this hip hop guy Daz Dillinger. I mean, there's not even any comparison! He's loud and nasty and his songs are all about guns and dealing and child support and fucking lots of women. I said that to Brandi. But she just shrugged her shoulders and said, "So what? He's got a great sound and he raps about real stuff. Enrique Iglesias is a wimp."

I got so furious that I couldn't even talk anymore! I guess I know what she means — Daz Dillinger's music is wild and in your face and more about real life. But sometimes you don't want that kind of real life. Sometimes you want something *different*. I'm not a drooling idiot, I know I'll probably never meet Enrique Iglesias and even if I did he wouldn't be the way I imagine him. Plus I know I'll get older and probably he won't matter to me anymore. But I bet all my life when one of his songs comes on the radio I'll remember being young and how good it felt to daydream about him. He's, like, thousands of miles away but the daydreams are so intense that he seems close by, just around the corner or in another room, and that makes everything sort of magical and special. I'll never forget that. I'll never say he bores me.

Like, today, I imagined he'd be waiting for me outside the school, I'd open the back door and there he'd be standing by the bicycle rack in all that soft summery air. When he saw me he'd smile and straighten up and watch me coming toward him. And he'd act just the way you'd want a guy to act. Because of him every pebble, every weed, every cigarette butt, every street sign, every brick in every building would have a sort of golden sheen, and we'd walk together, side by side, talking, our arms bumping together. We'd go slowly, street by street, through the beautiful city.

Of course in real life I opened the back door and there was Karko. He said, "You know, I was thinking, instead of an amulet, it should be a laser stun-gun that they find."

Honestly, he has the dumbest ideas imaginable. I couldn't believe my ears. I said, "That won't work at all. It has to be something mysterious that they don't know the meaning of. Plus, it has to change them without them realizing it. How is a laser stun-gun supposed to do that?"

"But an amulet's *boring*," he said.

Boy, am I ever sick and tired of hearing that word. "Well, a laser stun-gun is just *stupid*," I said.

He doesn't have a clue, and not only that, he's as stubborn as a mule. I was so busy yelling at him, trying to make him pay attention to what I was saying, that I forgot to worry about whether anybody saw us leaving the school grounds together.

At the corner of Logan, we saw some police cars blocking the street. There was a lot more garbage than usual and a lot more graffiti, including a big "Fuck You" in red letters across the front of Andromache's Bakery. I had to look twice because I couldn't believe that graffiti was there, the old lady who runs that place wouldn't usually stand for it, she'd be out there with a pail and a scrub brush in about one minute. There was a car at the curb and its doors said "Chicago Police Department." For a second you think maybe you're losing your mind and having hallucinations or something, until you figure out that they're just making a movie. You see that kind of thing quite often — signs saying "City of New York" or "Cincinnati Public Library" or "Philadelphia Municipal Authority," because lots of Americans come up here to make movies and Toronto stands in for dozens of other cities. But no matter how sad and ugly we thought our neighbourhood was, I guess they weren't satisfied, they had to make it worse, more garbage, more broken glass, more weeds, more swear words painted on the walls.

There were a lot of vans parked around, and they'd set up lights in front of the doorway of Yanni's Place, except they'd changed the name to "Joe's Bar and Grill." Of course Karko had to stop and watch, and I must admit, I got a little excited too, because sometimes an actual star is involved. Once on Bloor Street I saw Matt Damon. The door of his Winnebago flapped open for a second and he was just sitting there, drinking a coke. Nobody would believe me when I told them that.

A guy was standing on the curb with a clipboard, looking as if he knew what was going on. Karko asked him what movie they were filming. It turned out to be something for pay-TV called *Stone Cold Dead* starring nobody we'd ever heard of, which was kind of disappointing. Still, quite a few people were standing around, so we did too. Even if you're not interested in the subject, you never know what's going to happen. Once I saw them filming a scene from a murder mystery, two people struggling on a balcony until one gets pushed off, and this stunt woman dived from ten stories up, right onto a great big air mattress. Another time on Yonge Street when they were filming a scene for this cop series, an actress fired a gun and an actor fell down on the ground with some very red, real-looking blood dripping out the corner of his mouth.

Karko asked the guy with the clipboard what this movie was about. The guy said it was a docudrama about this big drug bust that happened in Chicago a couple of years ago. Two actors came and stood in the doorway. The guy with the clipboard looked at us and put his finger to his lips and the director said, "Action." For a second there was such quiet that you could hear a dog barking and traffic from blocks away. Then one of the actors grabbed the other one by the arm and said, "Are you sure you can trust her?" The other one pulled his arm away and said, "Forget it, motherfucker, this thing is going down tonight!" The director said, "Cut!" and that was it.

Boy, I think even Karko could write a better scene than that. Still, I just about died when he said to the guy with the clipboard, "We're scriptwriters."

The guy looked around with a smirk. You couldn't blame him — here's this big dumb-looking teenaged geek wearing a toque and a dirty T-shirt, saying something like that. Why did he have to bring me into it, for God's sake? I felt like pretending I didn't even know him.

Karko said, "We're working on an *X-Files* episode right now." He wasn't even embarrassed. I poked him. I laughed and said, "Come *on*." God, I was just as geeky as he was.

The guy with the clipboard said, "Is that so."

Karko said, "Are you guys from Hollywood?" I don't know why I kept standing there. I felt like sinking through the sidewalk.

The guy said, "Isn't everybody?" He was probably some local guy the movie company hired for a couple of days to stand around holding a clipboard. But in Karko's tiny mind, if you're working on a movie you've got to be Steven Spielberg or somebody. He just wouldn't shut up. He said, "Do you know Chris Carter? He created *The X-Files*. Before that he was a complete unknown."

"No," the guy said.

"That's the way it is, right?" Karko said. "You just have to have one great idea."

"Uh huh, right," the guy said. Then he yelled, "Hey, Frank, are we saving the shootout till tomorrow?" and bustled off after the director.

I could see Karko was ready to stand there for another hour, talking to whoever would listen, asking dumb questions and making a total idiot out of himself, so I said, "Look, I have to go."

"Oh, yeah?" Karko said. "Hey, I was thinking, maybe you should come over and we can work on the script some more."

I didn't know what he meant by "come over." I stared at him. "Where?" I said.

"You know, to my house," he said. "Where we were before."

He meant that big empty house near Bloor and Avenue Road. He called it *my* house, like he owned it. I couldn't believe it.

I told him I was babysitting and after that I had lots of homework to do. As if. But he bought it. Anyway, he pretended to. "Okay, well, so you don't think we should use the laser stungun then?"

"Oh, do whatever you want," I said. But for some reason, I couldn't stop myself, I had to add, "But a laser stun-gun will just ruin the whole thing, that's all." I don't know why I had to say that, why did I even *care*?

"Okay, okay," Karko said. "We'll keep the amulet." Like he was doing me a big favour.

I started to walk off. I'd only gone a few steps when I saw this familiar-looking car coming down the street, going very slow. It took me a minute to remember where I'd seen it before and then, I don't know why, the slow way it moved made this sort of chill go over me. I turned my head. Karko was standing at the corner waiting for the light to change. The car pulled up to the curb and Karko's father got out. He seemed a bit unsteady on his feet. He tripped on the edge of the sidewalk. He wasn't smiling, or acting dirty or sarcastic like the time before. He just kept his eyes fixed on Karko and it reminded me of the way a cat's eyes look when they focus on a mouse, that kind of fierce white-hot stare. It sort of froze me. I just stood there. Karko started to shake like a leaf. I could actually see him shaking from half a block away. His father said something in Lithuanian. Of course I couldn't understand it, but his voice was so totally quiet that it was spooky. I've never heard a voice so totally quiet before, like the tone and expression were sucked out of it and there was nothing left but words coming out like stones. Karko stammered. At school he never stammers; no matter what happens he acts as if nothing fazes him. He said, "I'm s-sorry, — I f-forgot." His father kept staring, the same burning cat's eyes. Then he opened the door of the car and stood there, waiting for Karko to get in. Karko didn't want to. He looked around, as if he was hoping someone would help him. I saw the expression on his face. I thought maybe I should try to do something but I was too stunned, I couldn't move. Karko kept stammering, "I c-can't, I've got to . . . uh . . . there's . . . I'm s-supposed to . . . for school, like . . ." His father wasn't even listening. He just kept standing there staring, with his hand on the car door. Karko took one last look around. His eyes landed on me for a second, but it was like he didn't even see me. Then he got into the front seat. His father shut the door, very softly. Click. In a minute the car was pulling out into the intersection. I saw the back of Karko's head, with that stupid toque sitting on top of it, all crooked. People were bustling along, none of them paying attention. The whole thing was so totally quiet that I was the only one who even noticed. I kept standing there watching that old grey car slide through the traffic like a slow-moving cloud. I had this weird feeling that a shadow was spreading out all around it and sending a chill over everything, even the sun.

I keep telling myself that maybe I should have done something, but what could I do? It all happened so fast and I wasn't even sure what was going on.

God, what must it be like to be Karko? I can't stop picturing him with that crooked toque planted on his head. The big sad freak.

But it's not my problem, why do I keep *thinking* about it? As if I don't have enough to worry about in my own life. I'm probably totally overreacting. After all, what happened, really? Karko got into his father's car and drove away. Big deal. But I can't forget about it, I've tried to go to sleep and I can't.

At least our Dad isn't scary. The worst he ever does is sit without talking. Sometimes it goes on for days and drives you up the wall. But when he is talking, he's usually okay. He tries to show an interest and gives you a couple of bucks — if he has it. Most of the time he doesn't have it. His jobs never last long, something always goes wrong. Either he's laid off, or he says something to piss the boss off and gets fired, or he starts feeling fed up and quits. Once in a while he still gets a gig playing music, but that never lasts either.

Becky always says, how pathetic. What a *zero*. But at least he's never stared at us with tiger's eyes. When things are bad he just stares at the wall and daydreams.

I guess the most awful time for us was after we first came to Toronto. His drug problem was at its worst then so he couldn't work at all. I still remember how bad he looked, all pale and twitchy and sick. I was really young and I was sure he was going to die. I thought if somebody looked as bad as he did and had to go to "detox" it meant they were done for. I remember how huge the city seemed, and we were like tiny little insects in the centre of it. It seemed to me there were so many streets that they must have spread out across the universe, and no matter how long you walked or how far you drove, you could never, ever get out. Sometimes I felt as if I could hardly breathe.

Then Mom had the accident. That's the way it is, just when you figure everything's as bad as it can be, something even worse happens. She was crossing the street and a guy on a motorcycle ran into her and broke her arm. She had to have her arm in a sling, the whole bit. It was just bad luck, but it seems to me that's the only kind of luck this family ever has. It could have happened to somebody else, somebody walking right in front of her or right behind her, somebody with more money and a house and sick pay. But no, that motorcycle zeroed right in on her. So then she couldn't work. I remember sitting with her in some office, I don't know what it was, unemployment or welfare I guess, something like that. I remember she cried. That made me feel frozen inside because she didn't cry very often, she always laughed and acted like everything was okay. But that day she cried and said to the woman behind the desk, "You've got to help me, please help me, what are we going to do?" I wanted to cry too but I was so frozen it was as if all my tears had turned to ice. That seemed weird, to feel so icy cold inside, because it was a hot summer day, I remember there was a fan buzzing on the women's desk. She wasn't a nasty woman, in fact she seemed sad and upset, but she said, "No," anyway. I don't know why, but they always have reasons and no arguments or crying or begging will change their minds. So afterwards we were back on the street, walking fast even though we had nowhere to go. Mom was still crying, but I couldn't cry, all I could do was pant in the awful blazing heat and try to keep up with her.

That same day Dad got out of detox. That's how I remember it, anyway. It would be just like him, perfect timing, as usual. We waited till after dark to sneak away from the motel because we couldn't pay the bill. The gravel on the driveway crackled so loud it sounded like firecrackers and I was sure someone in the motel office would hear and come running out to stop us. But no one did.

I don't know why I'm remembering all this now. I'd rather forget about it, but I can't. Every so often it comes into my mind.

We drove through lots of streets, to me it seemed like hundreds of streets, hundreds of street signs and cold white lights and dark buildings and black shapes, all floating by, never stopping, never ending. Finally we parked in a big empty lot behind a warehouse. Sometimes I still have dreams about that parking lot. Nightmares, actually. Where I'm trying to cross it all alone, casting a shadow so long that it stretches out of sight. No matter how many steps I take I don't move at all, and something is behind me, I don't know what, I'm afraid to turn around.

Mom said not to worry. She said Dad would get a job and her unemployment would come through and her arm would heal, and she'd find a better job than she had before, and we'd find a great place to live and everything would be fine. Dad hadn't been saying a word. You could tell he wasn't so sure. But then he seemed to pull himself together. Maybe he thought he should help Mom out.

"Yeah, that's right," he said. "Now that I'm clean I'll get my guitar out of hock and I don't think I'll have any trouble finding lots of gigs. This is the big city, man, there's plenty of action. You can make some serious money. And then you know what? I'll take us all on a holiday. Somewhere with a beautiful beach. We'll just lie around in the sun."

He sounded so confident that for a second I actually felt better. But Becky wasn't buying it. She said, "What about tonight? Are we supposed to sleep in the *car*? God, I'd rather die! Why did we ever come here? It's all your fault! I hate you!" She just yelled that at the front seat, I don't know which one of them she was yelling at.

Mom said it wouldn't be so bad. She said, "Let's pretend we're back home in Saskatchewan and we're camping out. We're in a big field. Look at all those stars in the sky. Let's turn on the radio." When she pressed the button the radio lit up, it looked like a little glowing box of red and yellow, the only light in the parking lot, the only sound. She said, "Oh, this one's your Dad's favourite."

"Man, you hardly ever hear this version anymore," he said.

A bunch of loud guitars and drums screamed and boomed for a while, then settled down. Mom said to Dad, "I don't mind the slow part so much now." He gave a little smile.

The radio announcer said the time. It was only midnight. I couldn't believe it. I'd thought surely the night was almost over, but it was only starting.

There was no room to stretch out, no room to do anything. Becky said, "I can't stand this! I'm going to go insane!"

Another song came on. Mom said, "We know this one. Let's sing along. Come on. Becky, you know it."

Becky said, "Are you out of your mind? Do you really believe I'm going to sit here in this lousy car and sing now? What are we going to do tomorrow? You have to think of something, you're the one who got us into this mess! You're such a loser!"

"Come on, Cory," Mom said.

I was petrified. Singing was the last thing I wanted to do, I wanted to lie down and cry or run away screaming. But there was nowhere to lie down, nowhere to run to. And it made me feel better to do something ordinary. My voice still worked, I still remembered the words, I could make believe that everything hadn't fallen to pieces, that everything was normal.

"That's right, Cory," Mom said. "Good girl."

I don't even remember what song it was. But we all knew it. After a minute Dad started tapping out the rhythm on the dashboard. "Hey, remember how Titch Austin always said you could make a drum out of anything? The beat's always there. Remember?"

Mom laughed. "Yeah, good old Titch. The beat's always there." She knocked on the windshield. "Sure enough, there it is." Dad thumped against the roof with the palm of his hand. Mom slapped her knees. Dad pounded the steering wheel with both fists. "There it is!" They kept looking at each other and at us, grinning, pretending so hard to be having a good time that they almost convinced themselves. I was just a kid, they almost made me believe it too. Or at least I pretended to believe it. Becky was the only one who wouldn't pretend.

I remember thinking how it might look to anyone driving past, this car sitting all alone in an empty parking lot, a couple of doors open, the radio playing, the people laughing, singing, making the chassis rock. You'd have thought those people were on top of the world, wouldn't you?

MONA   One night last winter we were all at home. I was off work and since Wayne had gone out of town, even Becky was there. It hadn't been a good day. We'd got a notice that our rent was going up. The furnace didn't work properly most of the time, the fire escapes were rusty, all the taps dripped, the hallways smelled, the stairwells were filthy, but they claimed that because of "capital expenditures" they needed to raise the rent $100 a month. I had to take Becky aside and ask if she could contribute $50 more a month to the kitty. I said, "Just for a little while. I can do some extra shifts at the café too. And I'm going to start looking around for something better. And at the warehouse they told your Dad they might take him back in a couple of months. So . . ."

Becky just stared at me. Her blue eyes were so shiny-bright that it almost hurt to look at them. "Sure," she said. "Let's count on that." Then she went into the bathroom and slammed the door.

I didn't blame her for being upset. She was a young, beautiful girl, she deserved to have a good time and own nice things. She'd only just been given a raise at the store and there I was,

207

asking for most of it to pay the lousy rent.

Later we were sitting around watching television. The weather had been stormy all day, you could hear the snow blowing against the window panes. It reminded me of Saskatchewan. I thought, we left almost ten years ago. I looked around the room at each face lit by the flickering screen. It struck me as kind of amazing that we'd survived everything and were still all together, sitting side by side on a bitter winter night, fairly warm, fairly safe. Even Joey was there, in a photo on a shelf by the door.

We watched the CBC a lot because we didn't have cable. There was a documentary on about a Canadian rock group who were making a name for themselves. The lead singer looked something like Jesse used to, fast-moving and lean, with spiky yellow hair. I wondered if Jesse noticed the resemblance too. While scenes went by of the band playing guitars, leaping around onstage, grabbing the microphones — scenes so familiar that they seemed to come out of my own memory — the yellow-haired kid said in a voice-over, "I know this is why I'm on the planet. It's still as much fun as when we were playing in Earl's basement, making up forty-minute songs and turning into balls of sweat, me in my T-shirt and jeans, Earl in his Burger King outfit, just playing for the love of it, because it was our one release, it was the one thing that made us feel like we'd never be fifty and stuck in a rut."

Jesse laughed. "Right," he said.

Becky flashed him a contemptuous look. "But they're young," she said.

If Jesse was hurt he didn't show it. He gave a kind of small, twisted smile. "Beck, you're never too old for rock and roll," he said.

That shut her up. But not for long. She was trembling; she glared at him with her shiny blue eyes, so much like his. "They've had hit records, they're on television," she said. And of course, he couldn't answer that.

Later we lay in bed, listening to the wind and snow. I knew he wasn't sleeping. He said, "Remember that night at Club 13 when we played till 3 A.M. and they still didn't want us to stop?"

"Yeah," I said.

"It was like the music just came pouring out of me," he said. "I didn't even have to try, it was just there, just flowing. And the crowd was with me. No matter where I took it, they were right with me. I really connected, they really got it. I almost felt as if I was changing their lives, you know, like I could do that. Almost like I was healing them or something. And myself too. Crazy. Man, if you have a few nights like that before you die, you can't complain." He thought for a minute. He said, "I guess once I had it in my mind that someday I'd make shitloads of dough and get famous and all that. But I didn't think about it too much, actually. Mostly I just wanted to connect. And be — great, you know?"

I remembered him that night, the way he moved, the way he laughed and threw his head back, the sounds that radiated from him, waves and ripples and arrows of music, coming straight from him to you, rocking you, piercing you, lifting you right off the earth.

"You were great," I said.

WINNERS

JESSE

Let's say that this is our chance
Let's say that we can change
Let's say we're finally gonna live
Let's say there ain't no chains

Let's say that they can't stop us
Let's say this world is ours
Let's say we'll fly straight up to heaven
And grab us a handful of stars

— "LET'S SAY," BY JESSE MAVERICK, 1985

MONA   We decided that Wednesday would be the day we told them. We were waiting at the kitchen table when Becky came out of the bathroom in a cloud of talcum powder, towelling her hair. I was excited and nervous, the way I used to feel at school right before I had to give a speech.

"Hi," I said. "Is Cory awake?"

"I doubt it. She never wakes up till you go in there and shake her. Why? It's still early."

"We have some news," I said.

Becky sighed and rolled her eyes. "I knew it," she said. "What now?"

"No, this is good." I couldn't keep my voice steady, you could hear the rising note of excitement in it. "Good news, honest. We want to tell both of you at the same time."

Her eyes moved from my face to Jesse's. He was grinning, nodding. She was wary, she didn't trust us. I can't blame her, we'd never had much good news to report in the past. Maybe she thought we weren't even capable of distinguishing good news from bad.

"Oh, come on," she said impatiently. "Why do you have to make everything into a big deal? Just say it."

Jesse wouldn't give up his moment, though. He wanted to orchestrate it, to have both of them sitting in front of him, waiting breathlessly, wide-eyed, to hear what he had to say. So I went into the bedroom to get the final member of the audience.

Cory slept the way a lot of teenagers do, completely abandoned, her blankets kicked off, her legs sprawled, her mouth wide open, a gleam of saliva on one cheek. And she looked sweet anyway. I shook her, I pinched her nose, I said her name three or four times, and still she refused to open her eyes. "No," she groaned into her pillow. "No-o-o-o."

I finally got her to stagger out to the kitchen, but she slumped in her chair with hair in her face and her chin resting on one hand as though her head was too heavy to hold upright.

"Are you awake, Cory?" I said.

"Yeah, yeah . . ." she sighed. "God, why do I have to get up so *early*? School doesn't start for another hour."

Becky sighed too. "Come on, come on, what's this big news?" she said. "Just tell us and get it over with."

Jesse started to tap his fingers on the tabletop. "Last week I bought a lottery ticket," he said. "A couple of days ago we checked the numbers, and . . ."

Slowly Becky's eyes lifted. Cory was still too sleepy to understand.

". . . We won," Jesse said. The words echoed in the room.

Who'd have believed you'd ever hear those words in a shabby old kitchen with rusty faucets and warped linoleum? We won, we won, we won.

"What?" Cory squeaked, sitting up straight, pushing her hair out of her face. Becky just looked at us, blank. "How much?" she said finally.

I let Jesse answer. "The jackpot was eighteen million."

"What?" Cory squealed again. Becky frowned. "How much do we get?" she said.

"There were three winning tickets," Jesse said.

"Yeah, yeah, so —"

"So our share is six million."

Cory stood up. "What?" she said. "*What?*" That was the sort of reaction we expected: astonishment, stupefaction, joy. But Becky just sat there, still frowning, her eyes open wide and glistening.

"Are you sure?" she said. "Let me see it."

"See what?"

"The ticket! Let me see it, I want to see it!"

"What for?"

"I want to check it! I want to make sure! I'm not going to get all worked up till I'm sure!"

"Your mom and I checked it," Jesse said. "Four times, and we called the hotline to confirm. We've got all the winning numbers, and there are three winning tickets, and each one's worth six million bucks. So that's it."

"Why can't I see it?" Becky said stubbornly.

"We've hidden it," I said. "It's in a safe place, don't worry."

"Where?"

"Well, if we told you it wouldn't be hidden, right?" Jesse laughed.

"Not here in this dump?" Becky asked. "Wonderful. Oh, that's really smart."

"Just until Friday," I said. "We're making some arrangements and seeing a financial adviser today and then on Friday we're going to claim the money."

"But Cory and I can't know where it is until then, huh? You don't trust us."

"It's just that the fewer people who know, the better, right? Don't worry, it'll be fine."

"Great. Sure." She folded her arms across her chest.

Cory had been jumping up and down. Now she looked at our faces, everybody serious all of a sudden. She said, "But we *are* rich, right?"

It sent a shiver down my spine to hear that out loud, I guess it was a sort of superstitious fear that being too happy or too sure of your good fortune was asking for trouble. But Cory apparently didn't have any such fear. Neither did Jesse.

"Shit, yes!" he said, slapping the table with the palm of his hand. "We're rolling in it! Goodbye to this fucking rathole!"

"Goodbye to Mrs. Ferrara and her screaming baby!" Cory said. "Goodbye to ten million cockroaches!"

"Goodbye to the Putnam Warehouse!" Jesse said. "Goodbye to all warehouses!"

"Goodbye to Pizza the Action," I ventured. "Goodbye to Dominic Villanova."

"Goodbye to wieners and beans!" Cory yelled. "No more leftover pizza! Goodbye to clothes from Goodwill!"

"Goodbye to supers!" Jesse said. "Goodbye to landlords!"

He held out his palm and Cory slapped it triumphantly. But Becky still wasn't smiling, she hadn't been won over yet, he had to draw her in as well. He looked at her and said, "We figure we'll divide it evenly, four ways. That's one and a half million each." It was such a long time since those days when he was the golden one they adored, the dispenser of songs and jokes and wonders. Such a long time had passed since he'd been able to give them anything they valued. You could see him expanding, feeling the old power and grace.

"What'll you do with your share, Beck?" he said.

She couldn't resist any more. She tried, but it was impossible. The frown faded, her face took on a softer, younger look. "I'd like to have a place of my own," she said. "I'd like to buy a whole new wardrobe. I'd like to take a trip."

"Where?" Jesse encouraged her.

"Mexico," she said, "Or — Saint Isaac. Nobody knows about it yet, but it's going to be big."

Cory said, "I want a motorcycle! And I want to get front-row tickets for Enrique Iglesias in August in Las Vegas! If we're rich we can go to Las Vegas, right? And I want a new stereo and about five thousand CDs! And I want to travel all around the world!"

Jesse said, "First thing for me is, I'm going to sit down and write some new songs. I really think I can finally do it right. I've been completely clean for two solid years this time and I've got lots of ideas. With a little more material I'll have enough for an album. I'll rent a studio, hire some backup musicians, see how it goes. Make some demos, circulate them to a few people I know. I've been reading that with the Internet, you don't have to wait for a record company to pick you up anymore, you can release your music through your own website and your own label, market yourself directly. So if they don't like what I'm doing, fuck 'em. This time I'm gonna be in control."

I said, "Well, number one on my list is —" All of a sudden

the phone rang. We all jumped as if there'd been an explosion.

As soon as I heard Jimmie's voice, I wanted to tell him everything. "Hi, Jimmie!" I said and took a breath, ready for the next sentence. But Jesse shook his head urgently, so I had to gulp the words back. "Hi!" I said again, sort of inanely.

Jimmie claimed that his reason for phoning was to ask me what movie Paul Newman had won an Oscar for, a pretty thin excuse. A lot of times I think he called hoping Becky would answer.

"*The Color of Money*," I said, and almost laughed at the appropriateness of it.

If I sounded breathless or giddy, Jimmie didn't seem to notice. "Not *The Hustler*?"

"No, he was robbed that year. *The Color of Money* was the consolation prize. He played the same character but lots older. Listen, Jimmie, I can't talk right now."

"Oh, yeah? What's going on?"

"Look — I'll tell you some other time, okay?"

"Well, how are you feeling? Are you going to be back at work today?"

"Oh . . . no, not today."

"Don't tell me you're going to take the whole week off? I thought you'd used up all your sick days."

"Yeah . . . but it can't be avoided."

"Dominic's been having shit-fits."

"Good," I said.

"Hey, tough talk!" Jimmie laughed. "Are you sure everything's all right?"

"Oh, yes." I couldn't resist, I said, "More than all right, actually."

"Come on, tell me," Jimmie said. "You know you want to."

"In a couple of days, I swear I'll give you the whole story."

"I can't believe you're going to keep me hanging. Okay, I won't forget this. You'll pay. Well, say hi to everybody."

I hung up. "He says hi to everybody," I told them, looking at Becky. She was pretending to look out the window, pretending not to be paying the slightest attention. But I knew he could be the love of her life if only she wasn't afraid. I'd help her, I thought, I'd invite him to dinner and seat them side by side, and it would be a beautiful dinner in some beautiful place, with all the best food and wine, because I could afford it! And I could send for Mom from out west, and have her at the dinner too. She'd come first class, and I'd take her to have her hair done, and buy her a new outfit, and of course she'd act grumpy and unimpressed, but she'd like it just the same. I'd look so different to her, the kind of daughter she never thought she could have, stylishly dressed, full of confidence and charm, with money to burn. I'd be the one bossing her around for a change. It would do her good. At the banquet I'd seat her next to Sal Perez who ran the corner grocery store — he was about her age and full of jokes, just what she needed. She'd have to be grateful to me, at some point she might even say the words "thank you." That would be a red-letter day for sure.

"You know what we should do?" I said. "We should have a banquet for everybody we know!"

They gaped at me.

"A great big celebration!" I said. "We can invite Mom, and Jimmie, and Mr. Perez from the grocery store — Becky, you can invite Erika and Wayne" — I would have liked to leave Wayne out but that would have been a little too obvious — "Cory, you could invite Brandi, and that boy you did *The Glass Menagerie* with, and any of your teachers that you like — hey, how about

Majeska? I'll bet she and Jimmie would really hit it off!" —
I threw that in to give Becky something to think about — "And
Jesse, you can invite some of the guys at the warehouse, and
Barney I guess, and some of the musicians you've worked with,
hey, maybe we can track down Titch Austin, I'd really like to
see him again — and, oh, who else? Mrs. Ferrara and her
daughter — hey, we could put up signs inviting everybody on
the block!"

"Mrs. Ferrara!" Cory said. "Why should we invite her?"

"Everybody on the block?" Becky said almost at the same
time. "Are you crazy?"

The whole picture was flooding through my mind, just like
one of those European movies — usually Italian, usually in the
last scene — where long tables are set up on the grass, with
white tablecloths, flowers, shiny dishes, jugs of wine, plate after
plate of steaming food, and all the characters gather to eat and
laugh and have a great time. I heard the music, I saw all their
faces: Jimmie and Becky, Mom and Mr. Perez, Cory and Brandi,
that big gawky kid from the drama class — Carcoat or whatever — Miss Majeska, me and Jesse, the other waiters and
waitresses from the restaurant; and Dominic too, why not, so
he could see what real hospitality was like; and Mrs. Ferrara,
why not, so she could get a rest; even that lunatic from downstairs, as long as we could give him a pill to keep him under
control, why not, it was obvious he could use some fun for
once. The hookers on the street corner, always standing there
looking so glum. The little old man always sitting in the park
giving crumbs to a few scrawny pigeons. The little old lady at
the food bank, always saying, "I'll just take a couple of cans of
tuna, I can get by on that." Why *not*? For once in their lives
they could eat whatever they wanted, drink until they were

tipsy, dance, sing at the tops of their voices, say anything that came into their heads, and it would all be free, they wouldn't have to think about the cost because it would already be paid for. What a day that would be; they'd remember it forever. God, what a party, they'd say, wasn't that the best time you ever had?

The whole idea made me feel so good I couldn't sit still, I jumped up and said, "Yeah, that's exactly what we should do!" Everybody stared at me, amazed, skeptical, not really understanding what I had in mind. But I knew they'd see. Later on they'd get it.

"Don't worry," I said. "It'll be tremendous!"

REBECCA   I walked down the street and nobody guessed I was rich. I went into the Second Cup for a cappuccino and nobody suspected they were sitting next to a rich person. They might have glanced at me, they might have thought, hey, look at the cool blonde. But they didn't know I was a millionaire. Something really big had finally happened to me. Never again was I going to be one of those faceless zeros with their drab little lives. I felt like I'd been singled out from all those people trudging along through another day. I'd been selected, I was special, I was the lucky one. Millionaire. I kept thinking the word over and over. It sounded like a shower of gold coins falling all around. Millionaire.

Of course I didn't go to work. Those days were over. But I got restless in two seconds just sitting around our grungy apartment; that didn't seem like the thing to do either. Mona and Jesse had it all figured out; we had to wait till Friday before we claimed the money. If it had been up to me we would have gone straight down to the lottery office that morning. Why waste time? You might as well start collecting interest, right? But oh no, that was too sensible for Mona and Jesse. They had to hide the ticket in a secret place only the two of them knew about, that kind of thing. You'd have thought they were a couple of adolescents instead of a middle-aged man and woman.

We weren't supposed to tell anybody either. Not one soul. Of course I could see the logic in not blabbing about it to all the neighbours and passersby on the street. After all we didn't want to get knifed and robbed, or have people lining up outside our door asking for handouts. But on the other hand, what harm would it have done to tell one or two close friends? I had this desire to tell someone, to hear someone gasp in amazement, scream out loud, oh, Rebecca, that's wonderful! And then grab me and hug me. For some dumb reason I wanted to jump up and down for joy with someone's arms around me. But who would that have been? I didn't have any women friends except maybe Erika, and she was my boss so I couldn't tell her. Wayne wasn't the jumping up and down type, and not only that, I was still annoyed with him, so I didn't exactly feel like rushing to the phone to call him. Eventually he was going to find out, and then he'd have to look at me differently. I wouldn't be just a pretty little nothing anymore. He wouldn't be able to keep me in a neat package to open whenever he felt like it, in a separate compartment from the rest of his life. He'd have to respect me because I'd have my own money. It wouldn't be, she works as a clerk in a dress shop, of course I won't be with her long. It would be, my girlfriend is independently wealthy. My girlfriend just bought a car. My girlfriend's flying home from the Caribbean tomorrow.

I kept walking for hours, just walking through the city. The pavement seemed to bounce under my feet, the end of each street blazed with sunlight between tall glittering buildings, as if with every step I was travelling upward, everything cheap and sad was dropping away like mud from my shoes, and everything ahead was brilliant and easy and clean and new.

It's only luck, someone might say. It's just a random thing, an accident that those particular numbers came up. But I couldn't help feeling that I must have done something right; I tried so hard, I struggled so long, and finally someone, God or someone, recognized that I should get a reward. It belonged to me. I earned it.

CORY JUNE 14, 2000 I can't believe I had to go to school today. Mom was like, "Even if you're rich, you still need an education." Yeah, right. As if I was actually getting an education at that pathetic school. Mom didn't go to work, Dad didn't go to work, Becky didn't go to work, but I had to go to school. I said, "It's not *fair*! I won't be able to concentrate for one second! What's the *point*?" Mom said, "In a few more weeks you'll have your grade ten, why screw that up now? You'll have plenty of time to enjoy yourself later." Easy for her to say.

So before I knew it, there I was, tramping down the street as usual. I had to keep shaking my head, I felt as if I must have dreamed the whole part in the kitchen when Dad told us we'd won. It's exactly the kind of thing you dream, not the kind of thing that actually happens. I kept looking at people's faces, perfect strangers, wanting to say, "Guess what?" At the same time it was kind of exciting to have such a huge secret, to be walking along with a normal face, carrying a knapsack, on your way to school with all the other geeks, and nobody knows what's just happened to you. I keep thinking about what we'll be doing next. We'll move I guess, we'll have a house and a yard and a garage and all that stuff that rich people have. Maybe we'll take a trip somewhere this summer (as long as we pass through Las Vegas for Enrique's concert in August!), and next year I'll be in a better school probably, with better kids. But maybe they won't like me, maybe I won't know how to act, maybe they'll still think I'm a geek. But no, I'll have better clothes and a better haircut and I'll just be *better*, I know it.

I was thinking all that as I was walking, and all of a sudden I thought, what if it *is* all a dream? And then I was scared. But then I thought no, it's real, and I got excited all over again. My head started to spin, I felt as though I'd just got off the Fireball at the CNE. Then I remembered that Karko would probably be waiting for me at my locker, with more dumb ideas about the stupid *X-Files* play, and that reminded me about everything that happened yesterday with his father and all that stuff. It was insane, my whole life was changed and still I had to be worrying about Kreepy Karko! I thought maybe I'd just blow him off, go into the girls' washroom till the bell rang, because I didn't want to spoil my wonderful day thinking about him and all his dumb problems. But as I was crossing the schoolyard, all of a sudden I got this absolutely *brilliant* idea. It just kind of exploded in my brain and stunned me so much that I had to stop walking for a minute. I thought as soon as I got my money I could buy one of those Camcorder things — or something even better, a real movie camera even — and we could film the *X-Files* story! We could go all over town and I even knew a place that we could get to look just like the alien city in Area 51. The opening shot could be a sign saying "Extraterrestrial Highway" and behind it a dark sky full of stars, with something rigged up to look like Giant Rock all spooky and mysterious in the distance, and then we could zero in on a car speeding along with Mulder and Scully inside. I don't know how you work something like that on film, but I figured we could easily find out. Oh, it could just be so *amazing*!

I practically ran down the hall, I couldn't wait to give Karko the whole picture. But he wasn't at my locker. I guess it's just as well, because I forgot that we're not supposed to tell anybody about the lottery ticket until after Friday when we get the money. I was ready to blurt it all out, the Camcorder and everything, the second I saw Karko's dopey face. I thought if he was all upset about his father being so mean, this would really cheer him up fast. But I waited ten minutes and he never showed. He wasn't in English or physics either.

Then I started imagining that maybe something awful happened with his father last night. God, why do I always dream up the worst possible scenario? He probably just ate too many barbecue chips before he went to bed and today he's lying on his sleeping bag, farting and reading Superman comics. Anyway, it's not my problem, why should I even worry? I don't need to care about any of this shit anymore. I'm going to have one and a half million dollars all my own! I'll never have to be afraid again, I'll never have to do without anything or miss anything or be left out. If I want to go to university I can, I can be a lawyer or a doctor or a film director; if I want to take the train I can, or a plane or a boat. I can fly to Europe any time I want, I can sail to South America, I can do whatever I want and be whoever I want to be. Even my scummy little bedroom seems nice right now. When I look out the window I can see the moon through the fire escape railing and any second Enrique's going to come down the alley singing. Even that seems almost possible. Oh, I love the world tonight!

MONA The bank was kind of like a cathedral, a modern one made entirely of glass. When you walked in your eyes were pulled upward to this towering ceiling, all transparent arches; through them you could see blue sky, clouds, shimmers of light, you could feel the sun's warmth falling down on you from high above. It was sort of awesome — you felt small and shabby, but at the same time it made you remember there are things that have nothing to do with money. Kind of a strange message to get from a bank.

That all changed in about thirty seconds. There was a special set of elevators that only went beyond the eighteenth floor and when you stepped into one of them you immediately sank down almost to your ankles in soft carpet. You saw your reflection in a wall of mirrors, you smelled expensive cologne, your ears were soothed with quiet classical music, you felt yourself rising without effort, as if no machinery was involved and you were being lifted by air alone.

I couldn't help noticing that Jesse and I were the only ones in the elevator not wearing suits. A group of men — all about a foot taller than me, all with gold cufflinks, tie clips and embossed briefcases — stood around us speaking what sounded like German. I have to admit it made me a little nervous; I was in a blouse and flowered skirt that I thought looked nice at home but with those smooth guys around me suddenly it seemed like a pretty cheap, tacky get-up, and looking down I noticed a grease stain on my breast pocket. Even my toes looked tacky, sticking out big and bare through the straps of my cheap sandals.

But one thing about Jesse that never changed was his easy-going attitude with people. No one ever intimidated him, it didn't matter who they were, or whether they were better dressed, taller, richer, better educated — nothing like that worried him for a minute. He looked at me with his eyebrows raised and a smile on his face, as if to say, get a load of these clowns.

He was the same in the financial adviser's office, sitting back in a big plush chair as though it was the old threadbare rocker we had at home. I couldn't feel quite so relaxed; the office was about the same size as our whole apartment — the desk alone looked bigger than our bathroom, and there were giant windows on all sides. You could see the lake with sailboats on it, Skydome, Exhibition Place; you could see towers and streets and ravines, the entire city spread out all around like a tremendous carpet.

The financial adviser seemed like a nice guy though, not pretentious or superior in any way. He was in shirtsleeves and right away he offered us a drink. Well, why not? It was the start of our new life, to be sitting on the twenty-fourth floor of the Toronto Bank, sipping wine from tall goblets while discussing future plans with our financial adviser. Walter Schroder was his name — it was in gold letters on his door — but he asked us to call him Walt.

"I'm not a wine connoisseur by any means," Walt said, "but I find this to be quite nice. It's Chilean. One of my colleagues brought it back for me, he has a client down there with a small vineyard. That wouldn't be a bad way to live, would it, grow grapes in the sun, make wine, walk in your fields . . . So tell me, how do you like it?"

It was good wine. I'd always had the cheap stuff before. You could really tell the difference.

"I understand from Barney that you're expecting to come into a considerable sum of money," Walt said. He wasn't sitting behind that huge desk, he was on the sofa across from us, having a glass of wine too. "Do you have any idea of exactly when that's going to happen?"

"Friday," Jesse said.

If Walt was surprised to hear such a definite date he didn't show it. He just nodded. "And if you can give me an idea of the general figure we're talking about . . ."

"Six million," Jesse said.

Again Walt just nodded. I guess he heard figures like that every day, no big deal.

"There are the two of us and we have two daughters," I said. "We want to divide the money equally four ways."

Walt kept nodding. He seemed to be deep in thought.

He said, "I understand that up to this point your financial situation has been a bit insecure."

Jesse and I both laughed. "That's for sure," Jesse said.

Walt leaned back against the plush sofa cushions. "Let me ask you this. What do you want from life?"

It's the sort of question you don't get asked every day. In fact, I'm not sure anyone had ever asked me that before. No wonder my mind went blank for a minute. Jesse recovered before I did.

"I want to concentrate on music again," he said. "For the last few years I haven't been able to spend much time on it, but now I want to get back to playing and singing and songwriting. I'd like to have my own studio and make some recordings."

"Right," I said, trying to collect my thoughts. "That would be perfect. As for me, well, I guess I'd like to take some acting classes. Not that I think I'm going to become a big star or anything. It would be just for the satisfaction." Suddenly it struck me with full force that maybe it wasn't too late after all, maybe we'd still be able to do all those things we used to dream about. Maybe not in the big way we'd imagined, but in some way. A shiver went down my back, I started to gather steam. "And I'd like to buy some cameras and try photography too. And maybe invest in a dress shop, something like that. And design clothes for it. My own line. I'd like to try all sorts of new things."

Walt took a sip of wine and set down his glass. While he was doing that his eyes passed very casually over us, as if he wanted to take a closer look without being too obvious. All of a sudden I wondered exactly what Barney had told him. Had he said we were kind of off the wall, he wasn't sure how serious this was, maybe it was all bullshit, but just humour us, as a favour? I thought I saw something like that in Walt's expression, a little flicker of skepticism or amusement. But I said to myself, okay, you'll find out. Later you'll see it was all true.

"And we want the best of everything for our daughters," I said. "We want them to have lots of choices."

"Yeah," Jesse agreed.

"So," Walt said. "What I'm hearing is that you have better uses for your time and talents than sorting through investment opportunities. You're going to have concerns you haven't really dealt with before, like tax minimization, estate planning, wealth management and preservation. But you want freedom from a sort of day-to-day, intense concentration on those kinds of things. That's where I come in, to take that burden from your shoulders so you're free to pursue your goals, and at the same time feel confident that your financial concerns are being handled properly."

"With the amount of money we're going to have, we could just put it in a savings account and live on the interest, couldn't we?" I said.

Walt smiled. "Well, of course that depends on how you want to live. It's true that you'd have a small regular income from a savings account, but of course that's not what I'd advise. Your money can do so much more for you than that."

"Like what?" Jesse said.

"Well, I'll just talk in general terms for now. Once you actually receive your money I can prepare a detailed plan, we can discuss it and you can make some decisions. But for now, I'll just toss out some ideas. One possibility is what we call our International Diversified Investment Portfolio. It's for clients who have a minimum of one million dollars to invest. Our strategy's based on two proven approaches, that is, global diversification and long-term planning. The International Portfolio lets you take advantage of investment opportunities in markets all over the world, and because of the diversification you're protected against economic and political instability. Diversification is the key, it reduces volatility without sacrificing return. How? By bringing together a collection of investments that go up and down at different times. So it's relatively simple to smooth out your cash flow. We've got offices in thirty-one different countries so we can offer services from any location that's convenient to you. But I'd be managing your portfolio myself and giving you regular reports showing all the activity and the current values, so without having to worry about it every day you'd still be kept abreast of everything you needed to know. And believe me, I'm very rigorous about selecting securities that I'm confident will really perform. I'll ensure that your risks are reduced but you still retain long-term growth potential."

The wine was making me light-headed. My brain was full of images; I saw Jesse in a recording studio, wearing headphones, playing his guitar with all the old dazzling speed; I saw myself on a sunny, foreign street, taking photographs, beautiful pictures of Becky running on cobblestones with her long pale hair blowing behind her, or Cory standing in a street market, biting into a ripe purple plum. I saw oceans, white buildings, people laughing, curtains flapping at windows, gulls wheeling through the air, boats gliding, waiters in white jackets standing at the lit doors of restaurants, plates piled high with meat and fruit. Every week Walt would be depositing more money in our account. We'd just have to go and get it.

"A bit more?" Walt asked.

I was surprised to see that my glass was empty. "Yes, please," I said.

"Now, as for your daughters," Walt was saying, "we have what we call a Universal Trust. It's an excellent way to preserve wealth for your dependents. You appoint a trustee who becomes responsible for managing particular assets and distributing them to the beneficiaries in accordance with the terms of the trust. Tailor made for people who want to protect their money against uncertainty, but still allow for plenty of flexibility. A trust can be a very powerful legal instrument and if it's located internationally there can be definite tax advantages."

I glanced at Jesse, expecting that he might give me a smirk, a wink or a discreet yawn to indicate how bored he was with all this dry financial talk. But he was nodding his head, staring solemnly at Walt, apparently absorbed in every syllable. He even seemed to have forgotten about his wine, the glass was still in his hands, half full. I felt like laughing. In all the years we'd been together I don't think he ever looked at our bank book or our account statements, not even once.

"What about you?" he asked Walt with a smile. "You wouldn't be doing all this just for the fun of it."

Walt smiled too. "Well, of course there are fees involved in these kinds of transactions. But with the kind of portfolio I was just talking about, they're all rolled into one inclusive figure that we call a 'wrap fee.' Normally it would amount to between one and four per cent of the value of your portfolio. The higher the value, the lower the percentage. I think you'll find it quite reasonable considering the returns you'll be getting."

I was drunk on wine and daydreams. Through Walt's windows I could see sunlight glinting on water and the long glistening ribbons of streets. For some reason that brought back a dim memory, the smell of french fries in the air on a summer night, coming out of the Starlite Theatre, walking along looking in the store windows, holding my father's hand. Music from a car radio, the pavement blue in the dusk, Dad saying what a nice evening. How happy I was that night, how ready and eager for all the great things I was going to do in my life.

"It sounds good," said Jesse.

"Yes," I agreed. "It sounds fine."

"On Friday when we collect the cheque we'll come straight over here, right?" Jesse said.

"I'll give you my card," Walt said. "When you come in, just show it to the people downstairs and they'll notify me. Once we've got the exact numbers, I'll work up a detailed plan and we'll talk it over. You can bring your daughters in too. But right now I have one suggestion. There's one thing I'd advise you to start arranging immediately."

We'd been standing up, smiling, but he looked very serious. We stopped smiling.

"A vacation," he said. "Get away from everything, take as much time as you need, make sure you know what you really want. Last year I went to the Virgin Islands for three weeks, walked on the beach, climbed a mountain, went sailing, far away from all my usual concerns. Gave me a whole new perspective. Make sense?"

He ushered us solicitously into the hallway. We'd become delicate, special people who had to be cared for and handled with deference. We were the kind of people who had to take a vacation to prepare ourselves for the heavy responsibility of spending all our money.

In the elevator going down there were two tall women with sculpted hair, gleaming stockings and perfectly tailored outfits, but I didn't care anymore. I didn't care if I had grease all over my blouse, or if my toes were black as coal. I looked at Jesse and said, "I can't wait to diversify. Won't it be wonderful to reduce volatility?"

"Hey, this is no laughing matter," Jesse said. "You'd better wipe that smile off your face and keep a close eye on your long-term growth potential, baby."

The two women stared at us coolly. Apparently they weren't finding us very funny. That made us worse.

"I love it when you say 'growth potential,'" I told him. "Please, one more time."

"Maybe later when we get home. Right now all I can think about is smoothing out your cash flow."

The two women got off the elevator at the eighteenth floor. Neither of them looked back. We were alone, floating downward as softly as we'd floated up.

"You were sitting there with such a serious look on your face," I said. "Like you were just drinking it all in."

"I was," he said. "Especially the part where he said he'd take the burden off our shoulders so we'd be free to pursue our goals. That's what I wanted to hear. After that, I thought, let him enjoy himself. All that other crap is what these characters live for. So okay, go to it, Walt, knock yourself out developing an awesome international portfolio. Have a ball, man. All I want is to be free to do my own thing without ever having to think about that shit. Yeah, Cherniak knows how to pick 'em. Old Walt's just the right type. Something tells me he's going to do really well for us."

A streetcar was sitting at the corner. The driver turned and smiled, as though he'd been waiting just for us. There were two empty seats near the door.

"Let's take it all the way to Broadview and then walk up," Jesse said. "We can stop at the Bacchus for a beer."

"Where shall we go for our vacation?" I said once we were settled. What a question to ask, what a problem to solve. There we were, sitting on the Queen Street car like we'd done a hundred times before — hearing the clang, watching as the doors flapped open so that more people could crowd on — everything just the same, and yet everything was completely changed, because now we had a question like that to ponder, and the answer could be Africa, China, Tierra del Fuego. No corner of the globe was beyond our reach.

"I'd like Cory to finish her school year first," I said. "She's only got a couple more weeks, no point disrupting it. But after that, what?"

"Do you think Beck will want to come with us too?"

"I don't know. Maybe." But I doubted it. She'd want to go off on her own, or with Wayne to some tropical paradise, that was my guess.

"I've heard that Greece is wonderful," I told Jesse. "Jimmie went there one summer while he was at university. A Greek island, Mykonos or Santorini or Rhodes, one of those. He said you could feel yourself slowing down and relaxing. You'd be sitting at a table beside the sea, watching the sun on the waves, and you'd realize you had no desire to move for the rest of the day."

"How about Cuba?" he said. "It's supposed to be fantastic too, miles and miles of beaches, and apparently the music is something else. There's a band on every street corner in Havana, somebody told me. Musicians in every club. They've got jazz, they've got salsa, you name it. That would be a blast."

"Oh yeah! That would be great! Remember that saxophone player at the Blue Note that time?"

"Yeah, exactly. That's what I mean."

"We could spend a whole month wandering around just listening and collecting music. And I could take photos, maybe I could collect them in a book. Maybe not only Cuba, maybe all over the Caribbean. We could check out the reggae, the calypso, the . . ."

"Yeah, the merengue . . ."

"And how about Italy? Remember *Roman Holiday*? Yes, you do, it was on *Saturday Night at the Movies* just after Christmas and you watched it with me. Gregory Peck and Audrey Hepburn?"

"Oh, yeah, where they ride a motorcycle to all those places and —"

"Yeah, I love that movie. It's the one that made Audrey Hepburn a star. I remember watching it on TV when I was about twelve years old and saying to myself that someday I'd go to Rome and do all those things, throw coins in the Trevi Fountain and walk up the Spanish Steps and dance on a boat on the river . . . Although I've heard that Italy is really expensive, so maybe —" Suddenly I remembered. "Oh — but who cares?"

"That's right," Jesse laughed. "Who cares? I wouldn't mind going to Africa either. You cross the Mediterranean, land in Morocco, that's supposed to be really wild. And gradually keep going south. I'd like to try one of those safaris. It'd be interesting to see a real jungle, what it's like. Where is it those Monarch butterflies go? You know, they migrate south every year, millions of 'em, and they all end up in the same jungle, so you walk into this clearing and all around you are these millions of coloured wings fluttering. That would be something to see."

"That's Mexico, isn't it?"

"Oh, now, Mexico, we'd better think about that, right? You know what we could do? We could buy a Winnebago and just start driving and see where we end up. I'd really like to see the desert again too. Before I met you, when I was bumming around with the Dirt Angels in the U.S., we had a gig in Las Vegas, and what you could do was, you could jump in your car in the centre of the city and ten minutes later you'd be in Red Rock Canyon. That was wild, first neon lights, traffic, crowds of people, then all of a sudden — silence. Dark. Empty space. Sometimes I'd turn the car radio on and leave it playing and walk away from the car. I got a kick out of hearing the music get fainter and fainter. Finally I wouldn't be able to see either the car or the highway, it would be just me out there alone, standing on the ground looking up. Once or twice I got a spaced-out feeling, like I was too small and all my molecules were going to dissolve or something. But most of the time it was great. The colours were really incredible; if the sun was setting the buttes in the distance would get all kind of burnt-orange like something from another world. Or if it was dark, the ground wouldn't be black, it would be sort of a deep, deep mauve. I swear you could smell the sand and the sun on the plants, because the heat stayed in the ground even when the air was getting cold. One night I heard a coyote howl, could have been a hundred miles away or just fifty feet, it was clear as a bell but there was no sign of him, and I could see a long way, but no shadow, nothing moving, just this howl from out of nowhere, echoing and echoing. It gave you the shivers. You knew you were in a universe, man. Sometimes I'd have a tequila buzz going and I'd feel like my mind was expanding so that in one more minute the whole galaxy was going to make sense."

"I know what you mean, that reminds me of the Big Muddy Badlands. You never saw them, did you? My Dad and I went there once, just spur of the moment, one afternoon. It was only fifty miles or so from Walbrook but it was like crossing a boundary into another country. I was so excited I could hardly sit still in the car. I kept saying it's just like *Stagecoach*! It's just like *Butch Cassidy and the Sundance Kid*! Because it was the Old West that you always saw in movies, the land and the rock formations and the buttes, just the same. Sitting Bull actually lived in the Big Muddy for awhile after the Battle of Little Big Horn. Plus it actually was an outlaw hideout, the real Sundance Kid did stay there. Dad and I got out of the car and all you could hear was our footsteps on the rocks and the wind blowing. We went into one of the caves, and there was an old, old trunk on the floor, you couldn't help daydreaming about who might have left it there. Oh, Jesse, it was amazing. And the most amazing thing was that it was so close to Walbrook, this whole other world, and I never even knew it until that day!"

"It sounds cool. I wish I'd seen it. Too bad we never went there together."

"We can do it now, why not? On our way back from Mexico and Red Rock Canyon we could stop in. We haven't been back for such a long time."

"That's true," Jesse said, but he didn't sound enthusiastic.

"I went for a walk the last night before I left," I said, without thinking, because suddenly the memory just flowed into my mind. "Remember how if you went out the back door of Mom's house and crossed the back yard, you could go right away from the town, right into the prairie? That's what I did. You should have seen the sunset that night. You remember what the sunsets were like there, right? The whole sky, in every direction, all colour? That night it was so red — blood red — all across the horizon, it just took my breath away, it really did."

"Yeah, I've seen sunsets that colour in Alberta too."

"Yeah, it's like you were saying before, you realize you're just a tiny little atom in this strange, colossal universe. Then I got to the top of that rise, you remember the one, where you look down and see Highway 35 going east? And I saw —"

Too late I realized where I was going. It was something we'd never managed to talk about; I'd always been afraid to; it was so painful, I didn't think he could stand it. But I'd gone too far to stop. He guessed what I was going to say; he looked down into his lap. My heart started to pound. But I plunged on, there was nothing else to do.

"I saw Green Hill Cemetery. You know how you can see it so clearly from that rise, the white gate and the trees and all that? And I saw the new part where the trees were still small; there was hardly any shadow there, it was all glowing, and even though it was so far away I'm sure I could see the place where his — where Joey's — little grave is, and I don't know, this is crazy, but I felt really close to him somehow, as if he was right beside me, not too far out of reach. He was such a sweet little boy. I knew he wouldn't blame us. He'd forgive us."

Jesse nodded, still looking down into his lap. I didn't know which one of us had reached out first, but I realized that our hands were clasped together, squeezing hard.

"And I remembered reading somewhere . . . you know that theory, that time doesn't just move ahead in a straight line, it's more like a dimension? That could be possible, couldn't it? We don't know so it could be possible. And I thought if it is true, then maybe in some other dimension Joey's still alive and we're all in Mom's living room, playing with him and laughing and singing just like we always used to do. It made me feel so much better to think that. You know?"

He nodded again, still looking down, squeezing my hand.

I said, "Maybe we could all go back to Walbrook and we could go for the same walk. Across that field, down the slope to the cemetery. Just to see it, all of us together, I think that might be a — a good thing, don't you?"

Jesse cleared his throat and spoke very quietly. "Yeah," he said. "That might be a good thing."

"Parliament Street," the streetcar driver called out. I looked up and saw the old corner grocery, the traffic lights, Marty Millionaire's Used Furniture Store that we'd passed so many times before. It was almost a shock, because I felt as if we'd just travelled ten thousand miles.

∽

Months had passed since the last time I'd been in the Bacchus Tavern, but of course it hadn't changed one iota — the same cool, musty air, the same cheap ashtrays on the glass-topped tables, the same opaque windows with the stained glass arches that made a sort of yellow glow, as though it was always five o'clock in the afternoon. I thought, maybe this will be the last time I ever have a beer in the Bacchus. That gave it a whole new aura, soft and dim and golden, as though it was already just a memory, something I could look back on with nostalgia because it was over forever.

The bartender, Wesley, knew us. "Hi, Jesse, hi, Mona," he said.

Two old guys, regulars who'd been sitting at the same table every day for ten years, turned their heads and nodded. A woman who looked about fifty-five, maybe even sixty, was alone at a table by the door. There was a scrawny guy with glasses standing at the bar, and two young guys with greased-down hair and leather jackets playing pool. That was the entire clientele of the Bacchus right then. But when Jesse said, "I'll buy a round for everybody," they all snapped to attention and stared in astonishment, as though he'd offered free drinks to a packed house.

"What's up?" Wesley asked. "Didja win the lottery or something?"

Jesse had been kind of quiet ever since Parliament Street, but that question made him snap out of it. He didn't miss a beat. "Right," he said. "I've got my driver waiting outside to take me downtown to the Four Seasons, but I thought I'd just drop in here for old times' sake."

They all laughed. "That's the first thing I'd do if I won," the scrawny guy at the bar said. "I'd rent myself a suite at the Four Seasons or the Royal York and stay there four, five weeks."

"I'd tell my boss what he could do," Wesley said, filling beer mugs. "Then I'd walk out onto the street and take a cab to the airport."

"Yeah? Where'd you go?"

"First plane anywhere."

"Anywhere?"

"Wouldn't matter."

"Rio," one of the pool players piped up. "No winter, carnivals, palm trees, and the chicks go topless." His friend laughed and raised his mug of free beer. "Yeah," he said. "Hasta la vista, baby."

"I read somewhere that most Canadians who win are pretty conservative," Wesley remarked. "Pay off their debts, put the rest in the bank, like that."

"Shit," the first pool player said disgustedly. "What's the fucking point then? Give it to me."

"Yeah, I saw this guy on TV once, he'd won a million but he never even quit his job cleaning out the stables at Woodbine Racetrack."

"You know, a guy like that doesn't even deserve to win."

"Remember Brownie Beggs?" one of the regulars asked.

"Who?"

"No, he was before your time, I guess. He used to come in here almost every night back in the eighties, didn't he, Mal?"

Mal agreed. "Yeah, he used to sit over there by the men's room so he didn't have to walk too far."

"Anyway, he won the lottery. Half a million bucks. And you know what? Three months later it was gone."

Wesley whistled. The pool players laughed. I looked at Jesse. He smiled and shrugged. The scrawny guy at the bar said, "What the hell did he do with it all?"

"One night he stood outside on the street handing out fifty dollar bills to anybody who walked past."

"He tipped a waitress at the City Grill five hundred dollars because he liked the colour of her hair."

"He went to Windsor one weekend and bought a house there, but later he couldn't remember the address."

"He gave a thousand dollar bill to a hooker on Sherbourne Street. She said she'd never seen a thousand-dollar bill before. He said, 'Keep it.' She had her picture taken with it."

"He bought cars for three of his best buddies."

"After three months he goes to the bank to make a withdrawal and they tell him, 'Sorry, sir, that account has been closed.' Not a dime left from $500,000. That night Brownie slept at the Sally Ann."

The scrawny guy with glasses shook his head in disgust. "Shit," he said.

"Well, that was Brownie. He was a drinker, that was one of his problems. And he'd never had so much money in his life. He couldn't handle it. Half a million bucks. He thought that much money would last forever."

"Whatever happened to him?" one of the pool players asked.

"I don't know, do you, Mal? Haven't seen him for years. Last I heard he was up north, working as a short order cook. So there you go."

"Yep," Mal agreed. "There you go."

All of a sudden the woman spoke up from her table near the back. I was surprised to hear her voice, I thought she wasn't paying any attention. She said, "What you'd hafta do is hit the road." She sounded drunk, the words came out too loud and slurred together. Everybody looked at her. She had short hair and a big face, her lipstick was a bit smeared. "Y'know what I mean, hit the road," she said. "Leave everything behind and start all over. Thass the only way, y'know what I mean? Otherwise you'll just screw it up as usual. So take the money, hit the road, and start all over someplace else. Right? Start all over like a brand new person. Thass the way. Y'know what I mean?"

Wesley and the scrawny guy with glasses smirked at each other. The two pool players returned to their game. The regulars sipped their beer and looked down at the tabletop. Only Jesse seemed to take the woman's advice seriously. He nodded, as if he was impressed. "Like a brand new person," he said. "Yeah."

REBECCA   On Wednesday night I could hardly sleep at all. Every police car and ambulance in the city had to drive by our street with its siren screaming. I'd doze off and then come awake in a panic, sweating. I kept thinking about that ticket, somewhere in the apartment. I kept imagining someone coming in and taking it. Or a fire starting, the whole dump burning down, burning the ticket into a spoonful of ashes. Cory was snoring. I leaned over and poked her. She sighed, rolled onto her side and started snoring again. A shadow flickered across the blind and I thought, here they are, the robbers. They know we've got it, they've come to kill us and ransack the place looking for it. We're not safe, I kept thinking, we're in danger. It was only toward dawn that I finally managed to drop off, and then I had crazy dreams — being chased down dark alleys, running so hard my heart was ready to burst; but then all of a sudden a gate opened, there was a garden, a fountain, the smell of lilacs, and suddenly Jimmie Glenn came out on the pathway in front of me and kissed me on the lips, a hard fiery kiss.

The next morning after Cory went to school I said to Mona and Jesse, "Look, this is ridiculous. What are we waiting for? Why don't we just go down and get the money today?"

But oh no, they wouldn't hear of it. For some ludicrous reason their brains were fixed on Friday morning, as if there was something mystical about that time, as if trying to go earlier would cause some kind of catastrophe. So juvenile. But what could I do, I had to accept it. It was really frustrating, though. I didn't know how I was going to endure another day of waiting, waiting, waiting. I knew I wouldn't be able to relax for one second until I actually had the money, until it was in the bank under my name. That was when my new life would start.

Then it occurred to me that I didn't need to wait to go shopping. What better way to celebrate and get my mind off my worries? Buy myself something extravagant, something beautiful, put it on my credit card (that I lied about my income to get) and pay for it later, when I had my share of the money. My share, a million and a half. Thinking of it made me feel almost dizzy. All sorts of things whirled through my mind, the whole city had opened up like a treasure chest and I could reach in and take whatever I wanted.

I went to a downtown dress shop that I'd noticed lots of times, called Elegance. It was at a whole different level from Artemis; they had only one dress in the window, with no price on it. Inside everything was white and grey. The mirrors had white frames with curves and scrolls. The carpet was grey and didn't have a mark on it.

A woman came up to me. She was wearing a grey silk blouse and a white skirt. She had an English accent. She said, "Can I help you with something, madam?"

I was on the other side at last. I wasn't the one rushing around with armfuls of fabric, thinking of flattering things to say, laughing, sweating. I was the one whose mood mattered, the one who said, "Do you have it in blue?" and, "Could you show me another one, please?" I was the one who didn't blink to hear the words "a thousand dollars," who simply nodded and said, "Do you have a matching scarf?" And when I didn't blink two other clerks came over to help, suggesting shoes, earrings, bracelets. All I had to do was murmur a couple of words and one of them was off again, running to get me whatever I'd shown an interest in, while the other two hovered around me, paying compliments, praising my hair, my skin, my figure, my height. I saw myself in the mirror, standing on the grey carpet in the white light, tall and blonde, my shoulders bare, in a long, sleek, silver-blue gown that looked as if it was liquid poured down over my body. I was like a goddess, like a model in *Vogue*. The caption would read, "It's What You Always Knew You Could Be."

As I was leaving the store, the woman with the English accent said, "Thank you, madam. Come again."

I used to promise myself that if I ever made it big, I'd never treat people like shit, I'd always be gracious and courteous. So I made a special effort, I looked right at her, I tried to put a lot of warmth in my smile and voice, I said, "Thanks for all your help." I think she appreciated it. I always appreciated it when customers acted as if they knew I was a human being, not a robot. Maybe after I was gone she turned to the other clerks and said in that English accent, "What a chah-ming gel."

Walking along I saw myself in all the store windows, my hair bright in the sun, carrying my white and silver bags with the word *Elegance* on them. I couldn't believe it, that was me. But I still had this feeling I wanted to tell someone. Just one person. I couldn't see how it could hurt to tell one other person. I wanted it to be a guy, a guy who'd be excited, who'd be turned on when I showed him the new dress because he could imagine how hot I'd look in it.And since I was mad at Wayne, naturally I thought of Jimmie Glenn. Say hi to everybody, he'd told Mona

and she knew — and so did I — who that message was really
for. She thought she'd worry me, saying she was going to introduce him to Cory's drama teacher. What a laugh. As if he'd ever
prefer someone like that over me. I knew he was still thinking
of me, he still had hopes. You have to like a guy who doesn't
give up too easily. I could picture the expression in those
blue-green eyes when he saw the Elegance gown, and maybe
he'd come up with some poetic Shakespearean compliment.
I don't know why but I was really in the mood to hear some
Shakespeare. I decided I might as well walk over to Pizza the
Action, see if he was around, take it from there.

All the cars that morning seemed to have so much colour in
them, all the trees looked so green, and for once the city didn't
look dirty, it looked shining clean. I felt so good I even started
to sing to myself, one of Jesse's dumb old songs called "Let's
Say." I was surprised that I remembered it at all. The words
came back to me as easily as if I'd been repeating them every
day for ten years. Who knows, I thought, maybe I could invest
in a play for Jimmie Glenn to star in — something good, not
Canadian — and it would be a huge hit and he'd actually make
some money. Maybe he'd end up on Broadway. I pictured
myself at a big New York party in my silver-blue gown, people
coming up to me to say how great he was and how great I was
for giving him his start. After that maybe he'd go to Hollywood
and make movies, maybe he'd win an Academy Award, he'd
stand up there and say, I have to thank one person most of all,
the woman I love, without her I wouldn't even be here: Rebecca
Masaryk. And the camera would turn on me while everybody
applauded, and I'd be looking amazed, shaking my head, my
hand over my mouth. And everybody would say, God, she's
beautiful enough to be a movie star herself.

If I don't control myself the most idiotic things go through my mind sometimes.

I turned the corner onto the street across from Pizza the Action and just at that moment Jimmie came out the door. He was looking in the other direction so he didn't see me. Some woman had left her credit card behind and Jimmie was holding it up and calling her. He was wearing his pizza waiter's outfit, white pants and a striped shirt with a big smudge of tomato sauce on one sleeve. From a distance he looked really short, and you couldn't see his beautiful eyes. I stopped walking, stood in a doorway until he'd gone back inside. I thought, for God's sake, what am I doing?

If you think about it, a million and a half dollars isn't all that much money. When I first heard the words I thought, wow, I've got it made. But in this city it's easy to spend a million and a half on one house. People spend a million and a half on one yacht. People can invest a million and a half in some development and no one bats an eye, it's small potatoes. It takes at least a million to mount a big Broadway play. A Hollywood movie that costs a million and a half is called low budget. It's not so much. A person still can't sit back and relax. It would be too easy to spend it all and end up with nothing, right back at the bottom. Especially with some artsy type on my back. What I needed was someone like Wayne, someone with his own money, someone smart, someone who understood the real world. I knew Wayne would be able to tell me exactly what to do with a million and a half bucks, how to double it, triple it. With him I knew I could have everything, for the rest of my life — the condo, the boat, the summer cottage, the winter vacations, the fast cars, the trips to Europe, the restaurants, the candles, the music, the clothes, the white sand, the palm trees, the sunlight, the wine in sparkling glasses, the penthouse, the ocean view, the first class seat. On the other side, what? Standing in a doorway, staring at a pizza restaurant, the shiny cars flashing past in between, rocked by this terrible longing, it surged up inside me so strong I thought it was going to break me in half. My legs wanted to move, I wanted to cross that street, the way I might have had an insane compulsion to throw myself off a cliff, jump into the blue. Why? Because across there, behind those glass doors, was a crazy guy who wormed himself into my mind one night and I couldn't get him out. Something stupendous happened and he was the one I wanted to tell; I wanted to see his eyes looking at me, it seemed as though if he touched me I'd feel this emotion that had been buried in me for so long it almost turned to stone. If he touched me the stone would crack, that emotion would flood upward like a tidal wave, so powerful that nothing could stand against it, and to feel it would be worth anything, anything.

Sure. After that there'd be a few good days, maybe even a year, maybe even two. But gradually it would fade away. He'd spend all I had and it wouldn't be enough. I'd have to go back to working as a clerk. I'd never go anywhere, never have anything, and he wouldn't care, wouldn't help; there'd be no money in the house, everything would be in ruins, all because of him. But he'd just go down in the basement and do his thing, reciting speeches, playing air guitar, practicing serenades, singing those poetic verses that I once thought were so exciting, while upstairs people cried and worried, couldn't sleep, couldn't rest, counted their pennies. But it wouldn't matter, those same Goddamn chords would come up through the floor until they made me sick to my stomach, made me want to scream, made me want to pull the house down.

I saw Jesse the day he left Walbrook. I never told Mona that, or anyone else either. I was walking home from school at lunchtime, and I saw our car coming along in the opposite direction, his arm resting on the open window, his blond hair blowing in the breeze. He honked at me. He leaned out and said, "Hi, Beck!" Just as if nothing had happened, as if it wasn't his fault that Joey died, as if nothing was his fault at all, and everything was the same as when we used to run across the lawn to meet him.

I didn't smile. I stared at him as if he was a complete stranger, and then turned my head and kept on walking.

And I'm glad. I'm still glad I did that. Probably it was already in his mind to leave us, probably he had the road map open on the seat beside him. It served him right.

I stood in the doorway across from Pizza the Action so long that my muscles got stiff. It started to rain, one of those sudden weird downpours that happen sometimes even though the sky is blue and the sun is still shining. Through a curtain of fine golden drops I saw people running, cars flashing, and the Pizza the Action sign blinking on, blinking off, dribbling away into the gutter.

As soon as the rain was over I started back the way I'd come. The faster I walked the stronger I felt. I heard my shoes on the pavement, clip clop, clip clop, brisk and sure. No need to look back. No doubts, no regrets. No time for anything like that.

I remembered what Jesse said about how he was going to spend his share of the money. The same old bullshit, renting a studio, making demo tapes, all that crap, he was going to take a million and a half dollars and throw it away. It didn't seem right. All those times when he was out of work, who paid for his food and his beers and his cigarettes? Mona and me. It was her choice but I didn't get to choose. When I was fifteen years old I was working at Zeller's after school and already their hands were in my pockets. I was the adult, they were the children, always needing more, always dragging me down.

My brain seemed to be working in rhythm with my feet. Clip, clop, it's Mona's fault too. Clip clop, she gets a windfall and her first thought is to have a dinner party for every deadbeat in town. Clip clop, what a waste. Clip clop, too stupid to live. Clip clop, always been that way. Clip clop, they had their chance. It should be my turn now. Clip clop, my turn. Clip clop, my turn.

CORY   JUNE 16, 2000   Tomorrow morning we're going to collect our money. Actually it's this morning because I just looked at the clock and it's after twelve.

When I got home in the afternoon the phone was ringing like crazy and I ran to answer it and it was Karko! Believe it or not, I felt sort of relieved, because he wasn't at school again today and I couldn't help being sort of worried, God knows *why*. What's it to me if Karko comes to school or not? As if I don't have enough other things on my mind! But he was so worked up over that *X-Files* script, and then all of a sudden to just not show up for two days, it seemed really weird. I kept thinking about his father and everything. So I said, "Where the hell have you been?" He sounded kind of out of breath and hoarse, as if he had a cold. He said, "I just wanted to tell you, I'm leaving town, I'm hitchhiking to California." Just like that. I said, "*What?*" and then I heard this loud thud from Mom and Dad's room, it almost gave me a heart attack. It was such a shock that I hardly heard what Karko was saying but it was something like, "The cops threw me out of my place and I'm sick of it here, so I'm going to California to sell the screenplay. Wanna go with me?" I could hardly concentrate, I was listening for more sounds from Mom and Dad's room. I said, "Are you nuts, you can't just go to California! What does your dad say?" Karko said, "Who cares? You're the only one I'm telling anyway, I don't give a shit about anybody else." He took a breath and all of a sudden I thought it wasn't a cold at all, maybe he was crying, or trying not to cry. He said, "I hate this lousy city. They don't want you anywhere. They just want to keep squeezing you until you disappear. In California the weather's always warm, you can sleep on the beach." I was sure I heard more noises from the other room. I thought about the lottery ticket, that maybe that's where it was hidden and somebody was trying to steal it. "Why don't you come?" Karko said. As if. I said, "That's the dumbest idea I ever heard! I have to go now! Forget it!" and hung up. I know it wasn't very nice, but what are you supposed to do when somebody just *springs* something like that on you with no warning at all? I didn't have time to think, and so much else was going on, I just blurted out the first thing that came into my mind. Then I went rushing into Mom and Dad's room and saw Becky standing on a chair, opening boxes on the top shelf of the closet.

I said, "What in hell are you DOING, Becky?"

She didn't even look around. It was as if she didn't care who saw her. She said, "Where's that ticket? I've looked everywhere I can think of!"

I couldn't believe it. Plus any minute Mom or Dad or both of them were going to walk in, and then I knew I'd get blamed too, it would look like I was helping her.

I said, "You'd better stop it! They said we were supposed to wait till tomorrow!"

She said, "I don't give a shit! I have as much right to that ticket as they do, more in fact! I'm sick of them destroying my life!" And she threw a box full of old Christmas cards onto the floor. I felt kind of dazed, it seemed so strange to see all those Santa Clauses and snowy fields and Virgin Marys on the floor in the middle of a hot afternoon in June.

"Where would those zeros hide something valuable?" Becky said. "Come on, think, don't just stand there with your mouth open! They might be back any second!"

"We should wait till tomorrow like they told us," I said. I figured that let me off the hook, later I'd be able to say I didn't go along with it, I tried to stop her.

"They don't have any idea what to do with that much money!" she said. "They'll screw it up for us just like they always do! We have to start taking care of ourselves! I'm going to find that ticket and I'm going to take it downtown right now and cash it in, okay?"

I was so stunned that I couldn't even move. Everything got very quiet. She was standing on the chair, looking at me.

She said, "I'm not saying we won't give them any of it, but they shouldn't be in charge. We can't trust them. Even you know that, don't you?"

I don't know why, but I felt like crying all of a sudden. My eyes got burning hot. "That's not fair, they try their best! They don't mean to do anything wrong!" I said.

Becky laughed. "Oh, no, they don't mean to do anything wrong," she said. "They just can't help themselves! They're so stupid they hardly even know they're alive!"

Then all of a sudden she went completely still. "Wait a minute," she said. It was as if she'd remembered something. She jumped down from the chair and ran into the living room. I ran after her. I didn't know what else to do. My heart was pounding so hard I thought my chest was going to blow up. It came into my mind that maybe I should phone 911. Yeah, right. What would I have said? "This is an emergency, my sister is acting really crazy!" "Yeah, what's she doing?" "She's tearing the place apart looking for a lottery ticket my parents hid!" Sure, they'd drop everything to answer that one.

She ran over to the shelf where Joey's picture always sat. The frame was lying face down with the back off. She grabbed it and the glass front fell on the floor and broke. Joey's picture drifted down and landed on top of the broken pieces. Becky screamed, "NO!" She was holding the cardboard backing in one hand. And of course just then Mom walked in. I was so worked up that I couldn't even think, and everything seemed to be happening so fast, but I saw that she'd been to the hairdressers to get her hair cut. She looked a lot younger and she was humming. But when she saw what Becky was doing she stopped singing, stopped smiling. She said, "Oh God!" and ran over and got down on her knees to pick up Joey's picture and shake the broken glass off it. Becky stood there staring at her, trembling all over. "Is that where it was?" Becky said. Her voice was so high and loud that she sounded like somebody else. "Was it there?"

Mom looked up. Becky said, "But now it's gone! Oh, you stupid assholes! You had to hide it in a fucking picture frame!"

Mom put her hand over her mouth. She was still holding tight to Joey's photo with her other hand. She and Becky were both panting. So was I.

Then Becky's face went rigid, starting in the jaw and moving upward until it looked like a statue's face. She said, "Where is *he*? How long has he been gone?"

Of course she didn't need to spell it out, who she meant by

"he." Mom and I both knew. My stomach flopped like a fish on dry land.

Mom said, "He was here when I left. He told me I should go get my hair done."

Becky said, "Oh, shit." She was quiet for a second and then she said, "Oh, shit, shit, shit, shit! He took it."

Mom said, "No, no, he wouldn't do that."

Becky said, "He's halfway to Miami by now."

Mom said, "He wouldn't ever do that. Somebody must have broken in and stolen it."

Becky laughed but it wasn't the kind of laugh where you really think something is funny. She said, "Oh God, are you ever going to grow up? Grow UP! Nobody broke in! He knew exactly where it was and now it's gone and so is he! What do you think that means?"

Mom said it again, "No, no, he wouldn't do that."

Becky said, "Why NOT? It wouldn't be the first time he left us! He did it before when he had nothing, what's going to stop him now? I know it, he's on his way and we can just eat shit!"

Mom kept kneeling there on the rug holding Joey's picture with pieces of broken glass all around her. She was shaking her head but I saw that she believed it, Dad was gone. I started to cry. I couldn't help it. I've never felt so terrible in my life. It was disappointment and shock and sadness and loneliness and anger and, most of all, feeling just so *sorry* for all of us, even for Joey, dead such a long time but still smiling in his little picture. We were all there in the same old ugly living room, and Dad was leaving us again, each second he was farther away, rolling down the highway, playing the car radio, smoking a cigarette, blowing the blue smoke into the air, slapping the steering wheel in time to the music, not thinking about us, not caring, ready to forget us and be rich all by himself.

"The selfish bastard!" Becky said. "He takes everything, he doesn't leave us one thing! I guess he's going to be happy now, I guess he's going to have a great time! He can rent studios and make demo tapes and have a website, he can even pay people to cheer, I guess! That's how he'll spend it, all sorts of stupid, crazy ways. He'll go through it in no time, it'll run through his fingers like water! He doesn't even know what it means, but oh God, he took it all! I hope he chokes on it, I hope he chokes and dies!"

Mom just crouched there on the floor, staring at her own hands holding Joey's picture. I had to sit down because I was crying so hard that I didn't have enough energy to keep standing. I never remember crying like that in my life before. It was like my whole body was full of tears, they were churning up and overflowing through my eyes, my nose, my mouth, and I couldn't cry enough to get rid of them all. I don't know why but I was thinking of all sorts of awful things in a jumble, the day Joey died, how that man down the street kicked his poor little dog last week and what an awful squeal it gave and how it huddled against the wall, how that old lady with the two canes always shows up on the corner of Broadview and Danforth with the sign around her neck, "old and sick, please help," how I yelled at Karko and hung up on him and I didn't mean it, how Dad got away but we didn't, how we'd have to go through the long sad months again, getting used to him being gone, hating him, dreaming about him, picturing him in Los Angeles or New Orleans, our hearts stopping when we saw a stranger on the street because from the back he looked just the same. I was thinking, no Enrique Iglesias tickets, no Camcorder, no new house, no new school, no planes or boats, nothing was changed after all, we were stuck in exactly the same place, the same losers we'd always been.

All that went through my mind in a few seconds, and I was still crying, and then I felt some cool air against my arm. I looked around, and Dad was standing there. I knew it was him, even though my eyes were all blurred. The late afternoon sun was coming through the kitchen window behind him, making a weird orange light around his hair and the shape of his shoulders. I was so stunned to see him that my tears dried up, just like that.

He must have heard some of the terrible things Becky said about him. He must have been opening the hall door while she was screaming them out. He must have heard me crying too. He could see Mom slumped on the floor with Joey's picture. It was obvious what all three of us were thinking. We all stared at him as though he was a ghost. But being Dad, he didn't try to deal with any of it. He wouldn't have had a clue how to start. Instead he just stood there smiling, as if everything was just fine.

"It's okay, I've got it right here," he said, taking the lottery ticket out of his shirt pocket. "I phoned the lottery office again this afternoon to check things out so we'd know what to expect tomorrow. They gave me a lot of advice. They said we were smart to keep the ticket hidden, but they told me we should have a photocopy of it, just in case, which made sense, so I took it up the street to the Mac's Milk and used the photocopier there."

"You just carried it up the street to Mac's Milk? A six-million-dollar lottery ticket?" Becky shrieked. "Are you nuts?"

"Beck, it's all right. Nothing happened, I've got it right here. And they also told me to write our name and address on the back. See, I put us all down."

I felt so drained I couldn't even get off the couch but he showed the back of the ticket to Mom and Becky. I looked at it later. There was a space for your name and address. This is what he wrote: "Masaryk" and then all our names: Jesse, Mona, Rebecca, Cory.

It was as if this huge tornado had blown through the apartment and thrown us all around and left us beat up and dazed. We needed a few minutes to recover, and Dad kept on talking to give us time. "They said they could give me the names of some financial advisers. When I told them we already had one, they were impressed," he said with a laugh. "Oh, and we might need an unlisted phone number, because once the news gets out, all sorts of types will be after us, phony charities and people pretending to be investment experts and friends we haven't seen for ten years, that kind of stuff. Tomorrow we have to take ID with us, something with a photo and a signature."

Of course Becky was the first of us to pull herself together. She said, "And we'll each have our own account, right?"

Dad smiled at her, as if he hadn't just heard her say she hoped he'd choke and die. "Yeah, Beck, that's the agreement."

"We'll divide it into four equal parts?" Becky said. She was staring back at him like a lawyer, not smiling.

Dad nodded. "Yeah, one a half million each, like we said."

Becky's eyes stayed fixed on his face, hard as blue rocks. She said, "I don't know if that's really fair. Maybe the ones who've been bringing in the most money should get a bigger share. That would be Mona and me."

After a second of silence Dad said in a light tone, "I bought the ticket, Beck."

"Okay, one dollar," she flashed back with a nasty laugh. "That was your contribution."

When she saw we were all staring in disbelief her face got red. "Well, isn't that right?" she said. "Mona and I have been paying the rent for the last two years! Doesn't that entitle us to something extra now?"

I couldn't believe she could be like that. "I can't help it if I have to go to school!" I said. "I give Mom almost all my babysitting money!"

"What does a fifteen-year-old need with a million and a half dollars anyway?" Becky said. "Some of it could go into a trust fund for her education or whatever, but why should she have her own bank account?"

"I deserve it as much as you!" I said.

"Look," Becky said. "Mona and I have made more of a financial investment, so now we're the ones who should get a bigger return, right? I'll bet that's what they'd say in court."

I glanced at Dad to see how he was taking it, that she was talking as if he and I were useless *parasites* or something. But no matter what anyone says to him he never shows if he's hurt. He just kept standing there, smiling his little easy smile, not trying to defend himself. He didn't even bat an eye when she said the word "court." Maybe he didn't think she was serious. But I knew she was. That would be just Becky's style, bringing a lawsuit against her own family. She'd think she was totally justified, as a princess she'd naturally deserve more than anybody else.

Mom was still sitting on the floor with Joey's picture in her lap. She didn't raise her head, but she said, "We're going to divide it in four equal parts. Period."

Becky's face got red again. She took a fast breath as if to argue. But it's not often that Mom talks in that tone of voice, so sharp and determined. It was kind of intimidating, even for Princess Becky. She shut her mouth — for about five seconds.

Then she said, "Okay, but if one of us spends their share and has no money left, they can't expect more, right? They can't come to the others moaning and complaining and asking for help. Right?"

"That's fine with me!" I said, glaring at her. "I'm never going to need *your* help!"

"Good," Becky said.

Mom stood up, holding on to Joey's picture. Dad said, "Hey, you got it cut. It looks nice." They stared at each other for a minute. Then she gave a sort of a weak laugh and fluffed up her new short hair.

Dad said, "So tomorrow morning we'll get up and go down there." He was still smiling, as if nothing had ever been wrong all our lives. "Let's just grab a cab," he said.

So that's what we're going to do.

III

RETURNS

JESSE

At midnight you feel wired,
By three A.M. flat busted and tired,
Not sure if you've got what it takes to go on,
But hey, the night ain't so long.

Don't know the last time that you got a good sleep
The dark's spread out so wide, so deep,
But come lie beside me, in one hour it's dawn,
Baby, the night ain't so long.

Baby, we're gonna be all right,
We're not ready yet to give up the fight,
We're gonna fix whatever's wrong,
I swear the night ain't so long.

I think we're gonna find our way,
Gonna open up our eyes some day
And see the place where we belong.
Sometimes the night seems long
but baby, it ain't so long.

— "THE NIGHT AIN'T SO LONG," BY JESSE MASARYK, 2000

MONA   We all got dressed up. I guess we were thinking about those scenes we'd watched on television, lottery winners being handed a giant cheque, standing there grinning at the camera. We all wanted to look good for that. I was glad I'd had my hair cut by a professional, instead of doing it myself, standing in front of the bathroom mirror and chopping off the split ends with a pair of scissors.

On the stairs we ran into Mrs. Ferrara. She had the baby fastened to her chest with one of those harnesses, and she was carrying two plastic bags full of groceries. She stared at us in amazement. I guess we looked different from usual. Or maybe it was just that we were all together, going out in a group as if we were going to a wedding.

The taxi was sitting at the curb. It wasn't unusual or luxurious, just an ordinary city cab, but the sight of it lifted me so high it might as well have been a pink Cadillac with Elvis behind the wheel. I felt like laughing out loud. We weren't trudging to the subway station, we weren't going to wait for a bus or a streetcar, we weren't going to pry open the sticky doors of our 1989 Ford, we were just going to sit back and ride.

"You know what?" I said, "I think this is only the second time I've taken a taxi since I came to Toronto!"

"Well, big deal," Becky said.

None of us had been able to look at her all morning. She'd been so harsh the afternoon before, and we hadn't figured out what to make of it. But all of a sudden I knew it wasn't her fault. She was barely twenty and she'd never had any money before. How could you blame her for getting a little carried away? I decided I was just going to forget everything she'd said, she hadn't really meant any of it. She was still my little Becky, the same one who cried so hysterically at Joey's funeral that Mom had to take her out of the church, the same one who used to look up at me with her clear blue eyes and say, Mommy, you'll love me forever, won't you?

She and Cory and I got into the back seat and Jesse got into the front. He said, "Thirty-three Bloor Street East, please." I'm not sure if the cab driver knew that was the address of the lottery office, but he gave us a look. Jesse turned around and grinned. And we were off.

The only other time I took a cab in Toronto, I was going to the nearest emergency clinic with a broken arm. The pain was excruciating, I was terrified about not being able to work, and I couldn't take my eyes off the meter. Every time the numbers went up more sweat broke out on my upper lip.

But when the circumstances are better, you can relax and enjoy yourself. The streets look different from a taxi. You're gliding along, easy and light, your head resting against soft upholstery, and the people roll past like extras in a movie, a transition scene or the opening moments before the real action starts. Everybody looks bright and exotic, even the crazies, even the bums. You float across the Bloor Street Viaduct as though you're on a yacht, and below you see the valley all in a green haze, you could swim in all that green, it couldn't be any greener in the tropics, in fact you'd hardly be surprised to see monkeys and parrots in the trees. Ahead of you are the city's glass towers, blue and gold and silver against the sky, they always made you feel so small before, but suddenly they remind you of the Emerald City in the *The Wizard of Oz*, you're going right in through the gates, the four of you, it's like you're at the head of a parade, flags waving, trumpets blowing, all those people with the cell phones and suits and briefcases are going to stand aside and stare as you pass by.

The lottery office was in a mall beside the Bloor Street subway station. Near the entrance were a whole bunch of hot air balloons showing the names of all the different lotteries: Super Seven, Lotto 649, Wintario, some others I'd never even heard of before. You went through an arched doorway under a sign saying "Prize Office" and saw a big room that looked sort of like a bank, except that the bottom of the counter was made of bubbly green glass, and on the ceiling was a long twisted green light, like a neon snake. There was a "Winners" wall with silvery etchings of various people: a bus driver, a construction worker, an Indian chief, other types like that, who'd supposedly won the lottery. Maybe they were going for a Las Vegas effect, but it was all kind of tacky, not what I'd expected. Just as we were walking in, they called a name and this guy who'd been sitting in a chair got up and went to the counter. A blonde woman came out from a back room and handed him a cheque. He looked at it, smiled, and strolled past us on his way out. There were three people lined up, waiting to turn in their tickets and get their money. That was something I hadn't expected either, waiting in line to collect our millions. I'd kind of thought our days of standing in line were over.

"Ours might take a couple of hours," Jesse told us. "With the really big prizes it's a little more complicated. Maybe while they're processing the cheque we could go somewhere for brunch."

He tossed that off as if he had "brunch" every day of the week. But Becky was ready. "We should go to the Park Plaza," she said. "It's not far. They make the best Eggs Benedict in town."

"Oh, yeah!" Cory said, forgetting that she was mad at Becky. "I'd like to try that!"

"I'm having a Russian omelette," I said on impulse.

"What's that?" Cory wanted to know.

"I have no idea, it just came into my head this second," I said. "I'll tell them to make a regular omelette and stuff it with caviar."

Everybody laughed, even Becky.

Finally it was our turn. Jesse stepped up to the counter, taking the ticket out of his breast pocket. "Hi," the blonde woman said with a smile. My heart started to pound with excitement. I didn't know what would happen, I thought maybe there was some special fanfare when you'd won a million or more, maybe bells rang and lights flashed and confetti fell down from the ceiling. I took Becky's and Cory's hands and for once they didn't pull away. And I had this flashback, just a second of memory, all of us walking hand in hand down the main street of Walbrook on a summer day and one of Jesse's friends, Mark Fahey, leaning out of a doorway to surprise us by playing a couple of bars of "Heart of Gold" on his harmonica.

The blonde woman looked at the ticket. She said, "This isn't a ticket."

I didn't understand what she meant. Of course it was a ticket, one glance was all you needed, anyone could recognize it from three yards away, it was on the right kind of paper, it was the right shape and size, it had the line of numbers, all there as plain as day. The four of us stared at her in confusion.

"What?" Jesse said.

"No, this is just a computer printout of the winning numbers for last Wednesday. See, it says so right here. I'm sorry, but you're not the first ones to make that mistake. We use these to notify the retailers and sometimes people get hold of one of them by accident. It does look a lot like a ticket. The next time, if you think you have a winning ticket you should go straight to your local outlet and have it validated, that way there's no mistake."

Jesse took back the piece of paper and stared at it dumbly. I looked too. Sure enough, right above the line of numbers were the words, THIS IS NOT A TICKET. The letters weren't big and bold, nothing in particular made them stand out. I guess if you were excited, if you were tired, if you wanted to believe it was your lucky day, your eyes could pass over those words without even seeing them. You'd be concentrating on the numbers, checking them over and over, thinking at last, at last something wonderful is happening to me!

Behind us someone laughed out loud. Someone said, "You idiots!"

I was so confused that at first I thought a stranger was laughing at us, making fun of us. But no, it was Becky. Her face was red. She opened her mouth and let out a hoot. She said it again, "Oh, you idiots. You are the most idiotic people who ever lived! This is *unbelievable!*"

Before we knew it, we were back out on Bloor Street.

REBECCA   Of course I laughed. What else was there to do? It was so typical, so completely, perfectly, absolutely typical of Mona and Jesse that it almost made me hysterical. Of all the stupid stunts they ever pulled, that was the pinnacle. I laughed so hard that my eyes filled up with water and their faces swam in front of me, dumfounded the way they always were, mouths hanging open, like a comedy team, the Two Stooges, Dumb and Dumber, the Hicks from Hicksville. The only amazing thing was that I fell for it. You'd think I'd have known better. But I let them suck me in, I let myself believe it, the day before when Jesse showed us the damn ticket with all our names on the back, I actually felt this rush of emotion, this little-girl voice rose up inside me wanting to say that old sweet caramel-candy word, "Dad!" I barely glanced at the front of the ticket, I didn't see any warning words, oh no, I was just as ready as they were to make a fool of myself.

Somehow we got out of the prize office. I was still laughing but I had an impression that everybody in the place was watching us with pitying, sneering looks. Out on the street it was hot already and people jostled against us, hurrying along on their way to someplace important. Mona and Jesse just stood there, lost and stunned. All of a sudden I lost the urge to laugh. I didn't even want to look at them, or Cory either. She was only a kid and it wasn't her fault, but the way she was going I thought she'd probably end up just like them. It came into my mind that I didn't care if I never saw any of them ever again. I didn't want them near me, I didn't want them touching me or talking to me. I turned around and started walking. I walked as fast as I could. If they called after me, I didn't hear it.

At first I only wanted to get away, but after I'd gone a couple of blocks, everything hit me and then my shoes felt like they had soles made of lead. I thought of all that stuff I'd bought and how I'd have to return it. And what if they wouldn't take it back? No, I decided I wouldn't even think about that. And I decided that I wouldn't tell them the real reason, I'd go in like a queen, I'd say the things just weren't satisfactory. People did that at Artemis all the time, and Erika's policy was to give them a refund without question. The customer was always right. That reminded me that I'd have to go to Artemis and beg Erika to give me my job back. I thought of the routine, the long hours, the endless smiling and pretending to be interested in other people's clothes, the sun fading on the plate glass and I'd still be there while the light evaporated from the street, but no matter how late it seemed, my watch would always say I had two hours left to go. And then, unless I had a date, it would be onto the subway, so crowded sometimes that I'd have to stand with my nose a half inch from someone else's smelly armpit, and then home, up the dark stairs to the cockroaches, the falling plaster, the leaky toilet, the blaring TV set, the cigarette smoke, sitting there with those three zeros I had to call my family.

I went into a phone booth. I dialed Wayne's office. His secretary answered on the third ring. She always pretended not to recognize my voice, the bitch.

"I'm sorry, he's in a meeting right now," she said.

"Tell him it's Rebecca Masaryk and this is an emergency," I said.

"Oh, really? Well . . ." She didn't believe that any emergency of mine could be that important to him, I guess.

"You'd better get him right now or you'll be sorry," I said. That got her off her ass.

Finally Wayne came on the line. He was a little peeved. He didn't think I could have anything very important to say either. "Hi, what's going on? I'm in the middle of something here."

"Well, so am I," I said. "So let's get right to the point. Do you love me or what?"

"Oh, for — you call me in the middle of the morning for this? Come on, sweetie, give me a break, I've got some very important guys sitting in my office right now waiting for me."

"Just answer me yes or no, then. Would you say that you're in love with me?"

"Well, sure, of course I am, you know that. I'll call you later. Now can I get back to work?"

"So if you're in love with me, we should live together. And if that works out, then we should get married, right? Do you see that happening in the near future, or not?"

"Look, I thought we settled this already."

"No, we didn't," I said. "I don't want to go home tonight. I hate it and I have to get out. So the question is, can I move in with you or not?"

He said, "You expect me to discuss this right this second? I'm standing here at Joanne's desk and there are three guys waiting for me. Come on, honey. I'll meet you after work and we'll have a drink, okay? Right now I have to go."

"If you go I'm breaking up with you," I said. "I mean it, Wayne. I'll find somebody else, wait and see. I don't want to waste any more time with you if you're not serious."

He said, "Look, this is a very complicated situation, you know, I can't just —"

I didn't hear the rest, because I hung up. I had tears in my eyes but I wasn't really sad. I should have done it months ago, Wayne was way too cautious and conservative for me, I should have seen that before. I needed someone stronger, faster, more daring and dynamic. I saw my reflection floating along in all the store windows, like a sort of dream of a woman, a streak of blonde, a slim silhouette in a soft blue dress, with a tasteful slit to show a long gleaming leg. There are always lots of men around to appreciate those things. I have everything they want, the height, the figure, blue eyes, naturally blonde hair, how rare is that? My looks are the only valuable thing I ever got from Jesse. If I'm careful I can make them last for twenty more years, maybe even thirty — look at Lauren Hutton, she's in her fifties and still in great shape. And while I have my looks I'm not a nobody and that's the time to grab what I want.

I kept walking, I felt my stride getting longer, as though I was being photographed, a *Vogue* model walking through the streets, proud and fearless and gorgeous. I didn't need any stupid lottery, I was going to have everything anyway; I was going to live in a condo high above the lake, clean and full of light, nothing to see wherever I looked but blue water and clouds, nothing sad or ugly to touch me.

On Bay Street a guy was getting out of a Lamborghini. He was wearing an Armani suit. He'd had his hair cut at Vidal Sassoon. His sunglasses were Ray-Bans. I stopped and shaded my eyes, pretending to be looking at something across the street, just to give him time to notice me. After a minute I let my glance fall on him, casually, as if by accident.

He was standing there jingling his car keys, smiling. "Hi, beautiful," he said.

The same thing Jesse said to Mona a thousand years ago in the light of the Ferris wheel. Ironic, huh? But this was different, this guy had something to back it up. And no matter what happened I was sure I'd never turn it into a legend. It wasn't romantic at all. It's just the way a man makes contact when he can't think of anything else to say.

I smiled back. "Hi," I said.

CORY   JULY 10, 2000   I keep thinking about Karko. I keep feeling like it's my *fault*, that I should have been nicer to him when he phoned or treated him better or something. The day before school let out for the summer, Majeska asked me if I knew where Jonas was. I forgot that his real name was Jonas, everybody always called him Karko or Kreepy. It took me a minute to figure out who she was talking about. Then I said, "No, are you kidding, why should I?" Majeska said, "It's such a shame, just when he was starting to get along better." I never noticed he was starting to get along so much better. But I didn't say that to Majeska. She wants to think that just because people are good in a scene from a play their whole lives are going to be different. Let her keep on living in her dream world.

The day we found out we didn't win the lottery I went over to the house where he used to sleep. That seems like a hundred years ago now, but actually it was only a couple of weeks. After Becky'd flounced off in a snit, Mom and Dad just kept standing there on the street as if they didn't know what to do next, and it was just too depressing, so I said I was going to school. As if. But they bought it. Or maybe they were just so stunned that they hardly even heard what I was saying. I walked over to Avenue Road. I think I wanted to find Karko and tell him the whole thing. If anybody would understand about being humiliated and feeling like a piece of shit, it would be him. I guess I thought it might make up to him for the way I'd hung up on him, to hear that I'd had something lousy happen to me too. But there was a new sign on the house saying "NO TRESPASSING" in bigger, redder letters, and the window at the back where he always climbed through was bricked up. So he wasn't kidding when he said they'd kicked him out. I sat on the back step for awhile, listening to the traffic from far away and looking at the weeds. That seemed like a good thing to do for someone who'd just lost a million and a half dollars. After the first shock I wasn't that surprised. The amazing thing would have been if we'd actually got some money. That sort of stuff never happens to people like us. After a few days I almost forgot about all the wild ideas I had. I'm still wearing my second-hand jeans and my cheap T-shirts and my sneakers from Zellers. I still flop down on our ratty sofa and watch TV, the same as usual.

I keep thinking maybe I'll see Karko on Yonge Street. When I spot some kid sitting on a sleeping bag, asking for money, I have to cross over to take a closer look. He said he was going to California, but that was probably just talk. Karko in California — yeah, right. I'll bet he doesn't get far. Maybe when I've given up looking for him, he'll just appear suddenly. Last year that happened with Suzanne Wong, she ran away for two months and then came back for one month and then ran away again. I keep imagining the poor geek standing on the highway with his thumb out. Who'd pick him up? The only way he'll ever get to California is if he walks all the way.

I keep thinking about the *X-Files* script too, for some insane reason. Scenes and dialogue keep going through my mind. Maybe I should write my own version. It would be a lot better than Karko's, that's for sure. Actually, maybe it wouldn't even have to be about *The X-Files*, everybody's getting tired of them now anyway. Instead of Mulder and Scully, I could have this guy and girl hitchhiking to California to sell their screenplay to Hollywood. They get dropped off somewhere in Nevada and it turns out they're on the Extraterrestrial Highway. In the ditch they find this mysterious amulet and it changes them, it gives them powers they never knew they had. They can see a hundred miles across the desert, they can run with long strides, cross fifty miles in one minute, get to a miraculous city like nothing ever seen on the earth before. Aliens and humans have co-operated to build it. It has buildings made of a substance that looks like silver but never tarnishes. There are taxis that fly through the air and every roof has a garden with all sorts of strange plants and exotic flowers. The guy and girl start walking down the street, staring at everything, and people bow to them as if everybody knows who they are, everybody thinks they're important. But of course they have enemies too, without enemies there wouldn't be much of a story. There could be some people who recognize them as outsiders, who are afraid they're going to reveal the secret city to the outside world. So in the last scene they're running, being chased and shot at with laser stun-guns (that'll make Karko happy) and they drop the amulet and then gradually the streets start to change, they stop hearing the buzz the laser makes, then they realize they're back in the city they started out from, maybe they never left at all, the whole journey was just in their minds. Wait a minute, I know! They're walking along, sort of dazed, thinking it was all a dream, and then the girl sees a flower in a window box, just one flower but it's very weird and exotic, with huge, velvety, purplish-red petals and emerald-green leaves, not like an earthly flower but like one of the flowers they saw in the alien city! So they look at each other, that's what tells them, like, hey! maybe it wasn't a dream, maybe their city is an alien city too! Fade out. Oh my *God*, it's perfect! I just got a chill down my spine! Wait till Karko hears this, he'll love it! (Or else he'll burp and fart and say it sucks, one or the other.) But who cares, it's going to be absolutely *brilliant*!

I know he'll be back. I'll be nicer to him after this, I really will. And we'll have the script to do, next fall we can act it out in the drama room, I'm sure Majeska will still go for it. While we're acting it'll be just as good as actually going to California. Better, even.

A couple of months ago Majeska was giving us one of her pep talks and she said something like, "Imagination doesn't cost a thing." Lucky for us, because otherwise we probably couldn't afford it, and we're the ones who need it the most.

MONA We walked a long way. I don't think we even noticed how far we were going. We just kept moving our feet. With some part of my brain I was aware of people talking and laughing in sidewalk cafés, of kids on skateboards, couriers on bicycles, delivery men with packages, women with shopping bags, teenagers talking on cellular phones — the whole city streaming past — but it was as if it was all happening behind a veil. I was in a world of my own, and so was he, I think. We didn't talk, we didn't look around, we just kept walking. If the lake hadn't stopped us we might have gone on for a hundred miles.

Harbourfront was full of music, reggae in one place, Latin jazz in another, rock in another, r&b in another. Jesse played there a few times. He'd come down with his guitar, put out his hat, and go for hours. Sometimes he'd make fifty bucks, sometimes only two. We were still fairly young then. We still thought everything was going to change someday. That was a long time past. I hadn't been down to Harbourfront for four or five years. It looked different, flashier, less casual, more developed and organized. But the lake was still azure-blue, still covered with thousands of sparkling waves, almost big enough to make you think of the ocean. A boat glided by, so smooth it seemed to be floating on air. There were lots of people aboard, all holding champagne flutes, laughing, some of them dancing and drinking champagne at the same time. The sight of them made me feel this sharp pain in my heart. I used to think that someday I'd be on a boat like that, floating along and having a blast at some great party, dressed to kill, tipsy on champagne and strawberries, dancing on the deck. The time had come for me to face the fact that probably it was never going to happen, I was always going to be standing on shore in my waitress uniform, my feet sore, some loose change in my pockets, wondering if I'd have enough cash to get through another week. Standing beside a man I'd been with for twenty years, a man who always fucked up somehow, who never had a dime, and sometimes I wasn't even sure if I loved him anymore.

I gave him a fast look, as if he could read my mind. He was staring out at the water. Maybe he was thinking the same things I was. But of course he would never say.

I knew I was going to have to humble myself, apologize to Dominic, hope he'd take me back at Pizza the Action. And if he wouldn't, I'd have to start looking for another job right away, and who knew how many days it would take me to find one? I had exactly fifty-seven cents left. I'd spent four dollars on marigolds earlier in the week. Why did I have to buy those stupid marigolds? What was the matter with me? I looked at the blue lake water; I imagined what it would be like to go under, sink straight down, feel the waves close over your head. What a relief to go down, down, down into the cold, endless blue. What a relief to be dead, and never have to worry about money anymore.

I felt so grateful that I hadn't told my mother about the lottery ticket. She would have split a gut when she heard how things turned out. Just another example of how I'd never opened my eyes, never learned what it meant to be an adult. Oh, Mona, how could you be such a fool? But she wouldn't have let me feel sorry for myself either. She had no patience with that. You should count your blessings, she would have said — sternly, like a judge handing out a life sentence.

I was so tired that it seemed like a huge effort just to hold myself upright. But Mom's voice wouldn't leave me alone. No self-pity, Mona. Count your blessings. Okay, okay, I thought wearily, I'm healthy. That's always a good one to fall back on when you can't think of anything else. Jesse's healthy and not on drugs. I have two daughters and they're healthy too. Yeah, we're all so damn healthy we'll probably live another hundred years, and never in all that time will we have two cents to rub together.

Once I had the sweetest little boy in the world, too, but I lost him so soon, in a hideous way that I can never forget.

Hey, come on, Mona, Mom's voice scolded, you're supposed to be thinking of blessings, shape up, you're not even trying.

Okay. I had Joey for four years and now when I dream about him it's usually sweet and tender, the bad part has faded a bit. I dream about his little head resting on my collarbone, warm and light, the feathery hair tickling my chin. I see him fall on his face in the grass but instead of crying he gets up laughing, he was always ready to laugh.

He laughs and bangs his spoon on top of his high chair, watching us play cards around the kitchen table — I think "Lambsley" is the name of the game — Jesse's thumb is resting casually on one of his face-down cards, Becky slaps his hand sharply and says, "Dad! You're cheating!" He blinks in pretend outrage. "What? I don't know what you're talking about." Cory and I giggling, Joey banging his spoon, Mom standing in the doorway with her rusty smile, saying, "Heavens, what's all the ruckus?"

Taking a walk on a winter night, Main Street quiet, muffled in white, no cars in motion, no other people. Mom's promised to have hot chocolate waiting for us when we get home, the old fashioned kind with cream, marshmallows and maraschino cherries, and brandy chasers for the adults. Christmas lights twinkle at the empty intersection, Jesse sings a few bars of "Jingle Bell Rock." Joey holds up his little hands in the snowy air. Cory dances ahead, bending her head back, sticking out her tongue to catch the snowflakes. "Mrs. Rogers said no two snowflakes are ever the same. I know! Let's pretend we're at the

North Pole. Let's pretend there's pole people and a town all made of ice!"

Becky comes walking out of the bedroom, wearing a rose-coloured dress, you'd think she'd been worked on by a team of cosmeticians, dressmakers and hair stylists but she did it all herself, sitting on the edge of her bed with a little greenish mirror in front of her. She glows like a candle, softening all the worn edges on the furniture, brightening the walls, her reflection floats in the dark window panes, nothing looks cheap or shabby with a girl like this in the room, she spins slowly so you can see her from every angle, she says, "How do I look?"

Cory and Jesse start clowning, even Becky joins in, they're singing with exaggerated accents, turning a love song into a comedy routine, Jesse makes the guitar twang and vibrate, Becky pretends to clutch a microphone, warbling, "I lo-o-ove *yew*, bay-buh, I really, really *dew* . . ." twang, twang . . . Cory screams, "Stop it, stop it, I'm going to pee my pants!"

He cleared his throat and took a breath. I waited but he didn't say anything. It didn't matter, I was on a roll. Memories streamed through my mind like a film unreeling, all sound and colour, and I didn't feel quite so tired anymore. I remembered a night when we were coming back from the Toronto Islands on the ferry, years ago when it was still only a dollar and we could afford it. The sun was setting, the lake was the colour of dark plums, lines of people stood at the rail or sat on the benches, Becky leaned out into the wind, Cory was beside me half asleep, her head resting against my arm. Jesse got out his guitar. It didn't take long for people to start paying attention, nodding their heads, swaying, tapping their feet. The music drifted back across the water toward the shore. He started to play "When the Saints Go Marching In." That was Jesse at his best, giving what he had, trying to connect. People smiled and joined in on the chorus. "Oh, I want to be in that number, when the saints go marching in." I saw them all in the dim, watery light, weary old men and worn-looking women, laughing teenagers and young couples holding hands, mothers and children, all their faces turned toward us, each one glad to be there with the others, each one wanting to sing, and I thought that sometimes it wasn't so bad to be a member of the human race.

Jesse hooked one thumb in his belt and rested his weight on one foot. Sometimes he stood in a certain way, or got a certain look on his face, or smiled with one side of his mouth, or bent over with one fast movement, or raised his big, beautiful, shapely hand, and for a second he was the same boy I saw at the Walbrook fairgrounds, the boy I fell for so hard that I never recovered. The day before, when I believed for a minute that he'd run out on us again, one of the worst things about it was that I knew I wouldn't go after him a second time, not even for the money. But then he walked in and showed us the ticket with all our names on the back, and I thought this is my guy.

I felt myself flying through the air, travelling two thousand miles in a second, I was in a car on Highway 35 in Saskatchewan, it was night, after a show, the upholstery was trembling with the beat from the car radio, air was pouring through the windows, smelling like clover, smelling like gasoline, before us the land stretched away, immense and endless, silvery waves of grass rolling to the horizon, rolling right into the stars, there were *no limits*, and he said, "You won't believe it, but this old jalop can do a hundred and twenty miles an hour on an open road." He looked at me, his eyes shining. He was the wild, free, dangerous one I'd always hoped for, his face flamed in the passing headlights with such intensity that I felt the heat on my skin.

"Let's go," I said. The car jumped forward and the sky came rushing toward us, opening like an enormous gateway, calling us on. Go, go, go, go! He threw back his head and whooped. Light flashed on the windshield, darts of blue and red light. I think right then we were as happy as people ever get to be on this earth. We had that, him and me.

He was still holding the piece of paper that we'd thought was going to change everything. He crumpled it up. "What am I holding onto this for?" he said with a laugh. He tossed it into the lake. It bounced on the waves, a little scrap of yellowish paper, nothing at all. "We really thought we'd won," he said, looking at me with another laugh. That was always his way; no matter how terrible the failure, how bitter the disappointment, how devastating the loss, he pretended not to care. Sometimes it drove you crazy. Other times it reminded you of one of those old movies from the '50s or '60s, with those beautiful, flawed men, Marlon Brando or Paul Newman or Steve McQueen, who end up with nothing but smile and shrug as if it doesn't matter, and it just pierces your heart right through because all of a sudden they seem so brave.

"What a joke, huh?" he said gaily. "Us, lucky."

"Oh, yeah," I said. "Often."

Today I bought another lottery ticket.

ACKNOWLEDGEMENTS

I would like to acknowledge the Ontario Arts Council and the Toronto Arts Council for providing much-needed financial assistance during the writing of *A Streak of Luck*.

Thanks to Marc Côté and Steven Beattie for their support, valuable insights and editing expertise.

And finally, I'd like to express my fervent gratitude to my family and friends for all the inspiration, encouragement and understanding they've given me over the years.